LABYRINTH

ALSO BY HENRY DENKER

NOVELS

I'll Be Right Home, Ma
My Son, the Lawyer
Salome: Princess of Galilee
The First Easter
The Director
The Kingmaker
A Place for the Mighty
The Physicians
The Experiment
The Starmaker
The Scofield Diagnosis
The Actress
Error of Judgment
Horowitz and Mrs.
Washington
The Warfield Syndrome
Outrage
The Healers
Kincaid
Robert, My Son
Judge Spencer Dissents
The Choice
The Retreat
A Gift of Life
Payment in Full
Doctor on Trial
Mrs. Washington and
Horowitz, Too

PLAYS

Time Limit
A Far Country
A Case of Libel
What Did We Do Wrong
Venus at Large
Second Time Around
Horowitz and Mrs.
Washington
The Headhunters
Outrage!

Labyrinth

HENRY DENKER

WILLIAM MORROW

AND COMPANY, INC.

NEW YORK

It is the policy of William Morrow and Company, Inc., and its imprints and affiliates,
recognizing the importance of preserving what has been written, to print the books
we publish on acid-free paper, and we exert our best efforts to that end.

Library of Congress Cataloging-in-Publication Data

Denker, Henry.
    Labyrinth : a novel / by Henry Denker.
       p.   cm.
    ISBN 0-688-13700-8
    1. Trials (Murder)—New York (N.Y.)—Fiction.   2. Lawyers—New York
(N.Y.)—Fiction.   3. Multiple personality—Fiction.   I. Title.
PS3507.E547533 1994
813'.54—dc20   94-19103
                                                                         CIP

Printed in the United States of America

First Edition

1   2   3   4   5   6   7   8   9   10

BOOK DESIGN BY JAYE ZIMET

TO EDITH, MY WIFE

LABYRINTH

One

David Kirk would never have become involved in the Cory murder trial if he had not been the intended victim of an assassination attempt.

As Kirk and his young associate stepped out of the elevator on the twenty-ninth floor of the New York City building where he maintained his law offices, he was assaulted by a hoarse accusation: "Murderer!"

A single shot rang out. Then a second. Immediately followed by a third.

Pressed against the closed elevator doors, Kirk cautiously turned his head in the direction from which the shots had been fired. The figure of a short, heavyset man was silhouetted against the window at the end of the corridor.

Instantly, Kirk took score: *Hit man? Hit men work close. With silencers. This is no Mob job. Besides, he missed. All three shots. Rank amateur. He's lowering his gun. Giving up? Or setting me up?*

The man's dangling gun hand began to tremble. With his free hand he brushed at his eyes.

Gerry Prince whispered to Kirk, "Is he crying?"

Gesturing Gerry to remain pressed against the wall, Kirk cautiously started toward his assailant.

As Kirk came close the man became less a silhouette. Kirk could not identify the man. But his tear-strained face did look disturbingly familiar.

Kirk had had enough experience defending murderers to know one thing. This man was no killer. Despite the hatred in his eyes, the cold killer's look was not there. Kirk figured it was safe to reach for that gun. He was right. The man seemed relieved to surrender the shiny chrome-plated thirty-eight.

David Kirk reached for the man's elbow to guide him toward his office. The man jerked free as if Kirk's touch would contaminate him, but he followed Kirk down the corridor. They passed the doors of several other offices, doors which, from tense curiosity, were slightly open. Doors that slammed shut as Kirk and his assailant passed by.

Kirk entered his outer office and led the man through the reception area. Greta Nissman and Louise Grant, his two personal secretaries, stared in terror. One glimpse of the shiny weapon in Kirk's hand and Greta knew.

She asked, "Shall I put in a call to nine . . ."

Before she could even complete 911, Kirk interrupted, "No! Not a word. To anyone!"

Once inside his private office, Kirk dropped the weapon onto his desk. With a single brusque gesture he ordered the stranger to be seated in the visitor's chair across from the imposing desk.

Kirk studied the hateful face. Broad. Undistinguished. Freckled, with the look of a man who had worked outdoors at some kind of physical labor. His black eyes, hostile still, were now teary as well.

"Had you . . . I shouldna missed," he reproached himself. Then, in a loud angry voice he accused, "Because of you she's dead! You're just as much a murderer as he was!"

Kirk glanced at Gerry Prince. The young black lawyer shared his puzzlement. This was clearly a case of misidentification. Or else the man was deranged.

Rising up from his chair, and with even more venom, the man accused, "Murderer!"

"All right, let's just calm down," Kirk urged.

Glaring, the man sank back into his chair.

"Now, tell me, just who am I supposed to have murdered?"

"You know damn well! My daughter!"

From behind the man, Gerry gestured, *He is out of his mind. Totally flipped out.*

"I murdered your daughter?"

"Raped her first!" the man accused.

Still puzzled by the stranger's identity, Kirk replied, "Mister, I'm sorry if that happened to your daughter. But I had nothing to do with it."

"If it wasn't for you it never would have happened!" the man shouted.

In the same instant he lunged for the pistol. Kirk was quicker. He seized the man's outstretched hand, and with a single strong twist he forced him back into his chair.

"Okay! Now, tell me. What the hell is this all about?"

"Sure! Pretend you don't know! The great David Kirk! You bastard! You got him off! Set him free to go out and rape and kill again!"

As he looked into the man's vengeful tormented face Kirk realized why it had seemed so disturbingly familiar at first glance.

Kirk had indeed seen this face before. The first time, it had covered the entire front page of the tabloid *New York Post*. Bitterly angry then as now as he glared at Kirk. Over the picture, the *Post* had run the bold black headline FATHER WARNS, STOP FREEING KILLERS TO KILL AGAIN.

The story had started at the bottom of the front page, reporting how this man's daughter had been raped and then murdered by a young man who six months before had been set free "as the result of a highly technical defense by the brilliant criminal lawyer David Kirk."

Guilty in the face of this demented man's grief, Kirk started to explain, "Under our system of justice every accused is entitled to a defense. The best defense a lawyer . . ."

"Bullshit!" the man interrupted. "He confessed! What more did they have to know?"

"His confession was thrown out. Obtained under duress," Kirk tried to explain.

"Duress, my ass! He was never beaten by the cops. You made that up! Bastards like you are no better than the criminals you defend!"

There was a knock on the door. A strong knock, and so sharp that Kirk and Gerry both knew it was a warning as well. Before Kirk could respond, the door opened. Behind his longtime secretary, Greta, Kirk spied the blue uniform of a New York City policeman. Behind him was the gray suit of a plainclothes detective.

Kirk's eyes rebuked, *Greta, I told you not to call 911.*

Her helpless shrug denied, *It wasn't me who called.*

No matter who summoned the police, Kirk had to deal with them now. And especially with Detective Dennis Palmer, whom Kirk knew well, having grilled him in the kind of tough cross-examination that tabloid reporters describe as "withering and unrelenting." From the grim look on the veteran detective's face, Palmer had not forgotten.

Trying to defuse the gravity of the situation, Kirk greeted him warmly, "Palmer! Hi. Come in, come in! What can I do for you?"

Dennis Palmer moved into the office, cast a quick glance at the man seated in the chair, then at the shiny thirty-eight on Kirk's desk.

"Nine-one-one received a number of calls about a shooting on this floor." Palmer reached for the weapon, asking, "Mind?" Not that it would have mattered if Kirk had objected. Palmer sniffed the muzzle. "A very *recent* shooting, it seems."

Before his attacker could incriminate himself, Kirk claimed, "That gun is mine. I have a permit."

"Authorizing you to take target practice in the corridor of an office building? And scare the hell out of every secretary on this floor? If not the whole building, to judge from the number of nine-one-ones that came in?" Palmer demanded.

Palmer turned to include the assailant in his inquiry. The man stiffened and glanced at Kirk, seeking some cue as to the proper response.

Kirk resumed command of the situation, explaining, "We were just carrying out a demonstration in the corridor."

" 'We'?" Palmer asked skeptically.

"Yes. My . . . my client and I," Kirk improvised.

Palmer did not respond. Instead, he broke the weapon to count the remaining shells.

"Counselor, would you explain to me what *kind* of demonstration one carries out in an office building that justifies firing *three* shots?"

"I would be delighted," Kirk replied, giving Palmer a momentary victory before he added, "However, as you well know, matters between attorney and client are confidential. So, much as I would like to cooperate, my professional oath forbids it."

"I'm sure," Palmer observed wryly, still holding the weapon. "Counselor," he began afresh, "are you aware that the identification number of this weapon has been scratched off?"

Once more the stranger felt compelled to respond. Once more, to protect him, Kirk was quicker and more glib.

"A gift," Kirk explained.

"From a grateful client, no doubt," Palmer observed, expressing his opinion of Kirk's practice as a criminal lawyer. "Counselor, unless you cooperate, I *could* charge your 'client' with possession."

"Which could become very messy, Palmer. Barging in. Seizing evidence without a warrant. Then trying to invade the sanctity of the attorney-client relationship. Very, very messy."

"And you're not one to pass up any technicality when it comes to defending a 'client.' Tell me, Kirk, exactly *when* did this man become your client?"

"Sorry. Confidentiality," Kirk replied.

"Naturally," Palmer conceded, boiling with suppressed frustration. "Just to get things clear, Kirk, do I understand that you, an officer of the court, refuse to cooperate with the police in a clear case of unlawful possession of an unlicensed weapon, on which the identification number has been removed?"

"Just to *keep* things clear, you should say that my oath as an attorney *prevents* me from cooperating," Kirk corrected.

"Have it your way," Palmer conceded. He put down the weapon in question, then turned to the man in the chair to say, "Good day, Mr. Trimble," indicating that he had been aware all along of who the man was, why he was here, what he had tried to do, and what Kirk had just done to protect him.

Once the door had closed, Kirk said, "Okay, Trimble, as soon as the coast is clear, you're free to leave."

"Clear?" Trimble asked.

"We have to give Palmer and his boys-in-blue a chance to leave this floor," Kirk pointed out. "So, would you like a cup of coffee?"

"Nothing," Trimble replied. He sat there glaring at Kirk.

Some minutes later, David Kirk said, "Okay, Gerry. Take him down in the freight elevator."

Trimble rose slowly, then tried to straighten his clothes to achieve some semblance of dignity. Gerry Prince held the door open for him. Trimble stopped in the doorway, turned back and said, "You killed Cecilia!"

"The thanks you get after you just shielded him from a felony charge," Gerry remarked, just before he closed the door.

With no one left to hear, David Kirk confessed, "He's right. Because of me Cecilia Trimble is dead."

Three days later, when David Kirk returned to his office after another day in court, Greta handed him the usual sheaf of messages. He took them in his usual perfunctory manner, trudged into his private office, dropped his messages on the desk without scanning them. If there had been anything of special urgency Greta would have said so.

He leaned back in his maroon leather brass-studded desk chair, taking time to review the day's session of a trial in which he was defending a society woman charged with running a high-class call-girl service. The district attorney had been very effective. But Kirk had more than compensated for that by his stiff cross-examination of the arresting officers. However, there was still that damaging question of the madam's little black book. He must find some way to explain that as other than a client list. He felt sure that he would.

Kirk always depended on what he called his four-o'clock shadow. Not the kind used to advertise shaving cream and razor blades, but his legal shadow. In the early hours of the morning, sometime between three and four o'clock, it woke him with sudden stabs of inspiration that solved the legal problems he had fallen asleep brooding over.

Feeling confident it would happen again tonight, he started skimming through his messages, intending to answer only the most pressing. His phone rang.

Irritated, he snapped, "Greta! You know I like a breather after a day in court. Get rid of whoever it is."

"Including Judge Malachi?" Greta asked.

"Aaron Malachi? I don't have a case before him," Kirk protested with relief. From Kirk's earliest days in practice, Malachi had been very helpful. But he was also notorious for being very tough on defense counsel in criminal cases.

"His secretary said he wants to talk to you. *Today.*"

"Okay," David Kirk relented grudgingly. "Get him."

Within seconds, it seemed to him, his phone rang again.

"Malachi," Greta announced in her clipped speech.

"Judge . . ." Kirk greeted him with forced enthusiasm. "How've you been? Long time no see."

Malachi cut him short. "Kirk! Get your ass over here!"

"Now? At a quarter past five?" Kirk demurred.

"Now! At a quarter past five!" Malachi ordered.

"What's it about? Something—" Kirk started to ask.

The old judge interrupted once more. "What it's about is I want to see you! So get the hell over here!"

On his way to the old Supreme Court building on Centre Street and all the way up the fabled courthouse steps on which he had given so many television interviews during trials, David Kirk kept grousing to himself.

That cantankerous veteran of the bench was either an icon of the law or a kook, depending on whether he was for you or against you. Most times in the dozen years of David Kirk's career as a criminal lawyer since leaving the DA's office, Malachi had been his tormenting gadfly. It often seemed that Malachi resented Kirk's quitting the role of prosecutor to become a defense attorney.

But what might be in the old man's craw this late afternoon was a total mystery to David Kirk. Nevertheless, he raced up the many steps of the courthouse on Centre Street and presented himself at the chambers of Judge Malachi.

Ida Bornstein, Malachi's secretary for more years than anyone could remember, had her own way of warning you about the old man's attitude. She did it in the way she addressed you, such as by not calling you "Counselor" or even "Mister" but simply by your last name. And also by the look on her aging and ageless face, which, at times, exhibited either pity or a scowl of contempt.

She gave David Kirk the full treatment by a look of pity and a brusque "Kirk, he's waiting for you."

However, once he passed her on his way to the judge's inner office, she thought, *Such a nice-looking young man. Handsome actually. And unmarried. One of the highest-priced criminal lawyers in New York. Why can't my granddaughter Melanie meet such a man? But she has to hang out with storefront lawyers and environmentalists.*

The old judge's wheelchair was turned away from his large desk, which was cluttered with files of pending cases. He was facing the window, looking out over the early-evening going-home traffic, which jammed the streets and filled the air with blasts from angry automobile and taxi horns.

Without turning to greet him, Malachi called out, "Kirk, what's this I hear about you being a hero?"

"Hero? Me?"

"From what I hear," Malachi continued without turning to confront him, "you overcame a mad assassin. Wrestled him to the ground, disarmed him. Bound and gagged him and hauled him into your office, all single-handed."

"A gross exaggeration," Kirk replied, not sure if the old man was having fun at his expense or if the story had become inflated to this ridiculous degree from sheer repetition in the rumor mill that thrived around Courthouse Square.

"Is it also an exaggeration," Malachi asked, turning now to confront Kirk, "that you refused to cooperate with the police? Lied to them to protect a would-be assassin? Admitted ownership of a weapon not your own? And claimed the potential assassin was your client?"

"Well, I can explain that—" Kirk started to say.

"Not to me you can't!" Malachi interrupted in a growl so strong it belied his age. "Sit down!" he ordered.

David Kirk dropped into the nearest empty chair, prepared to endure Judge Malachi's lecture.

"Damn it, this is one of those times when I resent this wheelchair. I would like to be up and on my feet, pointing my finger into your handsome face like a prosecuting attorney. Making you tremble at my accusations. But I can't, so I'll have to do what needs doing from this miserable chair."

He propelled his wheelchair from behind the desk to come closer to Kirk, then softened his tone somewhat. "Okay, Davey, off the record, you did a fine thing. Protected a tormented father from being arrested on a possessions charge.

And who knows, depending on the DA, maybe even from an attempted murder charge. Nice gesture. But was that to protect Mr. Trimble or to salve your own conscience?"

Kirk was about to protest, but Malachi cut him off with a sharp "Your sonofabitch client was guilty as hell. But you got him off on a technicality. So he was free to go out and rape and kill again. And this time, a nice, innocent young woman like Cecilia Trimble. I wish Trimble had had better aim!"

Kirk was up out of his chair, towering over old Judge Malachi as he defended, "I did what I was sworn to do. Give my client the best defense possible! If that called for having his confession thrown out, so be it! And I won't be criticized by anyone! Even you!"

"Finished?" Malachi asked indulgently.

Kirk felt suddenly foolish for having exploded at this veteran of the justice system. He replied quietly, "Yes."

"Good. Now shut up and listen!" Malachi turned his wheelchair about and started back behind his desk once more. "Davey, doesn't it ever get to you?"

"What?"

"What we have done to the system!" Malachi challenged.

"I think we've got as good a criminal justice system as exists anywhere in the world," Kirk protested.

"That's not what I'm talking about!" Malachi growled angrily. "I mean the way people *feel* about the law. They look on judges and lawyers as their enemies. Because we violate their basic sense of justice. It shows you how far we've come from any rational system of justice when a citizen like Edward Trimble goes out, illegally buys a gun, and tries to shoot down a man like you. He missed. But there was a mother out in California who didn't miss. Four bullets into the head of her son's abuser. Right in the courtroom. We're facing an epidemic of vigilantism.

"All because of lawyers like you, and, yes, judges like

me. We keep turning criminals loose on technicalities. Lawyers' tricks and judges' arbitrary decisions. So they are able to repeat their crimes over and over again. We can't keep doing that if we want the average citizen to feel safe and free.

"We have got to draw the line somewhere. Somewhere," the old man repeated, because he himself did not know where that somewhere should be. "The law has become a game. The more guilty defendants a lawyer gets off, the better his reputation, the higher his fees. You, my dear David Kirk, are a perfect example. You do very well these days, don't you? Nice plush office. Very fancy fees. Photographed every time you enter or leave the courtroom. Invited on television to give your opinion on every important case. You are a star! While the people's estimate of the law sinks lower and lower."

"Your Honor, I didn't make the rules."

"I know, I know," the impatient judge said, trying to staunch the torrent of justification Kirk was prepared to unleash.

But he did not succeed. For Kirk continued:

"And if you're hinting at what happened in the Corregio case, the Appellate Division cleared me of all charges! I had nothing to do with bribing that juror!" Kirk protested.

"Davey, Davey, no need to get so defensive. I wasn't even thinking of that. Though now that you brought it up, I've seen lawyers disbarred for less. Another scandal like that and you won't be so lucky next time," Malachi warned.

Still bristling, Kirk said, "You may not approve of the way I practice law, but never question my ethics."

"Damn it, Davey, I am not talking ethics. I am not talking law. Justice, Davey, justice! We cannot continue to violate the basic desire of the people for justice.

"Trimble's foolish attack was an expression of the average citizen's feeling of futility. For your contribution to that I am going to exact an act of penance. I am assigning you to a case for which you will receive a fee of possibly a few thousand dollars and a little extra for costs and disbursements."

"Judge, with all due respect, I've done my share of . . ."

Malachi interrupted, "Yes, yes, I know you've done your share of volunteering when cases of important legal principles are involved. But this time *I* am making the assignment."

"I happen to have a heavy trial calendar right now and I am not in a position to accept an assignment."

"I remember ten, twelve years ago when you first left the DA's office you were hungry for assignments. I gave you your first one, and more after that."

"That's when I put my name on the eighteen-B list as available to defend the indigent," Kirk explained.

"And never had it removed," Malachi reminded.

"My name is still on the eighteen-B list?" Kirk asked, surprised.

"It was at three o'clock this afternoon," Malachi pointed out. "I had Ida check it."

"I never realized . . ." Kirk admitted.

"So, since your name is on the list, you *are* available. And *I*, as presiding judge, hereby appoint you to defend . . ." The old man had to wheel himself to the desk to refresh his mind on the defendant in the case. "Ah, yes, to defend Christopher Cory."

"What's the charge?"

"Murder two," Malachi replied, adding, "and if I read the preliminary papers correctly, a pretty bloody murder two. I have set arraignment for two weeks from Wednesday. I expect you to be there, ready to plead your client."

"This is short notice. I am on trial now, with still another case scheduled when this one is over. . . ." Kirk protested.

A sardonic smile creasing his wrinkled face, Malachi taunted, "Surely a lawyer of your great reputation and eloquent powers of persuasion can convince that other judge to delay a bit."

Kirk knew it was futile to protest. He nodded and turned to leave. But Malachi's words followed him to the door.

"This may be a well-needed lesson in humility for you, my high-flying young friend. And this time I won't let you get away with any of your usual tricks. Remember that!"

Three

David Kirk ran a tight ship as successful law practices go. He had two secretaries. Greta Nissman, Secretary and Office Manager, had been with him since the day he opened his office. A devoted spinster, the stout little woman knew every mood and foible of David Kirk. She anticipated all his needs, professional and social, and she governed the office like a tyrant. All the respect she afforded David Kirk became a despotic rule she exercised over the others in the office.

There was also Louise Grant, Kirk's second secretary, who had been with him for six years. By her aloofness and her supercritical attitude, Greta always made Louise feel that she was still on temporary trial status. Even the two lawyers who did most of the research for David Kirk lived in fear of Greta Nissman. When she declared that a certain memorandum of law had to be ready for Mr. Kirk at a precise hour, it was always there. If she read it over and decided that more supporting cases were necessary, the lawyer went back into the library or over to the Bar Association and started his research all over again.

The only member of David Kirk's staff who was immune

to Greta's domination was Gerald Prince. Greta was always sensitive to the special relationship between Kirk and his young associate. The first encounter between Gerry and David Kirk took place when Kirk was an eager young assistant in the District Attorney's office. He had been handed the file of *People* v. *Prince.* Examining it hurriedly, he had concluded it was another run-of-the-mill case. A teenage kid from Harlem had been apprehended and accused of mugging and attempting to rape a woman on a side street on the Upper West Side of Manhattan.

David Kirk's first look at that teenage kid, with his Afro hairdo, confirmed his expectations. The boy was black, of course. He was scared. And he had a mother who loudly proclaimed her son's innocence.

To himself Kirk had commented, *If black people keep protecting their guilty ones, how will we be able to tell who the innocent are?*

In the Prince case there was a positive ID. The woman who had been robbed and almost raped was sure he was the one.

Armed with that testimony and other pieces of evidence, including a knife found near the scene, which Gerald admitted having seen but never touched, David Kirk presented the case to a jury of mixed color. He did it with sufficient vigor and sincerity to win a verdict of guilty.

He felt so righteous that afternoon that he went about his other prosecutions with added zeal.

Until five months later.

In grilling two defendants in another case, David Kirk uncovered that one of the two defendants was the young black who had actually robbed and molested the woman who had identified Gerald Prince. Confronted by this new suspect, the woman was not only willing but anxious to go before a judge and admit to her mistake under oath.

David Kirk was not only relieved but proud to return to Mrs. Prince her son, Gerald, after he had served five months in a correctional institution for teenage offenders.

Kirk's relief and his pride were short-lived. For after he had apologized profusely, Gerald Prince asked, "Who gonna give me back my five months?"

And his mother added, "How we going to take this stain offa his name?"

"I will see to it that it is wiped off his record," David Kirk replied.

"You going down the street of this neighborhood with him telling everybody it was a mistake? And when he go back to school, you going to go with him and explain to everybody that this here boy served time for a crime he did not commit?"

That day David Kirk walked down that Harlem street feeling far less righteous, far less virtuous, than he had expected. Not only had he committed a grave injustice by being overly zealous in his prosecution of fifteen-year-old Gerald Prince, he had expected gratitude and praise from the boy's mother for righting that wrong.

If prosecutorial zeal could be a fault, smug self-righteousness was at least as great an evil. Determined to make amends, David Kirk promised that he would personally visit the school, explain what happened, take the blame upon himself. More, he would see to it that Gerald Prince would be admitted to City College. He would personally supervise Gerald's work, and see that he graduated with grades good enough to admit him to a law school.

By the time Gerald Prince entered law school, David Kirk had long since resigned from the DA's office and gone into practice on his own. Attending law school at night, Gerald Prince worked in Kirk's office during the day. He accompanied Kirk to every trial. At the outset, that meant running out to get sandwiches and drinks during short lunch hours, or racing back to the office to pick up a law book Kirk needed or a new memo one of his law men had just prepared.

Once Gerald Prince was graduated from New York Law School, and passed the bar, David Kirk made him his full-time assistant. He was always at David Kirk's side at the counsel table, making notes, passing suggested questions to him. In the evening, when the trial was in recess, they would discuss the testimony of the day while planning tomorrow's attack.

It was known in the courtrooms of New York that Gerald Prince was being groomed to become the second litigator in the office of David Kirk.

In the opening stages of any new case, Gerry Prince would conduct the initial interview with the assistant DA in charge to discover the details of the crime with which their client was charged.

However, since in *People* v. *Cory* Judge Malachi was looking over his shoulder, David Kirk decided to handle this first meeting himself.

The People's case was being handled personally by veteran prosecutor Howard Stone. Because it involved the murder of a young actress by her previous live-in lover, it had all the lurid elements to attract heavy play from the city's tabloid newspapers and all the local television channels. Which would lead to on-the-courthouse-steps interviews before and after each session. During such interviews an unfortunate utterance by a young, less-experienced prosecutor could subject the case to charges of prejudice, motions for mistrials, or even a dismissal.

To avoid that, the DA of New York County had appointed Howard Stone, a man long experienced in dealing with the media. He was too facile and knowledgeable to commit such blunders.

David Kirk was not gun-shy about going up against Howard Stone in the courtroom. He had done so a number of times during the last dozen years, and won much more often than he had lost. It was the personal side of their relationship that always troubled Kirk.

In a strange way, the nature of his relationship with Howard Stone predated his relationship with Howard Stone. It went back to his first year at City College, when David Kirk made the discovery that would affect the rest of his life.

His father, Daniel, sixty-one years old, on the verge of retiring from his job as construction superintendent for one of the large builders in New York, left their modest but comfortable Bronx apartment one morning after kissing his wife, Claire, and his son, David, as he did every day when he went off to work. Sometime during the late morning, on a new construction site on Sixth Avenue in the Fifties, while in a heated argument with a union shop steward, Daniel Kirk keeled over. Before the EMS ambulance could arrive, he had expired from a massive heart attack.

It became the duty of young David to take care of the mundane matters that follow such tragedies. His mother was so distraught that he had to arrange for the funeral parlor, the burial and all the details involved.

All important family papers, such as the wedding certificate of Daniel and Claire Kirk, David's baptismal certificate, the deed to the funeral plots, had been kept in the cigar box which Daniel had acquired years before when he still smoked. That box had always been safely tucked away on the upper shelf of the closet in the Kirks' bedroom.

For the first time in his life, David Kirk had the responsibility of taking down that box to search for the cemetery deed. He had found his own baptismal certificate and two bank books for small savings accounts. But before he was able to locate the cemetery deed, he came across a document folded so long ago that when he opened it it came apart in his hands in three separate pieces. When he read it he was stunned.

It was the birth certificate of an infant named David Moorhead. Enfolded within it was a second certificate issued and signed by a Family Court judge purporting to be the birth certificate of David Kirk, father's name Daniel, mother's name Claire. David Kirk examined the first document to discover that his birth mother's name was Charlotte Moorhead. No father's name was listed.

Stunned as David was, he did not confront his mother, who was still suffering her sudden bereavement. But after the funeral, once the relatives and friends had departed, when the two of them were alone for the first time, she was the one who brought up the subject.

"Davey, I've been reading it in your eyes the last few days. You found it, did you?"

She had barely got the words out when she started to cry once more. This woman who he had thought was all cried out.

"Mama, it's all right," he tried to comfort her. But he could not resist admitting, "Only it shouldn't have come as such a . . . such a surprise."

"In the beginning we didn't know what to do. Tell? Or not tell? Some people said yes, some said no. It was your father who made the decision. 'Why burden a little child with a lifetime of wondering who and where and how? He's ours, Claire. That's all that counts. He's ours.' Was he wrong, Davey, was he?"

There are some questions to which there are no adequate answers. He did not love his mother and father any less. But there was now that nagging question—that woman, that other mother. Who was she? Where was she? And, of course, *why did she give me up?*

After pondering that for some days he realized the wisdom

of his father's decision. Why carry that burden through a lifetime, especially during the early years, when a child's mind had so much more with which to cope?

During the following week, after his discovery had become like a third person in the Kirk household, his mother brought up the inevitable question. She was serving him breakfast before he went off to college when she said, "Davey, I won't mind . . ."

"Won't mind what, Ma?"

"If you go looking. Your father and I, we used to talk about that. He always said, 'If the time comes and Davey wants to find her, we've no right to stand in his way.' "

David would have liked to say, "I never even thought of that." Truth was, he had, constantly, since his discovery. So he replied, "In time, Ma, in time."

"I'll tell you all I know. And where we got you, son. They must have some record. And I hope you do find her. And if you do and you want to . . . to . . . to move out or anything . . ." She began to cry again.

He took her in his arms. "Ma, Ma . . . please. No matter what I find, *you* are my mom. This is where I belong. So, please. You've done enough crying for a lifetime these past days. Let me see you smile for a change," he coaxed.

She tried, failed and started to cry once more. As she used to do when as a child he hurt himself and cried, he used his forefinger to stop the flow of her tears and guide them back up to her eyes. It was a game they played that had always made him stop crying and start to laugh. It almost succeeded with his mother. She did not laugh, but at least she stopped crying.

In the weeks that followed, while David worked at his night job, which was now the main support of the household, and attended City College during the day, he made time to call on that adoption agency. He presented his document, inquired about their records and asked for their help.

The woman in charge of family reunification was most

gracious and helpful. Everything, of course, depended upon finding the original parent. Which in Kirk's case, while possible, was far from certain. Nineteen years had elapsed. People die. People move. Especially in the last twenty years, when there had been such an enormous shift in population from the Northeast to the South and Southwest.

"Of course, we will do everything in our power to find her," the woman said. "But we don't want people to harbor any illusions about the possibilities."

Some weeks later David Kirk received a phone call from the agency. That same woman. This time she sounded more optimistic and less cautious.

"Mr. Kirk . . . David . . . I feel free to call you that . . . since you were one of our babies. I think we have found her for you."

"You have? Where is she? When can I see her?" he asked at once.

"It's not that simple, David," she tried to explain.

"If you know where she is, why not?"

"Before we can effect a reconciliation we have to contact her first. And get her permission."

"Well, for God's sake, do that!" he urged.

Another three weeks went by. He received another phone call. This time the woman sounded much more guarded and, at the same time, much more sympathetic.

"David, it seems, how shall I say it, it seems that she has made a new life for herself. She is married. Has been for the last seventeen years. To a man who knows nothing about you. She now has two daughters and a son. And . . . and she thinks admitting her past and bringing you into her life might destroy her family."

"She . . . she said that?" David Kirk asked very softly.

"I don't want you to think that she doesn't care. She was very insistent on knowing how you were, what you were doing. She sounded very concerned."

"Of course. Naturally," he said, refusing to admit his hurt. "Thanks for your help. And you . . . you tell her that she doesn't have to worry. I will never again try to find her. So she doesn't have to be afraid of me."

He hung up the phone. He found himself unable to cry, though he wanted to. He thought, *Thank God I had the parents I did. My job now is to take care of Mom. Get my degree. Go to law school, make good grades so I can get a great job and give Mom all the good things she deserves.*

Despite his righteous resolve, that experience had inflicted a wound. A deep wound which, though scarred over by his subsequent achievements, had created a festering fear that no matter how substantial his successes, they might all be snatched away with the same shattering suddenness he had experienced on the day he discovered that faded, folded original birth certificate.

Four

While going to law school David Kirk had worked two jobs. He studied when he could—between jobs, riding on the subway to and from work, or to and from school. He was driven by the need not merely to pass but to excel so that he could win one of those prime jobs in one of those big law firms that start men and women off at forty to fifty thousand dollars a year.

On the day he graduated from law school, cum laude, he had two overpowering feelings:

Dad, I did it. I can now give Mom what she deserves.

And also, *Charlotte Moorhead, or whatever your name is now, you'll never know what you missed.*

Claire Kirk did not live long enough to enjoy her son's success. Even before the bar exam results were published, she died.

That day at the cemetery, when they laid her to her final rest, David Kirk made a second discovery.

His young cousin Margaret said, to console him, "That darling woman, she was as good to you as if you'd been her own."

For the first time he realized that everyone in the family knew that he had been adopted. Everyone but him.

He walked away from his mother's gravesite feeling more alone than ever. He no longer had a mother and father, and he felt he had no family at all. He was a man alone.

On the day of the announcement in *The New York Times* of those who had passed the bar exam, he felt like a man freed from a long prison sentence. He was ready now to tackle the big law firms for one of those multithousand-dollar-a-year starting salaries.

However, after spending weeks going from large law firm to large law firm, applying by mail with an excellent résumé accompanied by very laudatory letters from several of his professors, David Kirk made a discovery to which he had closed his eyes during the last seven years.

Those dream jobs with the fantastic starting salaries were reserved for men and women who had graduated from Harvard, Yale, and Columbia law schools. Possibly a few such jobs trickled down to graduates from NYU and Michigan. But not graduates from Fordham, St. John's, or David Kirk's alma mater, New York Law, even graduates like David Kirk, with cum laude attached to their degrees.

Economic pressure afforded David Kirk little time to adjust to reality. He knew one thing for sure: He did not intend to start his life in the law at a menial salary and spend the rest of it in the Bar Association library hunting down cases so that he could write brilliant briefs for other attorneys to argue in court and reap the public renown for their own private gain.

He wanted to be on his own. In the courtroom. Where he was intended to be. He had the gift for it. He could think and talk on his feet. With no false modesty, he knew he was an attractive young man. He had a knack for making people believe he was totally honest, an attribute he had developed one summer when he was seventeen and earned a great deal of money selling Bibles door-to-door across the rural areas along the New York-Pennsylvania border. He could be charming when necessary, glib when it counted.

What he needed was courtroom experience.

The most practical way to get that was to wangle a place on the staff of the district attorney of New York County. His professor of Evidence, who had once worked in the DA's office, was instrumental in having him meet Howard Stone, elder statesman among prosecutors. District Attorneys changed, sometimes with every election, but old Howard Stone remained.

The first time David Kirk met Chief Assistant District Attorney Howard Stone he was impressed by two things: his lean, almost cadaverous look and the bottle of Tums, large size, on his desk alongside the stack of files of cases awaiting trial. Even during that first interview, David saw Howard Stone take two Tums. He wondered how many Stone took during the course of a trial.

He was soon to discover. Whether it was devotion to duty or the frustrations that went with his overtaxing job, Howard Stone lived on antacids. Twice in the course of their association, David Kirk would see Stone carried out of a courtroom on a stretcher due to bleeding ulcers.

Stone had one asset for a senior prosecutor: He could recognize a born litigator when he saw one. So he took young

David Kirk under his wing. Soon he made Kirk his own assistant. Every trial that Stone prosecuted, David Kirk was there in the courtroom at his side. He was there when Stone worked over defense witnesses and cracked many a cleverly concocted alibi. And he was there when Stone, as imposing as Clarence Darrow of old, summed up dramatically before the jury.

The relationship that grew between Howard Stone and David Kirk was more than teacher and protégé. There were times, after Stone had shared with him some special courtroom tricks that were purely his own, that David felt Stone was his second father. His second adoptive father. Whoever his real father had been, he couldn't have been better to him than Dan Kirk or Howard Stone.

After several years of such personal training, Stone began to assign important cases to Kirk, to prepare and try on his own. By the end of that year Stone loaded him down with cases, so that David Kirk went from one trial to another. At times judges had to hold cases over so that David could get to them.

It was after three years of such day-in, day-out trial experience, which honed his courtroom skills to a fine point, that the Gerald Prince case had been handed to him. He had prosecuted it with his usual determination. And his usual success. It became another in his unbroken string of convictions.

The shock of discovering that he had convicted an innocent young man, destroying that boy's reputation and possibly his life, caused David Kirk to rethink his own goals, his own life.

He made a painful decision. Having made it, he walked into Howard Stone's office at the end of a long, tough day and very quietly said, "Howie, don't get excited. And please don't fly off the handle. But I have decided to quit."

"Quit?" Howard Stone asked, as if the word were not in his vocabulary. Automatically, Stone reached for his Tums.

"Resign. Go into private practice," David Kirk said.

"Private practice, eh?" Howard Stone repeated, by his very inflection of distaste passing acid comment on David Kirk's announcement. "You mean you are now going to defend the same crooks, mobsters, drug dealers, whores, pimps, embezzlers and child molesters you have been prosecuting? I have wasted six years training you to join the enemy? Okay, boy, go on! Get out! Get the hell out of my office!"

"Howie, no, you don't understand," he began to protest.

But Stone overrode his attempt. "Don't tell me! I know. You've seen those high-priced criminal lawyers with nowhere near your ability make all that big money. Have big offices in the new high-rises. Pull up to the courthouse in their limos. Have their pictures in the papers and on television. Own spacious apartments on Fifth Avenue or Central Park West. So, you figure, why not you? Well, if that's what you want, go! Grab it. Become a Mafia stooge!"

"Howie, you don't understand."

"Of course I don't understand," Stone shot back. "After all, this is not the first time in my career that I have worked to develop a bright, capable young prosecutor and seen him lured away by the money. The greed."

"Damn it, Howie! Listen to me!" David Kirk declared, half angry, half pleading.

His intensity, the look in his eyes, caused Stone to grant him a moment to state his case.

"Howie, it's . . . it's the Prince case. Gerry Prince. I almost destroyed his life."

Stone tried to brush that argument aside. "We're none of us perfect. Not even you. But it's a shock when you first discover it."

"Howie, you don't get it. I've got that fire. That fire to prosecute. I caught it from you. I go for the kill. Each time.

34

Until it almost doesn't matter if the defendant is guilty or innocent. Once you hand me that file it's like a hunting license. Don't come back without a dead deer slung over my hood. I've become a one-man vigilante squad."

"Come on, kid, stop dramatizing it," Stone replied. "Or the next thing, you'll pull that old refrain on me, 'Better ninety-nine guilty men go free than one innocent man be condemned.' I think that nice-sounding line was invented by criminal lawyers who have figured out those are pretty good odds. Ninety-nine guilty clients each at a good fat fee is surely much more profitable than one innocent one. And, once you get the guilty ones off, think of the repeat business. Kid, you're probably overworked and need some time off. And maybe a frequent roll in the hay with the right woman."

"Howie!" David Kirk exploded. "What I am trying to say is that I want to defend people from prosecutors like I've become! Prosecutors like you!"

That outburst was followed by a long, deathly quiet, after which Howard Stone took two more pills, then said, very softly, "I accept your resignation. Now get out."

Once David Kirk had left the district attorney's office he started his own practice in a one-room office that he sublet from a small firm of lawyers in an old office building near City Hall and most of the courthouses. A far cry from the elegant quarters that Howard Stone had accused him of coveting. He had the part-time services of one of the secretaries in the office pool. She was Greta Nissman.

When his modest practice, consisting of defending small-time hoods, prostitutes and the indigent assigned to him by the court had grown to the point where he could afford an office of his own, he took Greta along with him.

The thrill of hanging up his law-school diploma and his

license to practice law on the walls of his own office, in his own small suite, made him wish that Mom and Dad could have been there to share that moment with him.

Dan Kirk would have said, "Son, you make your old man proud." There would have been an embrace and a kiss on the cheek. An embarrassed kiss. For Daniel Kirk, with all his love, had always been awkward at such moments.

Within a few years David Kirk's practice had begun to flourish. His reputation grew steadily in the legal community, and, as important, in the criminal community as well. Cases of a more serious nature, involving defendants of means, began to be referred to him. Large law firms, which preferred not to have their names appear in criminal cases, referred their clients to him. Some of those firms were the same ones that had refused to hire him years ago.

In addition, his reputation for success had attracted many cases of worthy but penniless defendants who could not afford a lawyer of his ability and reputation. Though he could not take them all—no man could—he did his share, resulting in days when Greta Nissman complained, "Surely there must be worthy defendants who are also well-to-do."

Kirk did not openly agree with her, though he shared the sentiment.

He could be said to have truly arrived at his present prominence after he defended the young son of a wealthy Long Island builder, who was on trial for murdering a girl he had been going out with. There was overwhelming proof that the young man had indeed committed the act. The question was one of motive and circumstances.

David Kirk had presented what was considered at the time a novel, if not revolutionary, defense: accidental death in the course of consensual sex, heightened by resort to violence.

With unlimited funds at his disposal, Kirk had been able to introduce days of psychiatric testimony to that effect. In the end he had raised sufficient doubt in the minds of the jurors so that the legal requirement of proving guilt beyond a reasonable doubt could not be sustained.

On the day of that acquittal, David Kirk, who had refused to comment on camera during the trial, gave New York television the most exciting and impressive opening segments to the six o'clock news in many months.

Handsome, fluent, graceful, charming, he became a well-known personality overnight. From that time on David Kirk was a man immediately recognizable wherever he appeared. He was sought out for his opinion on cases of interest, whether he was involved in them or not.

In circles where crime was the principal business, even those who could not remember his name would say, "Hey, dis time I think we better get that good-looking TV lawyer."

He had finally arrived at the point in his career where he could pick and choose his cases. He made his own rules now. No drug-bust cases. No preponderance of organized-crime cases. He was determined not to be beholden to and eventually dominated by Mob interests.

If he now had his choice of cases, he was even more successful with women, when he found the time. With his prominence came requests and demands to lend his name to civic and charitable causes. He was delighted to be able to comply. More than once he made substantial contributions to worthy causes in the memory of Claire and Daniel Kirk.

Charities were always run by women of means who had time and money to give. And many who had more than money to give. Some were divorcées of husbands who had been too involved with their own businesses. Some were women of means who chose never to marry. Some were career women who were as eager for success as was David Kirk himself. But almost all of them were the most attractive women in New York, whose candid photos, taken at charity and public-service affairs, were featured in newspapers and magazines the country over.

But the demands of his career came before all else. His life as a sought-after criminal lawyer was hectic and all-consuming, especially when he was on trial, which was most of the time. It was a seven-day-a-week, twenty-hour-a-day grind. Few women had the patience to wait it out, as he discovered in a very painful way. Any woman, especially a wife, was entitled to more than "Darling, you have to understand . . ." Perhaps he should have been more understanding. *Next time,* he promised himself. *Next time I'll do it differently.*

If, after many hours spent preparing arguments, grilling witnesses, framing cross-examinations, going over reams of the previous day's testimony, he arrived at his Fifth Avenue apartment late at night or early in the morning, he could admit to a twinge of loneliness. But he consoled himself with the thought that at least he owed no one explanations, apologies or the obligation to make love when he felt too tired to.

He liked his life. Liked his freedom. Liked being alone. Even liked being lonely.

It did not occur to him that he was a little too defiant about it.

All this was part of the history that David Kirk carried with him as he called on Assistant DA Howard Stone to learn about the crime with which his new client, Christopher Cory, was charged.

"Good afternoon, 'Counselor,' " Stone greeted him as he entered the office, which was still in the same disarray Kirk recalled so vividly. Stacks of files. Bottle of white pills. Obviously Howie had switched antacids.

He noted that Stone had deliberately pronounced *Counselor* in much the same way as some of his criminal clients. Kirk smiled as pleasantly as he could under the circumstances and returned the greeting. "Hi, Howie, how's it going?"

"Same as usual," Stone responded, shifting in his same old swivel chair that creaked in the same old way. Pretending he had no inkling of Kirk's mission, he asked, "Well, Davey, what brings you here on this sunny afternoon when you should be out enjoying the fruits of your arduous labors in the vineyards of the law? A little golf, perhaps? Or basking on the beaches of East Hampton surrounded by a bevy of bare-chested beauties who dance attendance upon you? Is that where I read in *People* magazine or *Vanity Fair* that you go when you can snatch a few days off between very profitable trials? East Hampton? Bermuda? Palm Beach? Or is it Palm Springs?"

Ignoring that jibe at some recent publicity that had been showered on him after his victory in defense of a man reputed to be the current godfather of a Mafia family, Kirk responded in crisp, businesslike fashion, "You are holding a man named Christopher Cory. I have been appointed to defend him."

"So, old Malachi is trying to make an honest man of you," Stone replied, smiling. "Well, Davey, you may be sure I will do my best to cooperate. Where would you like to start?"

"The charges against Cory. May I see the file?"

As if it were sheer coincidence, Stone replied, "I just happen to have it here." He pointed to the single file on the center of his otherwise cluttered desk.

Apparently, Kirk realized, his little skirmish with Judge Malachi had gotten around the legal fraternity faster than he had expected. He reached for the file, started to thumb through it. Before he had finished the second page he looked up at Stone.

"Do you mean to say that in a homicide case this man was questioned without the presence of an attorney?"

"Seems he was offered an attorney but refused," Stone explained, pointing in the direction of the file. "It's all in there. What's more, 'Counselor,' he does not particularly want a lawyer now."

Kirk allowed that to pass as so much tactical jockeying. He read on. As he turned another page, the very first item on the top caused him to glance at Stone. "Without his being represented by an attorney, you drew his blood for a DNA? Come on, Howie!"

"I told you, he did not want an attorney. When we asked for a blood sample, instead of refusing, he volunteered."

"What the hell is going on?"

"Just what I told you. He refused an attorney. He volunteered his blood sample. If you don't believe me, ask him yourself."

"He must be out of his mind!" Kirk replied. "You took advantage of an insane man!"

"If you are thinking of pleading insanity, I can assure you Christopher Cory is as sane as you or I," Stone replied.

"I've got to talk to him. Now!"

"Before you do, wouldn't you like to read that whole file?" Stone suggested.

"I don't have to. I can imagine what your boys did with a suspect so naïve," Kirk replied.

Stone smiled. "I will save you the trouble, 'Counselor.' What we have on your man is a positive ID from a neighbor of the victim. Who is very familiar with the situation, since your man was living there with the victim some months before the killing. The neighbor saw your client enter the apartment on the day of the murder. And if that is not enough, we have a print at the scene. Not a fingerprint but a palm print. Left when one of the surgical gloves your client was wearing at the time ripped during the commission of the crime."

David Kirk was about to respond when Stone continued: "And how do we know the glove was ripped? He evidently got pissed off that it ripped, so he tore it off and flung it halfway across the room, where Homicide found it."

"That's it?" Kirk asked casually, trying to trivialize evidence that he knew would prove overwhelming in the courtroom.

"No, 'Counselor,' that is *not* it," Stone replied. "They

also found a spot of blood the size of a Kennedy half-dollar. Blood that did not match the victim's. If your client's DNA matches that, we will have what we consider a very strong case. Or is the proper word *conclusive* case?"

"Weapon?" Kirk asked, resorting to the one definitive element Stone had not mentioned.

As if reminded, but actually delighted that Kirk had taken the bait, Stone replied, "Oh, yes, we did happen to find the weapon. A carving knife. Very appropriate, considering the gruesome nature of the crime. In the trash can at the foot of the stairs outside the brownstone where the victim lived . . . and died."

"Prints?" Kirk asked.

"All over it. Don't forget he ripped off one surgical glove at the scene," Stone reminded.

"I want to see him. Right away," Kirk said.

"Frankly, 'Counselor,' if he were my client, so would I. Though, I told you, he doesn't want a lawyer. Not really."

"We'll see about that," David Kirk replied.

Five

David Kirk paced impatiently in the small conference room set aside for private consultation between accused and their counsel. Over the years he had spent many hours in such rooms. The furniture was always the same. A small bare table with burn marks where abandoned cigarettes had fallen out of ashtrays. A few chairs, straight-backed and spindly. The stench of old tobacco smoke, although the sign declared NO

SMOKING! The stench, not as oppressive as it used to be, was still powerful.

Kirk had laid out his yellow pad and his gold pen, a gift from a grateful client. When he received it he would have given it away, but he couldn't. It had not merely his initials but his full name engraved on it. He always used it with a sense of guilt suspecting it had been bought and mono-grammed with the proceeds of the crime from which he had been able to exonerate that client. As lawyers do, he had resorted to the ethics of his profession: *It is not your obligation to judge your client, only to defend him.*

The sound of the door brought him alert to his present situation. He rose to meet his new client. Instead of the man he expected, who would commit a bloody crime, Christopher Cory was a nice-looking, clean-cut young man, blond, in his mid-twenties. He was quite lean but well proportioned. His blue shirt and dark slacks hung loose on him. He must have lost considerable weight during his four days of incarceration.

Kirk invited him to an empty chair. Cory started forward, faltering just before he reached it. Kirk jumped up to catch him, but Cory made it without help. Instead of sitting down he gripped the back of the chair, stood breathless for an in-stant. The muscles in his lean face tightened as if it took great effort merely to sit down.

"You okay, Cory?"

"Yes, sir," he replied; then, unable to conceal his pain, he admitted, "except for the headaches. Do you happen to have some aspirin with you? I've been begging for aspirin, Tylenol, anything, for four days now. They won't give me any."

David Kirk thought, Naïve *is a small word for this young man. He has certainly never had any contact with the police or the jail system in this city if he thinks you just ask for medication or a doctor and get it. He's in for quite an education.*

"I'll see that you get some aspirin."

"Right away? Please? I don't like to complain, but you have no idea how bad these headaches are," Cory said, embarrassed at having to admit to such need.

"Soon as I leave," Kirk promised. "But first, a few things I need to know."

"I'll do the best I can," Cory said, gripping the edge of the table in response to a surge of fresh pain.

"First, at the time of your apprehension, did they notify you of your rights?"

"Yes. Said I could have an attorney. Didn't have to answer any questions. Didn't have to give any blood. They did all that! Now, what else, please? Because this pain is killing me!"

"At the time of your apprehension—"

"Mr. Kirk, why do you keep calling it 'apprehension'? They came in and arrested me. I'm at work. In the middle of developing the most fantastic set of prints of scenes I'd shot earlier that morning. . . . Dawn at Battery Park."

Kirk interrupted sharply. "Cory! Forget the semantics! Apprehension, arrest, the question is, at the time they took you into custody, at the time you waived your rights, gave that blood sample, were you suffering from these severe headaches?"

"The headaches started from the time they brought me down here," Cory said.

"*Before* they questioned you?" Kirk said, wanting to pin him down.

"Not before, during," Cory replied.

"During," Kirk evaluated. Not so helpful a response as he had hoped to elicit. But, with a little suggestion, that could change.

Funny how a client's memory could become clearer and more accommodating once the attorney "explained" the legal pitfalls in the original answers.

"Look, Mr. Kirk, I'm sorry. But unless I get something

for this headache I can't go on. My head is splitting in two! Like it's going to explode! So, please, please!"

"Okay, Cory. Just tell me one thing, and it's better if I know it now than later," Kirk said.

"Anything. I have nothing to hide," Cory said.

"The truth! Did you kill her?" Kirk asked bluntly.

"I didn't do it. I couldn't have done it. I was never even there. I swear to God, I swear," Cory insisted.

David Kirk had heard that denial, in almost those same words, many times before. Usually he discounted it as a self-serving lie.

This time the earnestness in Cory's blue eyes convinced him. They reminded him of the look in the eyes of fifteen-year-old Gerald Prince when he had persisted in his innocence. David Kirk would never be able to resist that look, that plea.

"Okay, kid, I'll do my best for you."

To comfort and reassure him, Kirk reached out to pat him on the shoulder. As he did, Cory's eyes turned upward until only the whites were visible. He slid to the floor.

Kirk dropped to one knee, turned Cory faceup to make sure he was breathing. Slowly Cory came to to find David Kirk leaning over him.

"What . . . what happened?" Cory asked.

"You just blacked out for a second. How do you feel?"

"I don't know. All right, I guess."

"Tell me, Cory, this ever happen to you before?"

"Yeah. Sometimes," he admitted.

"Look, kid, I'll drop some aspirin by for you right away. And I'll have my own doctor see you before the day is over," Kirk promised. "Meantime, one last question. Why were you so quick to surrender your rights, answer their questions, give them a blood sample?"

"I'm innocent. If I refused to answer, refused to give them blood, that could be considered a sign of guilt. Couldn't it?"

Man, Kirk thought, *talk about naïve. Give me an experienced criminal for a client anytime. Better go back and have another look at that file on Howie Stone's desk. But first, call Dr. Heldeman.*

———————————

At a quarter past seven that evening, while Dr. Julian Heldeman was examining Christopher Cory in his cell, David Kirk and Gerry Prince were in the DA's office poring over the file that Assistant DA Stone had made available to them in accordance with the Criminal Code of the State of New York. All incriminating, as well as exculpatory, evidence in the hands of the prosecution must be made available to the defendant's attorneys.

With the entire file before them, Kirk and Gerry were able to draw a complete picture of the case against Christopher Cory.

An actress named Alice Ames, twenty-two years old, very pretty, sexually attractive, was found murdered in her small apartment in Greenwich Village.

The murder was bloody. There was evidence of a bitter struggle, leaving the small one-bedroom apartment in a shambles.

Neighbors told of hearing a struggle and the young woman's voice being raised.

Forensics had picked up a palm print on the victim, on the knife the murderer used and on several articles in the apartment, which lent credibility to the suspicion that the murderer came prepared to kill. He was wearing surgical gloves at the start of the attack. One of them ripped in the course of the commission of the crime, exposing part of the palm, the print that was picked up by routine dusting.

Questioning of neighbors and friends of the deceased led Homicide detectives to a young man named Christopher

Cory, who had lived with the deceased for some months preceding the murder. Cory was now being held pending presentation of the case to the grand jury of New York County.

Homicide also discovered that Cory had left some clothes at a dry cleaner's a few days after the murder. Clothes that had previously been washed, though they were wool. There were still traces of the victim's blood on those clothes.

Opportunity, weapon and other forensic evidence being present, the only missing element to prove and convict was motive, which was satisfied with a little more digging.

Alice Ames had met Cory in acting class. They had started going together. Then they started living together.

A few months before the murder Cory had left the acting class. At the same time their affair ended and she forced him to move out.

Friends of Alice Ames told the police that Cory had made several attempts at reconciliation, but she would not relent.

That had supplied sufficient motive for Howard Stone to present the case to the grand jury.

Kirk was about to close the file when Howie Stone ducked his head in the doorway. Even before he spoke, Kirk knew the news was not good.

"Thought you guys would like to know. Just got the lab report on your client's DNA. It's a match with the blood we found at the scene."

Before he closed the door, Howie directed his last words to Gerry Prince: "Kid, anytime you get the urge to go straight, let me know. Can always use a bright young man around here."

Howie left the two attorneys alone.

"Doesn't add up, Gerry. The facts and the Chris Cory I met just don't match. He's not like any killer I've ever represented."

"That's hardly a defense," Gerry Prince pointed out.

Later that evening, David Kirk met with Dr. Heldeman, who reported that he could find no etiology for Cory's headaches. He had left with him a very strong pain reliever, and he felt sure that the pain would respond to it. But it was only a temporary measure. The cause was likely neurological, which included the possibility of brain involvement, possibly a tumor that could present as a first symptom just such severe headaches. Further medical investigation was indicated.

Heldeman recommended the neurologist to whom he referred his own patients, a Dr. Ramon Lipsky. The equipment necessary for a complete neurological exam not being available in jail, it would be necessary to have Cory released for several hours.

Since they had to wait until morning to apply for such permission, Kirk decided to make the most of Cory's pain-free hours to continue their questioning.

With Cory seated opposite them, Kirk realized how much more self-possessed he was once free of pain. Kirk allowed Gerry to open the questioning while he himself studied their client.

"Chris, you are fully aware of the crime with which you are charged?" Gerry Prince asked.

"They say I killed Alice," Cory replied, "which is impossible since I wasn't even there. So how could I have killed her?"

"They also say you attacked her body after she was dead."

"I raped her after she was dead? Man, that's crazy. I would never do such a thing. Never!" Cory protested.

"Not raped her," Gerry corrected, "inflicted a wound on her. The kind of wound that indicated you started to dismember her but stopped. As if interrupted. Or you changed your mind."

"Oh, I get it," Cory replied. "This is your idea, Mr. Kirk! I know about you from TV and the newspapers. You're the best. You come up with defenses that other lawyers would never even dream of. So this dismembering thing is one of your gimmicks. Right? You are trying to make me out to be crazy. Well, you've got the wrong client. I never killed Alice. I never saw her on that day or for months before that. I don't know what you're talking about, any of you. Not the police, not the DA, not you!"

Cory began to breathe laboredly, his hands clutched the table. Kirk realized his headaches had returned, so he came directly to the point.

"Chris, if you weren't anywhere near the scene on the night of the murder, where were you?"

"That's the strange part," Cory admitted slowly. "I can't remember."

"With friends? To see a film? At home watching television?" Kirk suggested.

"I can't remember," Cory replied. "That's the truth. If I was guilty, you can be damn sure I would have an alibi. I just can't remember."

Gerry glanced at David Kirk, a look that said, *I can just see Howie Stone take that one apart.*

Silently, Kirk agreed. Aloud he said, "Well, maybe it'll come to you. Work on it."

"The fact that I can't remember . . . I hope that won't discourage you."

"Discourage me?" Kirk asked, puzzled.

"I mean, that you'll continue to represent me."

"Of course we'll continue to represent you," Kirk reassured him.

"Thanks. Because I've never felt more alone, never needed someone to believe in me, more than I do now. I'm just getting my life together after Alice and I split up. I'd made up my mind, given up the acting. That's such a hit-or-miss career.

If you don't get that big break, that part that can make you a star, you become one of the herd. Subject to the whims of directors and producers. Work a week at a time, go unemployed for weeks, or months. So I gave it up. Matured, if you want to call it. Decided to go into photography. And I'm getting good at it. Real good. The day before I was arrested, the art director at *Vogue* called my work terrific. She's lining up a shoot for me. Even said she might want me to do a cover for them. I've got a whole new life waiting for me, Mr. Kirk. So, you've got to get me out of this. You've got to! I've got a life now. I want a chance to live it."

Recalling his own early years, and the passion of a young man on the verge of a career, David Kirk promised, "Kid, we'll do everything we can for you. The main thing, be honest with me at all times. And don't give up!"

"I hear you, Mr. Kirk," Cory replied, obviously enormously reassured.

Six

The next morning, before court sessions began, David Kirk presented himself at Judge Malachi's chambers to ask for an order granting prisoner Christopher Cory permission to visit Dr. Ramon Lipsky at his office up at the Neurological Institute of Columbia Presbyterian Hospital on Washington Heights.

Malachi wheeled himself to his desk to sign the permission while remarking in his low gruff voice, "This better not be one of your tricks, Davey, my boy!"

Relieved to obtain permission with less trouble than he had anticipated, David Kirk refrained from responding.

Dr. Ramon Lipsky was a frail man, not from age but from abusive treatment he had received in his youth in the Central American country from which he had been liberated through the intervention of the International Rescue Committee.

Lipsky said very little, speaking only when necessary to elicit some information from Cory. Occasionally he stopped to give thoughtful consideration to some affect he had just witnessed. But he said nothing.

When Kirk thought the examination was finally completed, Lipsky said, "Now the EEG." He pressed the buzzer on the intercom on his desk. "Miss Murphy, time now."

The nurse entered, led Cory out.

Once alone, Kirk had a chance to ask, "Well, Dr. Lipsky, what do you think?"

"Frankly, from my own personal experience in jail, if this man did *not* have a headache he would not be normal."

"Are you saying there is no physical or neurological cause for his headaches?" Kirk asked.

"Not that I could discover. And I can promise you now that his EEG will not reveal any brain abnormalities."

"Which, from a legal point of view, means what?" Kirk persisted.

Lipsky looked up from making his notes on Cory's chart to say, "Mr. Kirk, back in my old country, I did not get into trouble for practicing medicine. I was what they call politically active. So I am an inveterate reader of newspapers. Therefore, I know who you are. And what you are famous for. Also, I know why you brought your Mr. Cory here. To find some neurological basis for his defense. Sorry. When the EEG comes back, I will show you why."

In half an hour the nurse brought Cory back, and with him a sheaf of graph papers on which were tracings indicating the condition of his brain.

Lipsky held out the papers to Kirk. "If you know about these things, you can see for yourself. Otherwise, what I said before stands. No brain abnormality. And if that means no legal defense, sorry."

"To hell with that!" Cory exploded. "My headaches! Do something about my headaches!"

Lipsky did not respond to Cory but addressed David Kirk. "His headaches may be entirely psychosomatic. Probably are, considering his situation and the fact that there appears no other cause. I would suggest consulting a psychiatrist."

"What about a brain scan or an MRI?" Kirk urged.

Lipsky shrugged. "You could try. But I doubt it would reveal anything we do not already know. But let a psychiatrist decide that."

"Can you recommend one?" Kirk asked, then qualified his request. "A *forensic* psychiatrist?"

"Naturally, one with courtroom experience," Lipsky responded. "Dr. Wilson. Charles Wilson. A very good man."

Lipsky scribbled the name on a prescription pad, tore off the slip and handed it to Kirk.

For five days—one hour on each of the first four days and three hours on the fifth day—Dr. Charles Wilson met with Christopher Cory. He asked questions, evaluated Cory's responses. When he had gathered all his data and arrived at his conclusions, he met with David Kirk.

Kirk's first question was, "His headaches, have you been able to do anything about that?"

"They seem to have diminished somewhat," Wilson reported. "But they are still present. However, he presents a very strange picture."

"Enough to justify a defense?" Kirk asked at once. "I have to know as soon as possible. Because, according to the criminal code—"

Wilson cut in, "Yes, I know. If you are going to plead mental condition you must notify the DA within thirty days after his arraignment."

"Which is set for this coming Wednesday," Kirk pointed out. "So your findings are crucial right now."

"That's not the problem, Mr. Kirk," Dr. Wilson replied. "His reactions to all my tests are as normal as yours or mine. But there is something strange."

"If strange is the same as not quite normal, that's enough for me," Kirk said seizing on Wilson's words.

"I could not testify that this man is insane or deranged or even somewhat abnormal. All I can say is, his case is baffling."

"Baffling?" Kirk repeated. "*Baffling* is not a word that will impress a judge or a jury."

"Exactly," Wilson agreed.

"Can you suggest what I do now?" Kirk asked.

"I was just about to do that," Wilson said, then recanted. "No, I was really about to say, 'See John Beaumont, he's the best.' I've been so used to saying that over the past twenty-two years. Except that Beaumont is gone. But his assistant is excellent. And, like Beaumont, highly expert in hypnosis."

"Hypnosis?" Kirk was puzzled.

"It might be indicated in a case like this. And Dr. Scott is as good as they come. As I said, trained by Beaumont, who was the best."

"Dr. Scott," Kirk repeated.

"I will have my secretary call your office and give them the phone number," Wilson promised.

"Thanks," Kirk said, resigned to his frustration. As he started for the door he could not resist the need to ask, "Doctor, what about his terrible headaches?"

"Most definitely of a psychosomatic origin," Wilson replied. "The best we can do is try to ameliorate them with various medications. But unless the deeply rooted cause is uncovered, his headaches will persist."

"Nothing more can be done?" Kirk asked.

"If it can, Dr. Scott will be the one who can do it," Wilson said. "That is, if my suspicion proves correct."

"Tell me, do you believe Cory? Do you believe he is innocent?"

"I believe that he believes he is innocent," Wilson responded.

"Exactly what does that mean?" Kirk asked.

"Have Dr. Scott see him," was all that Wilson would add.

———————

Two days later, while in the midst of dictating a motion for a directed verdict of acquittal in a stock-fraud case, David Kirk suddenly interrupted himself to say, "Disturbs the hell out of me, Greta."

After years of putting up with the quirks of his overactive mind, Greta replied matter-of-factly, "I'll run this through the computer. Read it over. If it still disturbs you, maybe let Gerry take a crack at it."

"Not this memo, but Cory. How the hell could he go totally blank like that?"

"You've had other clients who went 'blank' when it was convenient," Greta reminded him pointedly.

"Those were intentional. Cory really went blank. Total amnesia about that whole day and the next two days," Kirk replied, then snapped suddenly, "Get hold of Lannigan. Have him check out Cory's early background."

"Lannigan costs money," the penurious office manager Greta pointed out. "And this is an assigned case."

"So we'll bear the expense. I've got to help that kid. Get Lannigan on it right away," Kirk ordered. "Now, where were we?"

"Therefore, in the face of such undisputed testimony . . ." Greta recalled to him.

Kirk resumed dictating.

Several days later Francis Lannigan, retired New York City police officer, who was now putting his talents and experience to less hazardous and more profitable use, was in Kirk's office reporting, "I'll tell you, Dave, it's a strange picture." He referred to his pocket notebook. "For example, he is popular enough to be elected president of his senior class in high school. Then he is expelled before graduation."

"What for?" Kirk demanded.

"Lying."

"About what?" Kirk asked.

"That part is vague," Lannigan was forced to concede. "The teacher involved is no longer at the school. But according to the written record in Cory's file it had to do with a girl. The details were either lost or were left unstated, probably to protect the girl."

"Anything else?" Kirk asked.

"He got a job in the local supermarket. First as a packer. Then he was promoted to checkout. Again he was expelled. Though this time of course they called it fired."

"What for?"

"This is the funny part. Not for stealing. Not for short-changing customers. But for lying. That's what the record says: 'lying.' Seems this character is an inveterate liar."

"Inveterate liar . . ." Kirk rose from his desk chair and started pacing. "Cory's testimony won't be worth a plugged nickel if Stone ever gets hold of his record."

"He already has," Lannigan reported. Kirk turned to ask, but Lannigan anticipated him. "He had a man out there the day after Cory's arrest."

"He would," Kirk granted grudgingly. "*Thorough* is the word for old Howie."

"Sorry, Dave, but those are the facts. Anything else you want me to run down on him?"

"That's enough for now, Frank. Thanks. And send your bill to Greta."

David Kirk was pacing the length of his spacious office declaring, "Gerry, with his arraignment two days away I'd like to at least formulate a theory of a defense. What do we have? Overwhelming forensic evidence against him. Positive ID from witnesses who know him. His failed memory. And the fact that he is evidently capable, popular and he lies. What the hell kind of defense can we build on that?"

"Maybe the best thing is a deal," Gerry suggested.

"Deal? A sexy case, good for nightly leadoff on the TV news and with such solid evidence, Howie Stone would laugh me out of his office. Besides, old Malachi is watching me like a hawk on this one. He would accuse me of trying to duck out by making a deal. He expects a defense. A good, strong defense. Which we, unfortunately, do not have. Besides . . ."

"I know," Gerry anticipated. "Even if we could get him a plea, a young naïve kid like Cory, seven or eight years in jail, what would happen to him there, his life might as well be over."

"Can't let that happen, can't," Kirk said. He dropped

into his desk chair, picked up his messages. As usual, Louise, his second secretary, had arranged them in order of importance.

The top one read: "Dr. Michael Scott returned your call."

"Gerry, who the hell is Dr. Michael Scott, and why would I have called him?"

"Didn't Wilson suggest a Dr. Scott?" Gerry recalled.

"Right." Kirk lifted his phone. "Louise, get Dr. Scott for me."

Moments later his phone rang.

"Dr. Scott's secretary asked if you can come to the office at six o'clock Wednesday evening, next week."

"Next week?" Kirk protested. "We are working under a strict statutory time limit. Thirty days after arraignment, which is set for the day after tomorrow. Can't he do it any sooner?"

"His secretary sounds like a very nice woman. But she is also very precise and rather firm. She said it couldn't be any sooner."

Since no other doctor had been able to come up with a diagnosis that would even hint at a defense, in all likelihood neither would Scott. So time did not seem to matter all that much, Kirk decided.

"Might as well make the date. Get the address."

Seven

When David Kirk was on trial, his chauffeured limousine was on call twenty-four hours a day. It allowed him to concentrate on his case instead of on the minor inconveniences of living in a city as large and hectic as New York. It transported him to the office as early as five or six in the morning, and stood ready to whisk him off to court in time for the start of the ten o'clock session. If, during trial, he had need for some volume from his law library, the same limo could speed Gerry to the office and back with the vital legal tome in time for Kirk to use it in arguing a point of evidence with the judge.

On Wednesday evening, at a quarter to six, David Kirk slipped into the limousine. Tired after a long day in court, he was not looking forward to a meeting with Dr. Scott. He glanced at the name and address Louise had neatly typed out for him: "Dr. Michael Scott. 112 East Seventy-third Street."

The fact that the usually efficient Louise had not noted an apartment number meant that Dr. Scott had his office on the ground floor of a large apartment house. Or else he occupied one of the impressive private homes on Seventy-third Street, which were remnants of a time when the streets from Fifth Avenue to Park Avenue were a succession of impressive private homes of the wealthy.

When the limousine pulled up at number 112, Kirk discovered that his second surmise was correct. It was a sturdy, impressive white stone private residence, four stories high, with considerable frontage on the street. No doubt both the professional and the personal abode of the doctor.

Kirk was about to dismiss the driver but reconsidered. If it became apparent early in his meeting that Scott could offer nothing new toward a defense, Kirk would not waste time by extending the session and adding to Scott's undoubtedly high fee. Psychiatrists, like lawyers, insisted on being paid by the clock.

"Wait for me, Geraldo. I don't think I'll be long."

He approached the door of 112 with a suspicion that the house was locked for the night. Then he consulted the slip Louise had handed him. The date was right. The time, six o'clock, was right. Kirk stared through the glass panels along-side the solid front door. The entryway was dark. Perhaps Dr. Scott had forgotten about the meeting.

Kirk debated leaving, but figured that, having come this far, the least he could do was ring. He found the bell, pressed it once, waited, then pressed it again. There was no response.

He was about to turn back to the limo, thankful that he had had Geraldo wait, when a light went on in the rear of the entryway. A woman came out of the darkness to approach the front door. To avoid being caught prying, Kirk retreated behind the solid door. It was opened by a tall blond woman who was attired in a trim tailored suit of gray plaid. She wore a white shirt that, but for its ruffle, might well have been a man's shirt. Instead of a tie, she wore a red crepe bow at her throat.

"I'm here to see Dr. Scott."

"I know," the woman said.

Kirk detected a slight smile on her rather pleasant face. *In fact,* he thought, *if she weren't wearing such heavy-framed glasses she would be considered beautiful. Which, come to think of it, might be the reason she was so late answering the door. Could it be she is more than Scott's very nice, precise secretary, as Louise had described her?*

Dutifully he followed the woman to a tiny elevator that would carry them to the second floor. The elevator was so slow and the car so small that he had the chance to observe her very closely. She appeared to be in her early or mid-thirties. Her blond hair, neatly and intricately braided, hung halfway down the back of her tailored jacket. The odor of her perfume was quite feminine, but neither oversweet nor cloying. It was, like the woman herself, distinctive but not overly feminine.

When the elevator door opened, she led the way to a large private office. One look told Kirk that when this house was built almost a century ago, this had been the ballroom. It was large enough, with a marble fireplace occupying the entire far wall. The ceiling was ornately carved. The walls of linenfold oak were of a kind no longer produced for sheer lack of craftsmanship. Much of the paneling was covered by bookshelves lined with technical and professional volumes.

The side of the room opposite to and facing the fireplace was occupied by a large antique oak desk inlaid with red leather and adorned with gold leaf that had long ago begun to fade.

Most noticeable on the desk was a sterling silver double frame holding the portrait photographs of two men, one patrician and mature, the other young and ruggedly handsome.

He was studying those photographs when the woman said very briskly, "Mr, Kirk!" as she gestured him to the red leather side chair. He felt that in some way he had been rebuked for staring at the two portraits.

Once he was seated, instead of summoning Dr. Scott, she took her place in the high-backed leather desk chair.

"Well, now, about your client," she began.

Long unaccustomed to dealing with intermediaries, David Kirk replied, "It may be Dr. Scott's procedure to have a secretary conduct the preliminary interview. But, with no disrespect, I don't have time for preliminaries. I am a very busy attorney."

"I see that *your* secretary made the usual mistake. Did she tell you I am Dr. *Michael* Scott?"

"Yes," Kirk said, reaching into his pocket for the neatly typed slip Louise had handed him.

She glanced at it and said, "Happens all the time, Mr. Kirk. My father was a Bible reading Presbyterian. He named me Michal. Without the *e* and pronounced 'Me-call.' The bane of my life ever since. Through college, and medical school, my records were always being 'corrected' by some helpful person. In my freshman year I was assigned to a male dormitory. And rushed by four different fraternities."

"Did it ever occur to you that might not have been by mistake?" Kirk observed, smiling.

Instead of returning his smile, Dr. Scott reproved, "Mr. Kirk, there is no need to resort to what is obviously your usual line of flattery to women upon whose abilities you have need to depend."

That set the tone for the rest of the meeting.

Scott had been fully briefed by Wilson on his findings and suspicions, therefore she informed him, "Mr. Kirk, it's obvious a case like this will take considerably more than a single session or two. I will need to see your client every day for some days. So, the first thing will be for you to get him out on bail."

"Get him out on bail?" Kirk bristled. "A young man, unattached, no strong roots in the community, charged with not only murder but a particularly bloody murder . . . I don't know."

"I'd be willing to appear before the judge and explain," Scott volunteered.

"That's very kind of you," Kirk said, then warned, "Doctor, you realize in a case like this, assigned by the court, there isn't the money available for usual expert fees."

"I'm not interested in this case for monetary reasons. But because, from what Wilson told me, I think it might prove helpful for a new textbook I am working on. To complete the series."

"Complete the series?" Kirk remarked. "How many textbooks do you have to your credit?"

"Six," she replied.

"Being as attractive as you are, how do you find the time?" Her sharp look forced him to apologize. "Sorry. I shall never again say anything flattering or even faintly complimentary."

She did not respond with a smile, or even a glint of amusement in her gray eyes. She said firmly, "Get your man out on bail. It's the only way I can work with him."

"Do my best," Kirk promised.

Though she had given him the clear impression that the interview was over, he lingered long enough to ask one more question.

"Dr. Wilson said you were expert with hypnosis. Would you do one thing for me? Put Cory under. Make him recollect where he was at the time of the crime. It is crucial that he remember," Kirk emphasized.

"The fact that he *can't* remember is what is crucial to me," Dr. Scott replied.

She turned back to the manuscript she had been editing when he arrived. Kirk realized it was her way of informing him that the interview was over.

He rose, stopping only to take a last glance at the two photographs. She looked up, as if she treated his curiosity as an intrusion on her privacy.

He left without another word.

Eight

The hearing in the matter of bail for defendant Christopher Cory was held in chambers at the insistence of Judge Aaron Malachi.

Kirk's presentation was brief. True, his client was charged with murder in the second degree. But he had no previous criminal record. Had never proved to be a danger to the community. And had resided in the city and in the borough of Manhattan for the past six years. Since the purpose of bail was not punishment but to ensure that the defendant would appear for trial, his client was bailable by the usual tests. Even such a gangland boss as John Gotti had been granted bail the first two times he was tried on charges that included multiple murders.

Further, Kirk argued, in this case there was another reason to grant bail. His client still suffered severe intractable headaches. According to several doctors whose statements Kirk presented to the judge, these headaches were likely of psychosomatic etiology. The opinion of one well-regarded expert, Dr. Wilson, was that the defendant's condition was so obscure and troubling that specialized psychiatric exploration was needed. The doctor he recommended was Dr. Michal Scott.

"And Dr. Scott says that the treatment of the defendant will require a number of frequent sessions. Which would be impossible while he is confined. So bail becomes a matter of the defendant's health, possibly his life."

Howie Stone smiled, shaking his head in obvious amused disbelief. "Your Honor, please ask counsel if he is seriously arguing that his client is about to expire from headaches."

Stone had resorted to such formal indirect manner of address to emphasize his total ridicule of Kirk's argument.

"Your Honor," Kirk replied, "in his present condition my client will not be able to cooperate in his own defense."

Stone exploded in a burst of laughter. "So, now headaches are a form of mental incapacity sufficient to constitute a defense."

"Your Honor, I am not pleading insanity as a defense. But I do insist that Cory's headaches are of such severity that he cannot function with a clear enough mind to cooperate in his own defense. Therefore, he cannot receive the legal representation the Constitution guarantees."

"Sounds reasonable," Malachi conceded, turning to Stone to hear his reply.

"Your Honor, if ever I have seen a case in which the proof of guilt is clear beyond the shadow of any doubt, it is this case. Every piece of forensic evidence condemns the man. In my opinion this headache bit is a choreographed piece of playacting. Not exactly foreign to some of eminent counsel's previous defenses."

"I resent the imputation that I would attempt to foist on this court a false set of facts to secure bail for a client on a murder charge," Kirk shot back.

"I'm sorry," Stone pretended to apologize. "I did not intend to 'impute' anything. I damn well intended to say that I accuse counsel of cooking up this headache routine. Your Honor, consider the evidence. Defendant's prints at the scene. DNA blood match. Visual identification, entering the scene of the crime. This is a textbook case. Yet counsel has the chutzpah to plead that his client be granted bail. Come on, fellers!"

Malachi turned to Kirk. "Davey, what do you say to that?"

"Mr. Stone and I agree on one thing. This *is* a textbook case. Which leads me to believe that my client was framed," Kirk replied.

"Framed?" Stone snorted a derisive laugh. "Framed by whom? For what purpose? Tell me that!" He turned to Malachi to have him join in his response.

The old judge grumbled only, "Pardon me."

He turned his wheelchair toward his private lavatory. He was gone for some minutes, during which Stone said nothing but shook his head in amusement at what he considered Kirk's desperate and transparent gamble.

Eventually, Malachi came rolling back, took his place behind his desk.

"I do some of my clearest thinking in there. And what I thought was, here is this young man. Accused of Murder

Two. Has no family here. Has no job here. No real ties here. Here is also a case which the media have already latched on to. Suppose I do grant him bail and he skips. What kind of a schmuck does that make me? Of course I could go through the motions. Set bail at a figure he could never meet. That way I don't seem to be arbitrary. At the same time we've got him in jail until the day of trial."

The judge took a moment to set a figure in his mind.

"Okay. Bail in this case is set at one hundred thousand dollars! Ten thousand in cash. Davey, has your client got ten thousand dollars?"

"No, Your Honor."

"You see," Malachi said to Stone, inviting him to share his strategy.

"My client doesn't. But I do," Kirk said.

Both Malachi and Stone turned from each other to stare at David Kirk.

"You? A lawyer putting up bail for a client? Davey, are you sure you know what you're doing?"

"At least now we know whose sanity is in issue in this case," Stone said, chuckling.

Unamused, David Kirk replied, "I have complete belief in my client's innocence. This way he will be available for treatment. And he *will* show up for trial. I will post bail by certified check first thing in the morning."

Howie Stone shook his head sadly. With a farewell wave of his hand to the judge and a "Man, now I've seen everything," he left.

Once he was gone, Malachi conceded, "Davey, you really believe your client was framed."

"I believe him when he says he wasn't even there. He's not the criminal type. I would swear to that. So the alternative is that someone, somehow, put together this damning collection of evidence to frame him."

"Who? Why?" the old judge asked.

"That's what we have to find out," Kirk replied, troubled because he had no clue.

———————————

David Kirk personally picked up Chris Cory and drove him home. He wanted to see where and how he lived, and wanted time to talk to him away from the stress of jail surroundings.

He discovered that Cory lived on a single floor of an old loft building on West Thirty-ninth Street and Eleventh Avenue. The place was barely furnished. A modest combined living-dining area led to a single small bedroom.

The only large room had been converted into a darkroom devoted to developing, printing, processing and storing Cory's film. There was an imported enlarger and other equipment that Kirk recognized as being extremely expensive. Cory was not likely to abandon all this and flee trial for a crime that he insisted he did not commit.

The darkroom intrigued Kirk for another reason. Hanging from the drying racks was a series of nude shots. All of the same young woman. Photographically they were excellent. The beauty of the young subject was startling.

Once Cory was comfortable again in his accustomed surroundings, Kirk sat him down to lecture him.

"You understand, you are never to leave the county. Which means the island of Manhattan. You are to let my office know whenever you expect to be gone from home for more than a few hours, where you are going, when you expect to return. And you are to visit Dr. Scott's office whenever she calls. She said that at the start she will have to see you every afternoon at five."

"Every afternoon?" Cory questioned.

"Yes. It will take extensive work to get at the root of your headaches."

"She thinks it's pretty serious. . . ." Cory said grimly.

"She doesn't know what to think yet, so you just be there. If you miss a single appointment I will ask Judge Malachi to revoke your bail. You'll be back in the slammer! But fast!" Kirk said. "Understand?"

"Yeah. Sure. I understand," Cory said, his pale face betraying that his headaches had increased in intensity. "Just tell me one thing. Why do I have to see her every day? Be honest with me. Did she say anything about my being, you know, off my rocker? Because I can tell you right now, I am not insane. And I don't want you or anyone saying anything like that at my trial! You have to promise me you won't do that!"

"Okay. I promise," Kirk said to mollify him. "But it would help if you could remember where you were at the time of the murder."

"I've wracked my brain. I can't remember. Have no recollection at all," Cory insisted.

Kirk was ready to leave, but, intrigued by that set of nude photographs on the drying rack in Cory's darkroom, he could not resist asking, "Those nudes . . . of her?"

"Yes," Cory admitted. "Taken just before we broke up. She was up for a film in which there was a nude scene."

"Strikingly beautiful . . . a classic body," Kirk remarked.

"To think someone slashed that lovely throat . . . stabbed her so many times."

Cory shuddered and pressed his fingers against his temples, trying to assuage the sharp pain.

David Kirk had had Greta deliver to his Fifth Avenue apartment all the documents in two other cases he was defending:

the appeals brief in a case in which his client had been found guilty of securities fraud, and the motion for a change of venue in a federal case in which his client was accused of RICO statute violations and organized-crime activity.

He was deeply involved in editing the motion for a venue change when his phone interrupted. His first reaction was, *Who the hell could be calling at this hour? Must be past midnight.* He glanced at the antique clock on the wall of his tastefully decorated study. *Past midnight? Christ, it's past two o'clock.* He had been immersed in his work longer than he realized. *So who could be calling at this hour?* Only two possibilities: a client seized in the middle of the night (he had several who were subject to such impromptu arrests).

Or a woman lonesome for his company. He had several of those, too. Although lately, due to the pressure of his professional schedule, he had kept his social calendar to a minimum.

Whoever it was, Kirk was not in a mood to greet the intrusion with great enthusiasm.

"Yes?" he asked sharply, making it a habit not to identify himself when he answered his phone.

"Kirk?" a male voice responded with an air of familiarity. "I read in the *Post* you are the lawyer for Chris Cory."

"Who is this?"

The caller laughed. In a dry, crackling voice he replied, "That's right. Pretend you don't know me."

"Am I supposed to know you?" Kirk asked, assuming it was a crank call, to which he was subject whenever he defended some man or woman who had invited public disfavor. As when he had defended another lawyer who had been tried for child abuse and murder. The public was so outraged that he had been deluged with calls that threatened him with reprisals, as if he himself were the accused.

The crackling voice replied, "If you don't know me now, you'll wish you did. Once Christopher Cory is found guilty of killing Alice Ames."

"And why would I wish to know you then?"

"Because I'm the man who killed her," the man replied with great satisfaction.

"You . . . killed her?" Kirk asked, intent on extending the conversation for any clues the caller might inadvertently drop.

"Oh, yes," the voice replied. "And if you have Caller ID, don't waste your time. This is a pay phone." He laughed. "You don't think I'm stupid, do you?"

"No, no, I don't," Kirk played along. "But how do I know you're not lying?"

"Try me," he challenged.

At the same time as he pressed his caller-identification button, Kirk asked, "If you really killed her, then you'd know how she died."

"Oh, but I do," the caller boasted. "A big carving knife. Across that lovely white throat. The stab wounds. And all that blood. *Her* blood."

The caller could have learned that much from the stories in the daily press and on the television news. Kirk tried to take him a step further.

"You just slit her throat, stabbed her and left?" Kirk asked.

The caller laughed, that same dry cackle. "Everybody knows that. But what they don't know, that slash starting at the shoulder."

For the first time, Kirk felt sure he was indeed talking to the murderer. As in almost every other publicized crime, there are always cranks who call or even surrender at police stations, claiming to be the perpetrator. But always, under questioning, it turns out they are faking. This man, whoever he is, is no faker. He knows the details too well.

"Then tell me, once you started to dismember her, why did you stop?" Kirk asked.

The voice changed from vindictive and boastful to sad and sentimental. "So beautiful, such a perfect body. It would have been like defacing the Mona Lisa."

"Can we meet?" Kirk asked. "I'd like to talk to you some more."

"I'll bet you would," the caller said, laughed, then hung up abruptly.

David Kirk made a note of the calling number. He would check it out first thing in the morning. But, he had to admit, that call was scary. For two reasons: There was no doubt the man was the murderer; and it was equally clear that he took great enjoyment from Christopher Cory's predicament, intended to see him tried and convicted.

In the morning, first thing, Kirk had Greta check out that calling number. As the man had stated, it was a pay phone. Located in the South Street Seaport area of lower Manhattan.

As Kirk stared at the slip of paper Greta had given him, he was struck by his dilemma. The caller had verified his belief that Christopher Cory was indeed the victim of a frame-up, yet Kirk dared not report the discovery to either D.A. Stone or Judge Malachi. They would laugh him out of court with a story that seemed so deliberately concocted.

He could hear Stone crowing, "Unidentified caller in the middle of the night? Come on, Davey, a man of your 'brilliance' can do better than that. Like the rough-sex theory you invented to get that young murderer off. That was a beaut. But this phony melodramatic call, this is something I expect in the *Sunday Night Movie* on TV."

No, Kirk decided, there was only one person he might share this with. Dr. Scott.

Nine

Promptly at five o'clock the next afternoon, Christopher Cory presented himself at the office and residence of Dr. Michal Scott.

Following instructions, he rang the bell and was answered by a buzzer that opened the door. He let himself in, then entered the small waiting room. Soon he became aware of an earlier patient coming down the stairs and departing. However, the waiting room had been so planned that he could not see who that patient was. He waited some minutes before he heard a woman's strong voice summon, "Mr. Cory, you may come up now."

He started up the carpeted stairs expecting to find an older woman of imposing stature to match her voice. To his surprise he discovered, standing at the head of the stairs, a blond woman, younger and far more attractive than he had imagined.

He was not aware that the reason she stood there was to observe him very carefully as he climbed the stairs. She noted that he moved slowly, lifting his feet as if they were too heavy for him. She would study him in a brighter light for signs of drug abuse.

When he entered her office she observed that he was dressed neatly. Brown tweed jacket, white shirt, simple-figured tie. A bit too stolid and plain for a man of his young years.

He sat down opposite her, shifted position once, then

again. She expected he would be ill at ease. Many of her male patients were until they became accustomed to being in treatment with a woman.

Before she spoke, she determined that he displayed no overt signs of substance abuse. She held out a sheet of paper. "Just a history. Fill it out and bring it back tomorrow."

She deliberately made him reach for it so that she could discover if there were any telltale white scars on his inner wrists, which would reveal if he had made any suicide attempts, serious or not. She discovered small scars. Still red. Betraying recent, probably not serious, attempts.

While he folded the sheet and slipped it into his inside pocket she availed herself of the opportunity to study his face for any twitching. She found a slight hint of such involuntary movements.

The form safely stored away, he focused his attention on her, awaiting her first question.

"Well, Mr. Cory . . ." she began.

He smiled. A smile that Dr. Michal Scott had seen on almost every patient at a first session. Intended to be friendly and warm, it betrayed uneasiness, fear, and was a plea: *"Doctor, I'm really all right, aren't I? I'm just here so you can tell me that I am. Then I can go away without revealing any more than I absolutely have to."*

"My first questions, Mr. Cory, may strike you as strange. But just answer them. Do you know what day this is?"

Surprised by the irrelevancy of her question, he repeated, "What day this is?"

"Yes. Today. What day is it?"

"Day of the week? Or the month? Or the year?"

"All of them, if you know."

"Of course. April fourth, 1994. Monday."

"Good," Scott replied. "And where are we?"

Cory smiled, shook his head slightly. She waited. He finally answered, "We are in New York City. In the office of Dr. Michal Scott. On Seventy-third Street. And a very impressive office it is. Almost as impressive as the doctor herself."

Though she had not expected quite that response, it served her purpose.

He's very uneasy. As he should be under the circumstances. And, like most men, he thinks that flattery is the most effective weapon in dealing with a woman. He is so transparent that I feel sorry for him. Which means I am in danger of accepting him too readily. I had best put this first interview on tape for future review.

"Mr. Cory, many patients are disturbed by the doctor taking notes. They become more concerned with the doctor's observations than they are with answering questions. So I like to put interviews on tape. That way you won't be tense. And my attention won't be diverted to note-taking when I should be concentrating on what you are saying. So, would you mind?"

"Taping? Of course not," he responded at once. "We used to do that in acting class."

"Good, it will only take a minute to arrange."

She was up from her desk, crossing the room. Cory had a free, unobserved view of her body in motion. He found her to be not only attractive but, to his photographer's eye, totally womanly. When she turned back she caught him staring. He was embarrassed, almost like a young boy caught staring at a naked woman.

She returned to her desk.

"Now, Mr. Cory, a few preliminary questions. Do you have a history of headaches or are they recent?"

Cory did not reply at once, just stared until she became conscious of his concentration on her face and her blond hair.

She urged, "Mr. Cory . . . about your headaches."

He smiled, confessing, "You're not what I expected. You're more. A whole lot more."

"Mr. Cory—your headaches?"

"I've had them before. But never this bad."

"Any history of syncope?" His puzzled look made her explain, "Blacking out, loss of consciousness."

"Oh, yeah. Mr. Kirk told you about that, did he?"

Dr. Scott did not reply but asked, "Lapses of memory?"

"Not really . . . Well, yes, there have been some."

"Like not being able to remember where you were at the time of the murder?"

"Are you working for the DA?" Cory demanded sharply.

"Of course not. But Mr. Kirk, who is trying to defend you, is greatly troubled by your failure to remember," she pointed out.

"This is not the first time."

"Have you had recent chest pain, palpitations, choking or smothering sensations?"

"If you mean panic symptoms, Doctor, just ask me. I'm not a child or a fool. No, I have not had panic symptoms," he declared.

Despite his irritability, she continued, "Any unexplained nausea or abdominal pain?"

"Not that I remember," he responded, beginning to resent such questions.

"Pain in the genitals?" Scott asked. When he did not respond at once, she specified, "Pain in the penis? The scrotal area? The testicles?"

He hesitated, then replied, "No. None."

There was one more obligatory question. She did not necessarily expect a truthful response, but she asked, "Mr. Cory, have you ever made any attempt at suicide?"

He turned slightly so that their eyes were no longer engaged. Only then could he admit, "Yes."

"One? Or more than one?"

"More," was all Cory said.

"Now that we've covered the preliminaries, just sit back and tell me about yourself," she suggested.

The feeling of confrontation and resistance that had built up in his mind gave way to an earnestness that was accompanied by sudden tears welling into his blue eyes. "Doctor, first thing you must understand, I did not kill her. I couldn't kill anyone. Especially not Alice. I loved her. I loved her."

His hands went to his temples, his fingers digging in to suppress the pain. He was silent until he sighed deeply, then admitted softly, "Sorry. The pain, the headaches, they're back. Do you have anything—"

"Did you bring anything with you?" Scott countered.

"Ran out of the stuff Dr. Wilson prescribed. And used up the refills."

Scott avoided the obvious invitation to provide medication or to write another prescription. Instead, she said, "Do the headaches come and go? Or are they fairly persistent?"

"Come and go."

"And when they do, how long do they last?"

"Seems like forever," Cory said.

"Seems is one thing. But how long?"

"An hour, maybe two, sometimes more. Lots more. When I was in jail they never stopped," Cory said. "Just went on and on until I thought I would go crazy."

Scott nodded understandingly. That she had done so on his last word caused Cory to leap up suddenly and accuse, "That's it! Isn't it?"

"What's 'it'?" Scott asked.

"You tricked me into using that word."

"What word?" Scott asked, fully aware of the word he meant.

"I told Mr. Kirk I do not want him or anyone to say that I'm innocent because I am crazy. I am innocent because I did not kill her! Understand? *I did not kill her!*"

Panting, he was forced to lean against her desk for physical support. A slight gleam of sweat broke out on his lean face.

Without a word from Scott he slowly sank back into his chair, then resumed pressing his fingers against his temples.

"The pain . . . the pain . . ." he whispered.

Scott permitted him some minutes of freedom from interruption.

When he had recovered, he said, softly, "Sorry. But, believe me, Doctor, I am not crazy. I am just the unfortunate victim of circumstances."

"Suppose you tell me about yourself *before* all this happened," Scott suggested.

"There isn't much to tell," he began. "Not yet. I mean, I am just finding my way. I'm on the verge of a career breakthrough. People are just beginning to recognize my work."

"As an actor," Scott presumed.

"I started out to become an actor. In fact, that's how we met. Alice and I. We took acting classes together until we . . . we split up. I gave up acting, even though some people said I was damn good at it. I went back to my first choice of career. Photography. And people are just beginning to recognize my work. I have had some very good reactions to my portfolio." Assuming she might not understand, he explained, "A collection of my photographs that I take around to magazines, advertising agencies, publicity outfits. They like my stuff. They're not just being polite. I've been at it long enough to know when I'm getting a polite brush-off. I haven't had any big assignments yet. But I'm getting there, getting there. Then this had to happen."

He shook his head, drew some deep breaths and began to press his fingers against his temples once more.

"Before photography and acting," Scott resumed, "what was your life like?"

"Nothing much. I was born in a little town. Went to school. Wasn't a genius. I did all right. Never failed a course. In high school, I was president of my senior class. No sports activities. But I was good in art. I did the posters for the class play. Also played the lead. I tried college for a year. But I think I was too much into theater and photography. So I left. Got some odd jobs. Started acting class. Worked in a photography-equipment store at the same time to support myself. Saved enough to buy the best equipment. After I left acting school I went out to prove myself in photography. That's about it," he said. Then he added, "As I warned you, not much to tell."

"Your family, what about them?" Scott asked.

"Well, there was my father, my mother, of course, and my two sisters. He was a hard-working man. With his hands. A mechanic. Didn't like my acting and photography. Thought it was work for sissies. To tell the truth, I always had the feeling he was afraid I was gay."

"And are you? Gay?"

"No. Of course not."

She did not accept that his family life was as uneventful as he pretended. But for the moment she saw no need to probe further.

"Tell me, your relationship with the young woman . . ."

"Thank God you didn't use the word *victim*. Like the newspapers do. And the district attorney."

"What would *you* call her if not the victim?"

"I would call her . . . would call her . . . just Alice, that's all. Alice, the most wonderful woman I ever met. Tender. Loving. She understood me. The only person who did. And she loved me. Oh, we had our squabbles, mostly about acting. But we always ended up loving each other . . . and making love. Sometimes I think we quarreled so much because it was a prelude to making love."

"That last time," Scott said, "the time you quarreled and did not make up, the time you left."

"It was torture. But I knew that in the end it was the best thing for *her*. You see, I didn't want to stand in her way.

Because she was marvelous. She could have, would have been a star, except for what happened. Whoever did that to her was jealous. Wanted to destroy her and destroy me at the same time."

"Can you think of anyone who might want to destroy her? Or you?" Scott asked.

"No," he admitted. Then he seemed to recall. "Well, there was this one director, put a big move on her. Promised her all kinds of chances on Broadway. But she wanted nothing to do with him. He could have killed her," Cory said.

"About your family," Scott said, suddenly reverting to the subject. He seemed to resent being asked but she persisted. "You told me some about your father. But nothing at all about your mother."

Adopting the Germanic pronunciation which comedians often use to imitate Sigmund Freud, Cory smiled and said, "Verrry interresting, yes, Doctor? Well, the truth is, it is *not* verrry interesting. Which is why I said so little about her. She was a very good mother."

"If you had to sum it up, would you say your childhood was generally happy? Or unhappy?"

"Not happy. But not especially unhappy. I'd say un-eventful. It would have been better if I'd played baseball instead of doing acting in high school. That would have pleased him," Cory said.

"When you return tomorrow, Mr. Cory, I would like you to bring with you as many recollections as you can of your early years. Make notes if you have to. But everything you can remember."

"I've told you about all there is to tell," he protested.

"There's no crime in not remembering," Scott pointed out. "However, if you can't remember, there's always hyp-nosis."

"Oh, no! I am not going to let anyone play games with *my* mind! Not while I am helpless," he insisted.

"A little Sodium Amytal can't hurt you."

"If that's what you plan, I am not coming back here. Do you hear me? I am not coming back!" he threatened.

"Mr. Cory, you're not here as a usual patient. You are here as a man accused of the crime of murder. You are out on bail, for so long as you continue to come here," Scott pointed out. "So I expect you here tomorrow at five. And every day thereafter for as long as I deem it necessary."

He seemed about to rebel, but slowly the anger drained from his face. He was once more the compliant, ingratiating young man.

"Okay. I will be here. But, please, no . . . no hypnosis. I couldn't. I just couldn't let anyone do that to me."

"We'll see," Scott said. "We'll see."

Ten

That strange night call had haunted David Kirk for the next two days, at times even intruding on his thoughts during the current trial.

It was so weird that he did not even share it with Gerry Prince. If he told anyone, he would tell Dr. Scott. He had a second reason to call her. Her first two sessions with Chris Cory: What conclusions had she reached? Was there any possibility of a psychiatric defense in her findings?

As for Cory's resistance, faced with twenty-five to life, he might be induced to change his mind. Kirk had seen friend turn against friend, wife against husband, son against father, when the alternative was twenty-five years to life. If Dr. Scott could provide the expert testimony, Kirk would find a way to convince Cory.

So determined, instead of having Greta place the call as usual, he did it himself. He was rewarded by a recorded message: "I am busy with a patient at the moment. Please leave your name, time and purpose of your call."

As she was in her attire and her carriage, even her long, braided golden hair, Dr. Scott was precise in her speech. It made him wonder about her overdetermined need to strive for perfection. He himself experienced the same compulsion at times, but always when he felt most vulnerable. Did the lady suffer the same affliction?

He left a brief message: "I have something of great importance to tell you."

Shortly after eight o'clock that evening, Dr. Scott returned his call.

"Sorry I couldn't get back to you sooner. Now, what is your important information?"

"Actually, it is two pieces of information. Too important to discuss on the phone. Have you had dinner yet?"

"Mr. Kirk, I thought I made clear that ours is a purely professional relationship."

"Doctor, all I want to do is discuss a very startling development that might affect not only my case but your handling of Cory as well."

After a deep and, he thought, exasperated sigh, Scott relented. "Where? What time?"

"Now, if possible. And to make it easy on you there is a very nice, very quiet French restaurant on Third Avenue and Seventy-second Street. No more than a five-minute walk from your office."

"Le Chalet Français," she identified at once.

"Oh, you know the place?"

"I've eaten there before," Scott said. "It is now eight-fourteen. Shall we say eight-thirty?"

"Yes. Of course. Eight-thirty."

Kirk hung up, thinking, *How like her to say, "It is now eight-fourteen." Not a quarter after, or eight-fifteen, but precisely eight-fourteen. Did that mean she was allowing herself precisely sixteen minutes to freshen up, walk to the Chalet and be there at precisely eight-thirty?*

He left the office at once, to be there ahead of time. He was curious to see if she arrived at precisely eight-thirty.

By God, she did!

He noticed, too, that Emile, the proprietor, greeted her with that effusive courtesy lavished only on his most cherished patrons. He started to lead her to a table until she whispered to him. At once he changed direction and led her toward Kirk's table.

Though Emile asked Kirk what he would like for an aperitif, he brought her a concoction of several cordials that created pleasing layers of color. Kirk concluded that she not only "knew" the place, as she had said, but dined there often. Her customary table toward which Emile had started to lead her was a small corner table. Set for one. Obviously she dined alone. And often enough so that Emile knew exactly what she drank.

One sip of the drink and she came directly to business, as if she had allotted herself a limited time for this meeting.

"Well, Mr. Kirk, your 'startling' news?"

"First, your impression of my client?"

"I've only seen him twice. Unless a patient is an extreme case it is impossible to form a reliable impression in so short a time."

"Did you discuss the crime and his possible involvement?"

"He insists he is innocent. Was not there. Could not have been there," Scott reported.

"Did he say where he had been at the time?" Kirk asked.

"He has no memory whatsoever."

"The same routine he gave me."

"Mr. Kirk, you call it a routine. Meaning it is something that recurs?" Scott asked.

"I had him checked out. His history indicates that he may be a habitual liar," Kirk admitted.

Emile interrupted at that point to take their orders. Once he had retreated, Scott studied the colors in her now half-empty glass as she considered, " 'May be a habitual liar' . . ."

She was thoughtful but not at all disturbed, as Kirk had expected.

"Psychiatrists may expect that from a patient. Especially at the first few sessions. But a lawyer is forced to take a different view. I believe Cory is telling me the truth. But if I put him on the stand, the prosecutor, using his previous history, can rip him to shreds. It won't matter if he is telling the truth on the stand or not."

As if she had been impervious to Kirk's concern, she considered once more, "A habitual liar . . ."

"Doctor, as far as I am concerned, it does not gain anything by repetition," Kirk commented.

"Mr. Kirk, is that the nature of lawyers?"

"What?" he asked, somewhat irritated by now.

"To jump to conclusions," she said.

Provoked by what he interpreted to be her patronizing air, Kirk asked, "What conclusions have you arrived at, Doctor? By jumping or otherwise."

By that time their first course had arrived. Which only added to Kirk's frustration. Halfway through her coquilles St. Jacques, Scott said, "Mr. Kirk, what you consider a problem during the trial I see as a possible advantage."

"The DA can prove my client is a liar and you can see a possible advantage. Doctor, given a choice, I would prefer to practice your profession instead of mine."

"Mr. Kirk, I don't think you would qualify for my profession. You evidently become too emotionally involved in your cases."

Provoked, Kirk replied, "Superior people like you think an attorney is a trickster. All he has to do is ask a few sharp questions, make an emotional appeal to the jury and his case is won. On television, maybe!"

He thought he detected a slight smile on her face. Perhaps he had indeed betrayed too much emotion in defense of his profession.

"A lawyer, a good one, which I am, is an actor for whom no playwright has written the lines. A director who controls the entire performance—his own, his client's, his witnesses, the DA's witnesses and sometimes even the judge's reactions and rulings. In addition, after being up all night studying testimony, preparing witnesses, hunting down legal precedents, he must come into court the next morning looking fresh and spry. That, my dear Doctor, is one tough job. Because always a client's freedom, or his life, twenty-five years of it, is on the line." Then, realizing he had become more intense than he intended, he spoke more softly when he added, "And it exacts a price. Wives, it seems, would rather be free than pay it."

To ease the moment, Scott explained, "Mr. Kirk, I was only about to say, from a purely psychiatric view, Cory's inability to recall his whereabouts has some redeeming features."

"Such as?" Kirk asked, openly dubious.

"In the first place, a study released by Bradford and Smith in 1979 proves that amnesia after a homicide ranges from forty to seventy percent. Depending on the case, of course."

Kirk seized on that. "You're presupposing Cory murdered Alice Ames. I don't believe that."

"Mr. Kirk, you have a compulsive need to anticipate. And are almost always wrong when you do."

Kirk glared at her, which did not prevent her continuing:

"I was about to say, what you call lying may be something else altogether. Cory's case may turn out to be highly involved, possibly dangerous. I would be doing him, and you, a grave injustice by coming to an early diagnosis," Scott pointed out. "Now, if that was the important information you had to give me—"

Apparently she was terminating this dinner meeting, practically dismissing him.

It was suddenly obvious to Kirk that he had not even broached the other reason for his call.

"There *was* one other matter," he said.

Her reaction betrayed that she suspected this was a ruse on Kirk's part to delay her departure.

"Dr. Scott, this is the strangest case I've ever defended. I happen to *know* that my client is innocent. He did *not* kill that woman. Yet I can't prove it."

"You *know* that Cory is innocent?" she asked, considerably intrigued now.

Kirk proceeded to describe that strange telephone call at two o'clock in the morning. He described the voice, the words, the promise to call again.

"Fascinating," Scott commented.

"Fascinating, hell! It proves my theory. This is exactly what Stone himself called it. *A textbook case. A perfect case. Too damn perfect.* Cory *was* framed."

"Mr. Kirk, from a lawyer's point of view this must be very encouraging. But exactly how do you expect that to affect my professional participation in this case?"

"Despite his history of lying, it proves that Cory is being absolutely truthful when he swears he didn't do it. Wasn't even there," Kirk replied.

"As to Cory's veracity, I will come to my own conclusions. As a forensic psychiatrist and hypnotist I have only two questions to consider: First, is Cory mentally competent to stand trial and assist in his own defense? Second, was he sufficiently mentally competent at the time of the commission of the crime to have formed the required *mens rea,* the will or intent to commit the crime?"

"Doctor, if Cory wasn't there, the question of intent cannot come up," Kirk insisted.

"Counselor, we are too early into the process to make such dogmatic statements," Scott pointed out.

Before Kirk could give vent to his frustration, she continued: "Mr. Kirk, what you told me tonight is certainly pertinent to my ultimate conclusions in this case. But if you want my testimony to stand up in a courtroom, I have much more work to do with your client. And that is all you are interested in. Am I right?"

Kirk felt even more frustrated. Despite his earlier suspicions, this seemingly perfect woman, with her aloof attitude, her total control of the situation, her eminence in her profession, seemed to have no weaknesses.

With a curt "Mr. Kirk, it is late and I have an early patient," she rose to leave.

In recent years few people told David Kirk that a meeting was over before he decided it was over.

He rose with her, and across the table he asked, "Tell me, Dr. Scott, were you born beautiful? With golden hair perfectly braided? And such almost perfect features? Didn't you ever go through the awkward stage? Lose your front teeth? Fall off a bike and scrape your knees? Didn't you ever fail a course in high school? Have any family problems? Or did you live your whole perfect life in a magazine?"

It was an outburst of frustration for which he was immediately embarrassed.

He was even more humbled when she replied, and very softly, "All of that. And more, much more."

Instantly he regretted that he had tried to intrude on a

part of her life which she chose to keep private. He had pierced her wall of invulnerability and felt the worse for it.

"I'm sorry," Kirk said.

"Mr. Kirk, as soon as I reach any conclusion about your client I will report to you. However, based on my long experience in this field it may take quite a while to get to the bottom of this case."

" 'Long experience'?" Kirk commented. "You don't seem more than in your mid-thirties, Doctor. Am I right?"

Refusing to be drawn into any discussion of her personal life, Dr. Scott said only, "Some of us are privileged to have gained considerable experience early in our careers."

Later that night, before he fell asleep, her words echoed in his mind.

"Some of us are privileged to have gained considerable experience early in our careers."

Eleven

At five minutes to five the next afternoon, Christopher Cory appeared in the waiting room of Dr. Michal Scott. He waited until she summoned him up to her office.

Instead of the smiling, ingratiating young man she expected, this time she found him obviously disturbed. His hands were overly active, fidgeting with his tie one moment, avoiding it the next, aware he was betraying his discomfort.

Scott deduced that her mention yesterday of the possible use of hypnosis had created his considerable anxiety. She turned on the video camera to record the session.

"Well, how are we today, Mr. Cory?"

He stared down at his damp hands. Rubbed them against his thighs. Then, his secret too grave to bear alone, he blurted out, "I had a terrible night. Couldn't sleep. When I finally did, I kept dreaming. Terrible dreams. I was on the run. All night. I woke up several times. My heart was pounding. Like it was about to explode out of my chest. I . . . I thought I was having a heart attack."

"Palpitations?" Scott asked.

"Yes. That's it. Palpitations," he admitted. "And a choking sensation. Couldn't catch my breath. Of course my headaches started again. I've been up since a quarter to five."

"Ever experience such feelings before?" Scott asked.

"This is not the first time," he admitted.

"Are those times ever accompanied by numbness in the hands or feet? A tingling sensation?" Scott asked.

"No, that only comes with the panic attacks." Immediately he realized he had previously denied panic attacks. "Those panic attacks, they don't really happen often. I mean, once or twice."

"Mr. Cory, is it possible that you had such a terrible night because you dreaded coming back here?"

"No, I kind of . . . To tell the truth, Doctor, I like the idea of coming back here. You're a nice person. The most sympathetic person since this whole mess started."

"Even though I mentioned that you might have to undergo hypnosis?" Scott suggested.

His hands began to tremble. To conceal it he pressed them to his temples, though she knew he was not in pain at the moment.

"Why are you so afraid of hypnosis?" Scott asked.

"Afraid you might give away secrets you've been hoarding for years?"

"I don't have any secrets, not any big secrets," he protested.

"Yet the very suggestion of hypnosis gave you nightmares. And sweats."

He glared at her, his eyes demanding, *How did you know?*

"It usually happens that way," Scott explained. "Nightmares. Sweats. Trembling. Panic attacks. Abdominal pain. Nausea sometimes."

With each mention of another symptom he nodded. When she was done he realized, "You know about those, too?"

"Mr. Cory, your symptoms lead me to conclude that you are harboring some deep-seated problems that resist coming to the surface. Since we can't expect the courts to hold still for several years of treatment, we don't have time for a protracted analysis. So if you want me to help you, I strongly urge that we try hypnosis."

Cory turned away.

For all patients, opening their naked, defenseless inner selves through hypnosis was a difficult decision. If what she suspected was Cory's problem proved to be true, he had even more reason to be apprehensive. She decided not to press him. The decision must be his and his alone.

"The other day you spoke about sodium . . . that stuff."

"Sodium Amytal," she reminded him.

"That's an injection, isn't it? I don't like needles. But mainly I don't like the idea of being drugged."

"There is another way. Hypnosis by suggestion. We just talk our way into it. But to do that you have to trust me. Do you?"

He turned to her. Stared into her warm gray eyes.

"Before we do that I have to know . . . whatever comes out, will it help me? And I don't mean the damn trial. I want to know if it will end my other troubles," he said. Her look forced him to admit, "Yeah, I have other troubles. That began long before I was arrested. That have nothing to do with being arrested or charged with murder. If it can help to cure me of that, I think I would be willing to risk being hypnotized."

"Good. Because it *can* prove very helpful. But you have to give yourself to it. Wholeheartedly," Scott pointed out.

"I . . . I think I can do that," he ventured. "Let's try it next time."

"Why not now?" Scott asked.

"You mean right now? Without any preparation?" he demurred.

"It doesn't require preparation," Scott said.

"Now . . . ?" Cory considered. "Right now . . . ?" Finally he nodded. "I can't promise, but I will do my best. Because I trust you. I like you. I like you a lot."

"All right, then, close your eyes. Relax your hands. Let them fall to your sides. Now, just imagine that you are out in the country. You are at the crest of a long, sloping green meadow. Very slowly you start down. The soft grass under your naked feet. A cool breeze brushing your face. Soothing, relaxing. Eventually, at the end of the long meadow, you come to a flight of wooden steps. You start down. Slowly. One at a time. One. Two. Three. Four. Five. You continue descending the steps. Counting them off. Count them with me, Chris. Count. Seven. Eight. Nine. Ten. . . ."

Soon Scott stopped, but Cory continued counting, falling deeper and deeper into sleep, his voice growing softer and softer, until he appeared to be under.

Subjects of hypnosis have often been known to pretend being under when they are really not. Especially if they have something to hide. For such situations Dr. Scott used a technique which she learned from her mentor in hypnosis, Dr. John Beaumont. He had termed it Suggested Anesthesia.

Scott reached for Cory's hand. Holding it palm down, she traced a circle on the back with her forefinger.

"Chris, did you feel that?"

"Yes, ma'am," he whispered.

"Can you describe it?"

"A circle. You drew a circle."

"Right. Within that circle you have no feeling at all. Do you understand?"

"Yes, ma'am," he replied obediently, in the flat voice of a hypnotic.

"Now, I will touch several places on the back of your hand. When I touch you *outside* the circle you will feel it and you will say yes."

"Yes, ma'am."

"But when I touch you *inside* the circle, where you can't feel it, you will say no. Understand?"

"Yes, ma'am," Cory said, nodding, his eyes still closed.

A true hypnotic would implicitly accept her instructions, illogical as they were, and would respond as instructed, with a Yes or a No.

Dr. Scott began to make light touching tests on the back of Cory's hand outside the circle. At each touch he responded with a low whispered yes. Now Scott touched him inside the circle of no feeling. One touch. He responded, "No." She touched outside the circle. Cory responded, "Yes."

Another touch inside the circle evoked another no. She alternated, inside the circle, outside the circle. Each time Cory responded as instructed, either yes or no.

Having passed that test, Cory was now ready for deeper exploration.

"Chris, you told me yesterday you are on the verge of success with your photography. Is that true?"

He did not respond at once. He sat slumped, head down, hands clasped between his thighs.

"Chris," she coaxed.

"Not . . . not true," he managed to whisper. "Not much good at it. Not much good at anything. Not acting. Not even making love. Times afterwards I have crying spells."

"Do you ever find satisfaction or pleasure in *anything* you do, Chris?"

After a slight pause he admitted, "Not . . . not really. . . ."

As she had suspected, he was anhedonic, unable to experience pleasure. A significant clue, which, together with other observations, might lead her to a diagnosis. A rare diagnosis, but one that might have great relevance to his present precarious legal situation.

"Chris, Alice Ames, the woman they say you murdered, was she aware of these problems you had?"

"It's why she gave up seeing me," he confessed. "Couldn't blame her. What woman would want a man like me?"

"Did you ever see her again after you broke up?"

"No," he replied. "Once I . . . I went to her place. Not actually to it, but just outside. I saw this man come out. Tall man. Beard. Very close beard. Seemed about thirty, maybe thirty-five. I knew, somehow I knew she'd been seeing him."

"How do you know he was there to see her?"

"I . . ." He began to fidget, reluctant to continue, but she persisted.

"Chris, how did you know he was there to see her?"

"Once before I passed him on the stairs," he confessed. "I went down to the next landing. Stopped. Very quietly sneaked back up a few stairs. Saw his feet on the floor. They went to her door. Heard him knock. Heard her call out, 'Sandy? That you?' Heard the door open. Heard her voice again, but this time she was interrupted by kissing. She was glad to see him. Very glad. I heard the door close. I knew what was happening."

"Chris, did you ever go back there again? Spy on them?"

"No. Never."

"Tell me, Chris, *did you kill her?*"

"No, I swear to God, no!"

"Chris, you told Mr. Kirk, you told me, you don't remember where you were at the time that Alice Ames was murdered."

"That's right, I don't."

"Don't remember at all?"

"No," he insisted, still in a flat whisper.

"Did that ever happen to you before?"

"I never been accused of murder before."

"I mean, Chris, did you ever have periods of time when you couldn't remember what happened, or where you'd been?" Scott asked, phrasing her words very deliberately.

"Times I couldn't remember . . ." he considered. "Yeah, it happened."

"Tell me about it," Scott urged.

"Was this time. Was developing some stuff. There was this knock on the door. United Parcel with a package. I didn't buy anything, so I thought, Maybe someone is sending me a present. I don't know who, but someone. I took the package. Sure enough, was for me. I opened it up. Was a suit. Not exactly a suit. A jacket and some black jeans. But very weird stuff. Weird. Nothing I would ever wear. Inside was a sales slip. Seems I did buy that stuff. That was scary. I was so ashamed. I didn't take it back. Then it happened again. Several times. But I never, not till now, told anyone about it. It was too weird."

Scott had accomplished what she expected. But in order not to put undue significance on it in Cory's mind, she continued to the end of the session with a number of innocuous, unrelated questions, all of which he answered.

She brought him out of his hypnotic state as slowly as

she had induced it. He woke, comfortable and at ease, as she had instructed.

After Cory had left, Scott ran the entire tape of his performance under hypnosis. She lifted her phone and punched in the number of David Kirk's office. Though Kirk had gone for the night, Gerry Prince was still in the library. He referred her to Kirk's home phone.

She reached him as he was getting into his dinner jacket to attend a fund-raiser concert for AIDS research. She told him that she had a tape he should see at once since they had to determine the next step she would take in the Cory case.

"Doctor, I'd duck this benefit if I didn't have to praise a lot of contributors and make a plea for additional funds."

"No, you couldn't very well back out of that on such short notice," she agreed.

"Why not come along with me?"

"And find my picture in the *Times* or the *Post* tomorrow?" she countered. "No, thank you."

"Is that what you're afraid of?" Kirk asked. "That they'll say, 'Dr. Michael Scott'—spelled wrong of course—'and dashing man-about-town and brilliant criminal lawyer David Kirk'?"

"Mr. Kirk, I was well aware of your exploits before you ever consulted me. David Kirk, the eminent lawyer, whose picture somehow appears in the newspapers the morning after only the most really important charity affairs. Always, of course, with some charity groupie staring up at you adoringly. Mr. Kirk, the other night, your heartrending justification of your difficult life almost had me in tears. But not sufficiently so that I am willing to join your groupie corps."

"Now you're being unfair," he accused.

"Perhaps," she granted. "But I've had a long day and I

am not in the mood to endure some boring concert. Even for a good cause."

"Bobby Short doing Cole Porter. And Barbra Streisand doing numbers from her first new album in years—boring?"

She considered, then asked, "Do I have time for a quick shower and to do my hair?"

"I'll come and help you with both if you like," he joked.

"Kirk, knock it off!" she replied crisply. "I will be joining you for only one reason. I need to confer with you tonight so I am prepared for Cory's session tomorrow. Where shall we meet?"

He was tempted to say, "Eight-fourteen and a half in Avery Fisher Hall at Lincoln Center." Instead, a bit chastened by her cool attitude, he said, "I will be waiting in the lobby of Avery Fisher Hall from eight o'clock on. Take your time. I won't be offended if you're late. Oh, it's black tie. So dress accordingly."

He was tempted to add, "But don't wear a tuxedo." In the interest of professional harmony, he refrained.

From five minutes to eight on, David Kirk kept staring above the heads of the well-gowned women and well-groomed men who poured into the marble lobby of Avery Fisher Hall. He was watching for that golden braid, one of Michal Scott's distinguishing physical characteristics. But he could not find her. Not even among the late stragglers.

By the time she did arrive he could hear music strike up inside the hall.

At first he did not recognize her. She was not wearing her blond hair in that tight, precise French braid. It was loose and surrounded her face like the frame of a striking portrait. Her crimson off-the-shoulder evening dress, which from experience Kirk recognized as a designer original, revealed the

93

womanly body that her severe business suits conspired to conceal.

Any woman with a wardrobe that included such a gown must have a more active social life than I suspected, Kirk realized. *Who is the lucky man? Or is it men?*

He rushed to greet her at the door.

"Sorry I'm late. But just as I stepped out of the shower I had an emergency call from a patient."

"Everything turn out all right?" Kirk asked.

"It'll hold till morning," she said. She realized he was staring at her. "Something wrong?"

"Quite the contrary. You sure know how to dress if you don't want to attract attention and have your picture taken."

"I only dressed this way to maintain your social reputation, Mr. Kirk," she responded crisply. "Now may we go in? I'm dying to hear Bobby Short."

Once she was seated, Kirk took the stage to make his welcoming speech. He stressed the desperate need for AIDS research. He praised the talented artists who gave of their time and talent for the cause. He also made sure to thank by name those patrons who had made substantial contributions.

Michal Scott observed him closely. She could not deny that he was a strikingly handsome man. His voice and speech were impressive, as she expected, based on his reputation as a skillful trial lawyer. There was also a magnetism about him, which explained his appeal to women. She determined not to be influenced by it.

His speech concluded, the music resumed.

Between acts, Kirk's earlier prediction came true. While they were sipping cappuccino in the lobby, their pictures were indeed taken. Many times. When photographers asked for Dr. Scott's name, since they all knew David Kirk well, he volunteered, as if imparting a state secret, "The lady prefers that her name not be used. It could prove embarrassing. You guys understand, don't you?"

The photographers all gestured to Kirk, *Don't worry, trust us,* then immediately circulated through the lobby asking everyone who she might be. Speculation ran all the way from the wife of an important foreign business tycoon to a new model imported from Sweden by one of the better agencies.

One man did know. He had been a patient of Dr. Beaumont and later of Dr Scott. But he chose not to disclose her identity.

Twelve

It was just past eleven when his limousine dropped David Kirk and Dr. Scott at her residence on East Seventy-third Street.

She showed him into her office, then left to make some coffee. When she brought in the tray, she found him staring at the photographs on her desk. Though he was staring at the younger man, she chose to explain, "Dr. Beaumont. My teacher. The best man in the field."

Aware that she had ignored his curiosity about the younger man, Kirk nevertheless replied, "So Dr. Wilson said. But he never did explain which field."

"That will become clear after you've seen the tapes I'm about to show you," she said. "Coffee?"

"Yes, thanks. But I can't wait to see those tapes," Kirk said.

At the same time he could not resist admiring the way that crimson dinner dress complemented her body. Once shed of those formal business suits she was very, very feminine. Intelligent as well. But unmarried. And who is that young man she chose not to identify?

She had inserted a cassette into the VCR, then flipped the switch. David Kirk began to watch the videotape of Christopher Cory's first session with Dr. Scott. He found it interesting but hardly startling.

While she was changing cassettes, she remarked, "Notice the difference between that and Cory under hypnosis."

Kirk watched with keen interest as he heard the voice of Michal Scott on tape while he saw Cory gradually lulled into a hypnotic state. He watched with even greater interest as he saw for the first time in his experience the circle-of-no-feeling test being performed.

"What's the purpose?"

"Malingerers apply normal logic to such situations. They know consciously that if you can't feel you won't respond. But genuine hypnotics accept the illogical logic of hypnotic suggestion and do as they are instructed."

"Then Cory is not faking," Kirk concluded.

Once the tape had run its course, Kirk remarked, "Well, it proves he hasn't been lying. He did not kill her. Terrific! I can make excellent use of this tape during trial. Doctor, you deserve your reputation."

"That isn't why I asked you to view those tapes," Scott started to explain.

Smiling, Kirk remarked, "Good God, don't tell me that in the New Age, videotapes have taken the place of etchings."

Scott disposed of that with a slight, impatient shake of her head, which her loose-flowing hair complemented.

"We now have to make a very grave decision," she announced.

"You've just proved my client's innocence. What more is there to decide?"

"Mr. Kirk, did anything else strike you about those tapes?"

"What else?"

"He had told you he could not account for his whereabouts at the time of the murder," Scott pointed out.

"And under hypnosis he repeated it. Proving he was not lying."

"He did more than that," Scott pointed out. "He revealed *other* times when he could not recall."

"You mean buying those weird clothes," Kirk replied. "Perfect. It backs up his alibi. He's had several other episodes when he couldn't remember. Which means that he didn't just invent it as a handy alibi for his whereabouts at the time of the murder."

"Not quite so fast, Counselor!" Scott countered. "There may be a great deal more here than appears on the surface. Dr. Wilson suspected it. That's why he referred the case to me. You see, Dr. Beaumont was one of the nation's, if not the world's, leading experts. Not only on hypnosis, but on MPD as well."

"MPD? Like MS? Or Lou Gehrig's Disease?"

"Multiple Sclerosis and Amyotrophic Lateral Sclerosis are diseases of the nervous system. MPD is a disease of the mind, Multiple Personality Disorder."

"Multiple Personality . . ." Kirk started to repeat, but interrupted himself to ask, "Doctor, are you telling me you suspect Cory is afflicted with multiple personalities?"

"I can't say for sure. Not yet. But there are definite signs and symptoms."

"So?" Kirk asked.

"The question is, how much further do I go with him? Professional curiosity tempts me to press on. But he is your client before he is my patient."

"From a lawyer's point of view I have only one question: Will this help in his defense?"

"Aside from being a defendant, he may also be a sick human being who needs help," Scott pointed out.

"Doctor, a lawyer is a technician. Obligated to give his client the very best defense he can, guilty or innocent. He can't live his client's life. Or cure his ailments. Though I must admit I've grown rather fond of Cory. He's a nice kid. So I have to consciously put aside my personal concern for him and ask, if you discover he *does* have MPD, can it serve as a defense?"

"There is at least one case on record in which it served to win a man an acquittal in a serious criminal case."

"I'll have Gerry Prince track that down," Kirk said.

"It's the Milligan case," Scott added. "In Ohio or Illinois, if I recall correctly."

"Of course we will need to prove that legally the condition constitutes insanity," Kirk considered.

"According to the American Psychiatric Association, MPD is a form of mental disease," Scott replied. "The criteria are quite standardized. First, the existence within one person of two or more separate and distinct personalities. Second, at least two of these personalities or states recurrently take exclusive control of that person's behavior."

"If you can satisfy the court on those two counts, can you swear that in your expert opinion Cory is a victim of a mental disease?" Kirk tried to pin her down.

"Yes."

"Then, by all means, go for it. Bearing in mind, at all times, how I prove it in a courtroom."

"First, I have to prove it to myself," Scott pointed out.

"And how do you do that?"

"Meet and talk to his alter or alters."

"Alters?" Kirk asked, puzzled.

"In our terminology Cory is the host. Any other personality is an alter. Remember the terms. You may be using them often."

"Do you actually intend to meet Cory's alters, talk to them?"

"It's the only definitive way to prove my diagnosis," Scott declared. "After all, you don't think that prosecutor is going to accept my verbal testimony as the final word."

"Howie Stone?" Kirk replied. "He'll have half a dozen experts in court, all bought and paid for, to swear that Cory is as normal as Judge Malachi."

"I have to be ready for them. Sure in my own mind that Cory has what I suspect. Certifiable Multiple Personality Disorder," Scott declared. "Now, if you don't mind, I have an early patient."

"Of course. Sorry. Didn't mean to keep you up so late."

"I'll show you out."

She led the way. Passing her desk he noticed once more the two framed photographs and remarked, "He must have been an excellent teacher to have produced a psychiatrist like you."

"He was a remarkable man," she said, with deep respect and reserved affection.

"You almost sound as if he were your father," Kirk remarked.

She did not respond but instead asked, "Do you wish to ride down, or use the stairs?"

"The stairs will do nicely, thank you."

"Then, do lock the door on your way out."

Once outside, instead of availing himself of his limousine, Kirk decided to walk down Fifth Avenue. Because of the lateness of the hour and the prevalence of muggers along the avenue due to the easy escape afforded by Central Park across the street, Geraldo followed him, staying slightly behind and cruising at Kirk's sharp, striding pace.

Kirk had much to think about, and the relative quiet of late-night Manhattan, plus the stimulating night air, helped.

A whole new possible defense had been opened to him tonight. Of course he would have to fight Cory, who had resisted even a hint of an insanity defense. But once the alternative was pointed out to him, Kirk felt optimistic that he could bring him around.

Of course there was that sticky business of bringing out those other personalities, what Scott had called alters. If they really existed, that is. Then there was the challenge of convincing Judge Malachi and Howie Stone to permit him to file such a defense so late in the proceedings. The statutory thirty days would soon be over.

And, he found himself thinking, she never did explain who that younger man was. Not that it matters.

Thirteen

Aware of both the legal and the psychiatric importance of the case of Christopher Cory, Dr. Michal Scott prescribed and carried out an extensive battery of psychiatric tests.

Gradually she introduced certain specific physical tests.

Cory cooperated fully. He submitted to having his respiration and blood pressure tested under hypnosis while being asked questions that might prove incriminating. He betrayed no acceleration of respiration, no increase in blood pressure.

She had him subjected to a galvanic skin response test with electrodes attached to his arms and chest. If Cory were faking, his emotional state might reveal itself in changes in the humidity level and temperature of his skin surface. Cory evidenced no such reaction.

Cory having passed his GSR, considered by most experts to be one of the best detectors of malingering, Scott notified David Kirk that she was finally ready to explore the next and crucial phase in her diagnosis.

When Kirk asked if he could witness the experiment, she replied, "I will want you available but not present in the room when I first hypnotize him. Once he's under, you will become part of it. When can you be free so I can schedule him?"

"Thursday evening. Say, six o'clock?"

"See you then," Scott confirmed.

———————————

"This evening, Chris, we are going directly into hypnosis," Scott began.

"No more tests?"

"No more tests," she assured.

"Thank God," he said, confessing, "It's been a strange feeling. All those tests, not knowing what you're looking for. Not knowing if what I say might displease you. Some days I leave here, or leave those labs where they test me, and I think, I hope what I said today isn't going to make her decide that she no longer wants to treat me. Because . . . because you have come to mean a great deal in my life. Not just because you are the kind of woman I would fall in love with. If I dared. But because I feel that my freedom depends on you. Mr. Kirk is my lawyer. It's his job to defend me. But somehow you've become more important. I have days . . . days when I have these fantasies . . . it is a year from now or two years. This whole terrible business is over. Everybody knows I'm innocent. I come back here to ask you to . . . to see me . . . not as a patient but as a man. And you, you say yes. I take you out on the town. I am so proud to show you off to everyone and say, 'See, she thinks I'm pretty good. Good enough to date.' And then, then that fantasy becomes more . . . no, that's too much to ask, even of a fantasy."

He was silent for a moment, as if gathering the courage to continue. "We . . . we make love . . . I kiss you . . . your lips . . . your neck . . . your breasts. . . . I think about your breasts often. . . . I . . . I . . . I think I better not go on. Else you will throw me out."

Cory avoided looking at her, embarrassed by his confession.

"All right, Chris. Now close your eyes." He was relieved to comply. "You are in that familiar green field. There is a slight breeze blowing, bending the grass before you. You start across that wide field. Then down the slope, slowly. Very slowly. You feel you are floating on the tops of the moist grass. Being carried along by the breeze. Now you come to the steps. Which lead down, down. You count each step as you go. One, two, three. Count with me, Chris. Four, five, six."

He picked up the count at once, and though she ceased he continued: "Seven, eight, nine, ten, eleven, twelve."

It seemed he was under. It was time to try still another test. She must make absolutely sure. Especially since she would be called upon to testify in court about this particular session.

She went to the door and beckoned David Kirk into the room, pointed out the blue leather chair near the fireplace.

"Chris, you may open your eyes now."

Once he did, she angled her chair slightly, forcing him to look directly into the television camera.

"Chris, can you see Mr. Kirk sitting in this room?"

In his hypnotic state Cory slowly looked about until he spied Kirk near the fireplace.

"Yes. Mr. Kirk. In that leather armchair," Cory replied in a low, expressionless voice.

"Now, Chris, look at this chair near you. Isn't that Mr. Kirk, too?"

Cory glanced at the empty chair to his right, then replied, "Yes. Mr. Kirk."

In his hypnotic state the concept of two David Kirks in the same room at the same time was not a disturbing anomaly.

Scott whispered an aside to Kirk, explaining, "Trance logic. He accepts whatever I say. No matter how illogical."

Dr. Scott was prepared for the next step in what could be a hazardous venture.

"Chris, for days now you have been complaining about severe headaches. Twice you said, 'I feel like my head is splitting in two.' Did you really think your head was splitting in two?"

"Felt like . . ." the hypnotized Chris Cory replied.

"Could it have been something else?" Scott asked.

Cory did not respond at once, but after a long silence he shook his head.

"Chris, I would like to speak to whoever is responsible for the murder of Alice Ames."

Cory did not respond.

"Chris—" she coaxed.

Cory turned away. Kirk looked to Scott for some hint of what to expect. She gestured him to be patient.

"Chris, I would like to talk to whoever killed Alice."

Cory remained perfectly still, not daring to turn back to

face her. She waited. Kirk, his eyes fixed on Cory, detected no movement, no change. He was about to admit that whatever Scott had hoped to achieve, she had failed.

Suddenly Cory exhibited a slight tremor, first of his right hand, then of his left. Now his whole body erupted into a state of clonic convulsion.

In a whisper, Scott informed Kirk, "We call this process switching."

Kirk was startled to see Cory's face, too, begin to change. Around his eyes and mouth, hard tight lines began to appear. His chin, which had always been slightly weak, now protruded hostilely. What had been a soft, gentle young man had become a dangerous presence in the room. Even Cory's hands—hands of a person of artistic endeavor—became clawed, almost grotesque. They had turned into two gnarled fists. But as yet he had not uttered a word.

Kirk forced himself to turn from studying Cory to looking inquiringly at Dr. Scott. She gestured him to be patient. She waited until Cory's switching had been completed, then urged softly, "Chris?"

Instead of the usual, low, expressionless voice of a hypnotic, he burst into a hoarse, angry voice that accused, "Bitch! Couldn't leave it alone, could you? Damned sneaky bitch! What the hell are you doing, butting in where you don't belong?"

"Who are you?" Scott asked.

"None of your goddamn business! So split! Get lost! I don't have to answer to you for anything!"

"Who are you?" Scott repeated.

"Who am I?" He laughed in amusement at her question. "Who am I? I'm the one who runs this idiot Chris. He's only the dummy. I'm the ventriloquist! I pull the strings. He dances!" He laughed, a bitter, vengeful laugh.

"Do you have a name?" Scott asked.

"Of course I have a name. But the idiot wouldn't know

it. Because I never tell him anything. Why should I? He'd only blab it all over the place."

"Would you tell *me* your name?" she asked.

The evil, alter representation of Christopher Cory looked at her, leered, then smiled in his strange way. "Since you were smart enough and pushy enough . . . you know, you're a very aggressive broad . . . okay, I will tell you my name."

"Which is?"

"Max."

During this exchange David Kirk had left his chair to take a position just behind Scott for a better view of this new alter personality of Chris Cory. The distortions in his face were even more marked now. Especially the jaw, which jutted forward almost in Neanderthal fashion. It was a face full of hatred threatening to explode into open violence.

"Max, tell me, who killed Alice Ames?" Scott asked.

Max's face, distorted as it was, broke into a smile of smug, deliberate, enjoyable vengeance.

"Who killed dear, sweet Alice? Who indeed? That miserable, sniveling little coward Christopher, he wouldn't. Couldn't. Gutless little bastard. I had to do it for him. All his life I've been having to do things for him. But now he'll pay for it. No more running and hiding. I did one hell of a job of framing him, if I must say so myself. *He* is going to spend the rest of his life in prison for something *I* did!"

He broke into coarse, vindictive laughter.

"Isn't that perfect? *I* kill. *He* pays! That'll give him something to have headaches over. My idea, too. His headaches."

He laughed once more.

David Kirk felt a cold sweat break out on his brow and around his collar. He was no longer seeing his timid, frightened client, but an evil murderer who seemed to be outside the reach of the law.

"His headaches," Scott prodded.

"His headaches," Max repeated, laughing once more. "I

think that was the best joke of all. Once I killed her, I wanted to let him know who I was. So I sent a signal. I said, 'Idiot'—that's what I call him— 'Idiot,' I said, 'not only are you going to spend the rest of your life in jail, I am going to drive you crazy. I am going to give you headaches. Bad headaches. There won't be enough medicine in this world to cure you! And when you tell the doctors, 'It feels like my head is splitting in two,' that will be true. Because I will be the other one of the two. I had it all planned. Until that bitch Scott came along."

He turned on her. "Pushy bitch! I ought to give you the same thing I gave Alice!"

He rose up in a menacing pose, extending his clawed hands as if prepared to strangle her. Kirk moved forward to intervene, until Dr. Scott whispered, "No! Don't!"

Once Kirk drew back, Scott ordered, "Max! You will sit down!"

He glared at her, as if deciding whether to obey or to carry out his violent intentions. Finally, he relented, sank back into his chair, muttering hoarsely, "Bitch . . . no good bitch. . . ."

The moment of greatest danger having passed, Scott said, "Now, Max, before you go, tell me, are there any others?"

"Others?" Max asked.

"Others like you?" Scott said.

"Can't be others. I won't allow it. Won't!" Max proclaimed.

"You can go now. But we will be speaking again," she said.

"Bet your sweet ass we'll be speaking again! And you won't get away so easy next time," he threatened.

Fourteen

With the withdrawal of Max, the turmoil within Christopher Cory slowly began to subside. Gradually he switched back to his normal, placid self. Still under hypnosis he appeared to doze, unaware of what had happened or of his surroundings.

"I had no idea," Kirk whispered. "Poor kid, to live with a burden like that."

"That's the life of an MPD. Not knowing. Having periods of blackouts. Being accused of habitual lying because they cannot account for their time, their actions, each time an alter takes over."

"At first I didn't quite buy his story about not remembering," Kirk confessed in a whisper. Then he continued, "Dr. Scott, I once told you it's my job to defend him. Not cure him. Well, no longer. He not only needs help, he deserves it. And I intend to see that he gets it, not only in court, but out. Do you think he can be cured?"

"First things first, Mr. Kirk. Now I'd better bring him out of it." Lifting her voice, she asked, "Chris, can you hear me?"

He nodded gently, relaxed as he had been when he first passed into his hypnotic state.

"Chris, you are going to come out of it now. When you do, you will feel rested. Comfortable. So count backward with me. By the time you reach one you will wake. With no memory of what happened. Ten, nine, eight, seven, six, five, four, three, two, one."

His eyes opened, as if waking from a deep, restful sleep.

He was startled by Kirk's presence. Before he could ask, Scott explained, "Mr. Kirk is here in preparation for your trial."

Cory smiled. "Thanks, Mr. Kirk, for taking the time." Turning back to her, and rising, he said, "My hour's up, I guess."

"Before you go, Chris, I'd like to ask you something."

"Sure. Anything," he replied, his usual affable self.

Trying to make it appear a casual question, Scott asked, "Chris, do you happen to know anyone named . . . Max?"

"Max . . ." Cory considered. "Max? No." Then he caught himself. "Oh, yes. There was a man back home. Except his name was Maximillian. Of course, nobody called him that. Too fancy. So he was just Hig to everyone, his last name being Higgins. But, no, I don't know any Max. Why?"

"Chris, sit down again," she suggested.

Suddenly no longer at ease, he glanced at Kirk to elicit some explanation or assurance, then slowly sank back into his chair.

"There *is* something wrong with me, isn't there?" he asked softly.

"*Wrong* is not exactly the correct word, Chris. But something very important to your case, and to your life, has come to light."

He tensed visibly, glancing from Scott to Kirk and back to her.

"What we found is treatable. It will take time, but it can be treated," Scott reassured him.

"Well, at least that's something," Chris said, but his flicker of a smile betrayed his nervousness. "Okay. Lay it on me."

"Chris, there is a condition in psychiatry known as Multiple Personality Disorder."

"Multiple . . . personality . . ." he tried to absorb.

"It means that more than one personality inhabits the same body, the same mind."

"More than one personality . . ." he considered with growing uneasiness. "Why? How?"

"A young child facing circumstances too difficult to bear sometimes invents other personalities to cope with extreme pain and suffering," she explained.

"Extreme pain and suffering . . ." he repeated, then was quite relieved. "That never happened to me."

"You have no memory of it because you blocked it out by making that other personality suffer it for you," Scott pointed out.

"Oh, now I get it," Chris realized slowly, then exploded angrily. "You're just like all the other shrinks! You want me to blame my mother! Blame my father! Well, they were both very fine people. They loved me. I loved them. So what you are trying to make me believe now is lies, all lies! There is no other person inside me!"

He turned on David Kirk. "This is *your* idea! You don't believe I'm innocent. So you invent another of your 'brilliant' defenses. I told you before, even if I have to spend the rest of my life in prison, I will never say I am insane! Because I'm not!"

He was shaking with both rage and fear. Soon he began to gasp. He seemed to shrivel to half his size as he pulled back in his chair, weeping now, and pleading, "Don't do this to me . . . don't . . . please. . . ."

Kirk appealed to Scott to say something to ease his client's torment. But she chose to remain silent. Suddenly, Cory sprang from his chair and started toward the door.

Scott called, "Tomorrow, Chris. Tomorrow at five."

"I am never coming back here!" he shouted as he ran toward the stairs.

Kirk turned to confront Scott. Before he could ask, she said, "Don't worry. He'll be here."

"I never realized how dangerous it could be, dealing with an MPD patient," Kirk confessed. "Do they all react like Cory just did? And are alters always as angry and violent as Max?"

"Some alters hate their hosts. Seek to punish him. Even destroy him. Others protect him. The angry ones are expressing the hostility that patients like Chris have been suppressing since childhood. Max does all his hating."

"But wouldn't the child and, surely later, the adult be aware of that other person which he himself invented?"

"The host is totally unaware of any alters. Yet the alters are very aware of him," Scott explained.

"So the only one in the dark is the patient," Kirk realized. "But you did say he could be cured. I'd like to help."

"That won't be necessary. I'm so intrigued by his case that I'm considering taking him on as a patient at no fee."

"After seeing Max in action, that might be extremely dangerous. He threatened to kill you," Kirk reminded her. "And we now know that he *does* kill."

"I'm aware of that. But also of my ability to control him," she stressed.

"I hope you're right. Well, from a lawyer's point of view this has been a rewarding experience. I have all I need. Tomorrow we will file notice that we intend to plead insanity as a defense."

"Not yet," Scott warned. "The key to completing the diagnosis is uncovering the root cause."

"You said that was abuse in his early childhood."

"Yes. Now I have to regress him back to relive it. React to it and overcome it. Abreaction, we call it."

"Then, the sooner the better," Kirk urged.

"That doesn't apply here, Mr. Kirk. Regression is a slow procedure," she warned. "Abreaction a very dangerous one. It takes time."

"How much time?"

"Days. Weeks. Maybe longer. This procedure cannot be rushed. Because there are cases in which the consequences have proved fatal."

"Doctor, we have very few days left to file. And Cory is facing twenty-five years to life without parole if I fail him," Kirk warned.

Scott remained quite firm. "*I* must decide when to risk it."

"Keep me informed. So we can file at the first possible moment."

"Of course," she replied most professionally.

"Thank you," Kirk responded as formally. "Now, I'm sure you must have an early patient," he added before she could remind him.

As he reached the door, she called out, "Oh, Mr. Kirk, Max's voice, his laugh, his abrasive attitude, were they familiar?"

"Come to think of it, yes. That two-o'clock-in-the-morning phone call," Kirk realized.

"I suspected as much. It's what put me onto the possibility that Cory might have an alter," she said. "Please make sure the door locks behind you on your way out."

Kirk started down the carpeted stairs, thinking, *Damn it, how does she always manage to put me in the position of being dismissed like some underling? Nobody treats David Kirk that way. Certainly no woman. Except this woman.*

Fifteen

Days later, David Kirk's limousine made its way north along Park Avenue in the heavy early-evening traffic. It seemed all of working New York was headed in the same direction.

Considerably puzzled and annoyed, he studied the message slips Greta had handed him with a sense of great urgency.

Strange message, he thought. *She calls, leaves word with Greta. "Have Mr. Kirk at my office at seven-fifteen. No later." What's going to happen at seven-fifteen that I have to be so precise? Must be that compulsion of hers to be so damned prompt and exacting. Maybe she could stand a little psychiatric treatment herself.*

Heavy as the traffic was, his car arrived at Dr. Scott's office residence some minutes early. She was a long time answering the door. When she finally did, he discovered that she was not attired in one of her usual businesslike suits. She wore jeans and a light blue sweater of fine merino wool that hugged her body to great advantage. Her hair was loose. Yet, unlike the night at the concert, it betrayed that she had been interrupted during considerable physical activity.

She was obviously surprised at Kirk's appearance ahead of schedule.

"Your message said no later than seven-fifteen," he reminded her. "Nothing was said about earlier."

"Well," she relented, "in a way it's a good thing you're here. I could use the help. Come with me," she said briskly, starting away. She seemed headed for the small elevator but changed her mind and climbed the carpeted stairs.

Instead of leading the way to her office to the right of the stairs, she turned left and led him through a small hallway that was cluttered with furnishings that had been hastily and haphazardly removed from one of the rooms.

Strange time to be rearranging furniture, when she is expecting me for what I must assume is a professional conference.

"I could use a hand in here," she said.

Kirk followed her into a small room that had been stripped of all furnishings. To judge from the discolored geometric spaces on the walls, it had been stripped of all pictures as well. He noticed one other thing: The room had no windows. The only piece of furniture was a small upholstered love seat.

"Take the other end, Mr. Kirk," Scott ordered. "And be very careful not to damage the doorway or the walls outside in the hall."

"Yes, ma'am," he replied crisply.

She rebuked him with a glare. "Okay, now! Lift!"

He had to grant one thing, she did her share of lifting. With considerable care, together they moved the love seat into the hall, placing it against the wall so that it still left a passageway.

"Good!" she said. "Now I must freshen up before Chris gets here."

"Would you mind explaining what this is all about?" Kirk asked.

"Since we don't have much time, I will have to do that while I am getting freshened up. Come with me."

Kirk followed her along the hallway to a room at the end. While they walked, she spoke crisply.

"You made such a point of the importance of time as a factor in your legal plans. So I accelerated his treatment. Not too much, I hope. But we may discover that tonight."

113

By that time she had led the way into her bedroom. She continued talking while she retired to the dressing room, where, judging from her variations of voice and inflection, she was changing clothes.

"I've been regressing Chris for several sessions."

"Back to his early years when the abuse took place?" Kirk assumed.

"I haven't dared try that yet. Until tonight. That's why all furniture, everything movable or breakable, had to be taken out of that room. Abreaction can be an extremely traumatic event."

"Requiring a totally bare room?" Kirk questioned.

"In the hospital I would have two orderlies standing by with restraining sheets and a straitjacket."

"Patients become that violent," Kirk realized. "And I noticed no window. To prevent jumping?"

"It could happen," she admitted. "So, no windows. No exposed radiators, no bookshelves, no pictures. In a word, no sharp edges or corners. Even the TV camera is up high and out of reach."

By now she had returned to the room attired in a neat skirt and blouse, with her blond hair back in her geometric braid.

Kirk realized that he liked her better with her hair straggling a bit. She looked more . . . more accessible.

As they started back to her office, Kirk asked, "Any instructions for me?"

"Just observe. Take it all in. So you are ready to deal with Stone's so-called experts."

She was interrupted by the doorbell.

"He's here," she said softly, with an air of warning.

She buzzed to admit him, then went to the head of the stairs to call, "You may come up, Chris."

Kirk heard the muffled footsteps climb the carpeted stairs.

Cory was noticeably surprised to discover David Kirk

there. He smiled, nodded. Apparently he had trouble adjusting to that situation.

"Everything we do, Chris, will be the same as in the last half dozen sessions."

"Hypnosis," he assumed.

"Yes," she confirmed.

"Okay," he agreed, starting toward her office.

Once in his usual chair, he was ready for the procedure to begin. Scott took a place behind him. She softly suggested the familiar images of green fields, light breezes, stairways leading down, counting, making him count with her. Very soon he was under.

"Chris, I want you to follow me down the hall and into another room."

She started out. Cory followed. Scott led him to the bare room.

"Now, Chris," she continued, speaking very slowly, "we are going backward in time again. You are no longer twenty-six. You are now twenty-one. Do you hear me, Chris? And now you are eighteen. Eighteen, Chris. And now sixteen. Thirteen, Chris. You are now thirteen. And now twelve. Twelve, Chris. This time we are going even further back. To nine, to eight. Now you are seven years old. Seven. And now, Chris, now you are six. Six years old."

He nodded, eyes still closed.

"Chris, when I touch your hand you will open your eyes."

He nodded, responding to her suggestion.

"Chris, can you remember being six years old? Whom did you live with when you were six? Chris?"

"Mama . . ."

Kirk noticed that he pronounced that word not in the low, emotional voice of adult hypnotic Chris Cory. He actually sounded like a child, a frightened child.

"Are you afraid, Chris? Afraid of your own mother?"

His face took on a look of childish anguish. He turned away from Scott. In doing so he found himself facing Kirk. He turned from him too. Slowly he moved to a corner of the bare room. He sank to the floor, huddling there as if trying to hide or disappear. Suddenly he raised his arms to ward off a blow that he was in terror of receiving. He began to whimper like a frightened child of six.

Kirk looked to Scott for some sign, but she signaled him to remain silent and to move out of Cory's line of vision.

"Chris, who is going to hit you?"

"He."

"Who is he?"

"He," was all that little Chris dared reply.

Scott approached slowly until she stood over him. Once more he raised his arms to ward off new blows, crying, "Please, no, I won't look, I won't know. . . . Please, please?"

Cory was crying bitterly, wiping away the tears with the sleeve of his jacket, as a child would.

"Chris, who is 'he'?" Scott persisted.

"He . . . he come to see her every afternoon . . . every afternoon . . . since Papa died," six-year-old Chris responded.

"And what does he do, Chris?"

"Does things . . . things . . . to her . . . in that room. I looked. He catch me, hit me. 'You do that again and I beat the living crap out of you, I teach you a lesson you never forget.' "

"*Do* you look again, Chris?"

From his crouching position in the corner, Chris nodded, a terrified, guilty little boy.

"*Does* he catch you, Chris?"

Chris nodded, huddling even tighter within himself.

"What does he do, Chris?" Scott had to repeat it before Cory could bring himself to answer. "What does he do?"

"He . . . reach into my jeans, takes out my doodle . . ."

"What does the man do when he takes out your doodle?" Scott asked.

"Says he cut it off," six-year-old Chris said.

"He said . . ." Scott tried to repeat but she was interrupted by Cory.

"He did it . . . did it . . ." little Chris said.

Scott and Kirk looked at each other in shock and alarm. Neither of them had had any inkling of such a traumatic event in Cory's early life. Surely one of the doctors who had examined him would have noticed such a deficiency.

"Chris, tell me . . ." Scott asked very softly, very gently, "that man—does he really cut off your doodle?"

"Max . . . he do it to Max," little Chris said.

The reply sounded even stranger to Dr. Scott than Cory's original admission. She gestured to Kirk, *I must get to the bottom of this.*

"Chris, do you know Max?"

"My dad give me Max," little Chris said very proudly.

"He gave you Max? How did he do that?" Scott asked.

"Birthday. When I five. He bring Max home. He say, 'Son, he is yours. Let's give him a name.' "

The description of the event, bare as it was, gave Scott the hint she needed.

"Chris, is Max the name you gave the dog your father brought you for your birthday?"

"Dad . . . he says, 'Son, what's the funniest name you can think of for a dog?' And I say, 'Max.' " Little Chris laughed, recalling that day, that singular happy event.

"Chris, that man . . . who does things with your mama, things you watch, did he do something to Max?"

The laughter was gone. Terror had overtaken Chris again. He crouched, trembling, a frightened child.

"What does he do, Chris?"

"Like he said," was all that little Chris dared reply.

"You can tell me, Chris, I won't hurt you. No one will hurt you."

"*He* will!" Chris insisted.

"He can't hurt you now if you tell."

"He will. He will! He did it to Max!"

"Did what to Max?"

"Cut off his doodle," little Chris said, beginning to cry with all the pain that only a child can feel.

"Chris, did you *see* him do it?" Scott persisted.

"Pick him up. Like he said he do to me. Pick him up. Put him on the edge of the table. Take my mama's big kitchen knife. Put Max's doodle down and just . . . just . . ."

With a single sharp stroke of his outstretched hand, Cory brought it down on the floor as if amputating the dog's penis.

"Don't you do that!" Chris cried out with all the anger and terror of a child. "Max is mine! Don't you do that!"

Cory catapulted from the huddled position to thrust himself against the wall as if hurling himself against that man. He bounced off one wall and into another. Scott and Kirk moved swiftly to stay out of his way as he continued running into one wall, then another, to attack this brute of a man who had done such a hellish atrocity to the one thing six-year-old Chris had held so dear, the only surviving thing his father had left him.

He continued to thrash about, impervious to pain or physical injury, until he finally sank to the floor, exhausted.

"Chris," Scott persisted, "what he did to Max, he threatens to do the same to you?"

Chris nodded, without daring to look up at her.

"And does he ever do it?"

Six-year-old Chris did not respond at once. After a long silence, he said, "Once . . . once . . . he catches me looking again . . . drags me to the table. I am kicking . . . crying . . . I call, 'Mama! Mama!' He drags me just the same, takes the big knife, rips open my jeans . . ."

He pressed both his hands on his crotch protectively while turning his face away and shuddering in terror.

"Chris . . . what happens?" Scott asked.

"Rips open my jeans . . . takes out . . . my doodle . . ."

Cory unzipped his slacks, reached in and brought out his penis. He held it out, as if it were indeed stretched on the table. Then he brought his other hand down sharply on the floor like a carving knife chopping it off.

". . . brings that knife down . . . hard . . . real hard . . ."

"On your doodle, Chris?"

"Yes . . . no . . . I think he does. I think . . . I can't feel. . . . He cut it off . . . but he didn't. . . . Just to scare me . . . scare me . . . scare me . . ."

He began to cry bitterly again.

"Is that the only time that happened, Chris?"

He shook his head. Then, suddenly, he glared up at Scott. With hatred and fear repressed for twenty years, he accused, "And you let him. . . . You let him."

He leaped to his feet, then turned on Scott to attack her, trying to beat her with both his fists. His attack was so sudden and of such ferocity that she was momentarily surprised and defenseless. Kirk leaped in to seize Cory in an embrace that pinned his arms to his sides. Cory struggled with almost demonic strength, but Kirk held him prisoner until his fury passed and he sank to the floor again.

Kirk was free to turn his attention to Michal Scott, who was still stunned and breathless. He took her in his arms, held her close, so close he could feel the pulse in her throat throbbing swiftly against his cheek. He held her until gradually the throbbing slowed to a more normal, steady beat.

Regaining her composure, she became aware of Kirk's embrace. She extricated herself, explaining, "He identified me with his mother. I had not expected that. Now I must release him from his torment."

She left Kirk's side to join Cory, who was crouched, exhausted, in the corner.

"Chris, stand up." He obeyed the command. "Now, Chris, when you come out of this, you will not recall what happened. Nor will you feel any anger, or any sorrow. You will only feel rested. Very rested, ready to go home and have a good night's sleep."

Cory nodded.

"Now, Chris, wake up."

He opened his eyes, smiled, then suddenly realized his exposed condition. He turned away from her. When he was in a proper state, he turned back, embarrassed and puzzled.

"It's all right, Chris. It was part of the session. How do you feel?"

He smiled sheepishly. "Aside from embarrassment, fine, a little sleepy, though."

"You go straight home. Have a good night's sleep. And tomorrow, our usual five o'clock."

After Cory had left, Scott said, "Now you see why sometimes we need attendants and a straitjacket."

"God," Kirk remarked, "do people really inflict such torture on helpless little kids?"

"I've heard worse from patients," Scott replied. "But now we know why his alter is named Max. Why Max killed the Ames woman."

"She rejected him, like his mother did," Kirk added.

"To him rejection means castration. The threat with which that man terrorized him. Chris will have to relive that trauma many times before he can overcome it and we can consider him cured."

Kirk could not resist a faint smile.

"Are you amused, Mr. Kirk?" she challenged.

"I was thinking, this is ironic. You want him sane. I want him insane. At least until his trial is over."

"The difference between us, Mr. Kirk. My profession is

dedicated to finding the truth. Yours is dedicated to hiding it."

His smile, faint as it was, disappeared.

Almost by way of apology she added, "Thank you for helping out when you did. I have never lost control of a patient before."

"Maybe you should do it more often. It was a refreshing experience not to see you in such total control."

She chose not to respond. Instead, she said very crisply, "You are free now to file your notice to plead insanity, Mr. Kirk."

She was once again the self-contained professional, one of the best in her field, the Dr. Michal Scott he had first met.

Sixteen

Assistant DA Howard Stone examined the document a second time before he exploded to his assistant, "What the hell is Davey Kirk trying to pull this time?"

His assistant was Harriet Fielder, a young black woman. Despite women's lib, NOW and endless federal and state court decisions assuring her protection against exploitation, harassment and all the other evils visited upon her race and gender, Harriet never surmounted her fear of Howard Stone once he was outraged. As he now was.

"Fielder, get that sonofabitch Kirk on the phone! Tell him that notice to plead mental disease as a defense must, by law, be filed within thirty days after arraignment! Which in this case is long, long gone!"

"I already have," she reported.

"Oh, you have," Stone replied, always disappointed when he discovered that his decisions and orders had been anticipated by an alert assistant. As he reached for his pills, he asked, "Well, what did that genius have to say?"

"I didn't get to speak to him. I talked to Gerry Prince. Gerry said that in this particular case it was impossible to satisfy the time requirement in the law."

"Oh, so *Gerry* decided that the statutory provisions did not apply," Stone remarked caustically. "Did you have the audacity to suggest to him that in determining if the statute did not apply there is such a person as a judge, whose job it is to make that decision?"

"I did point that out."

"And?" Stone demanded.

"Gerry said they were ready to take the matter to Judge Malachi if you did not see fit to waive the statutory time limit."

"Very good, my dear. We shall have a very interesting meeting with old Malachi. Get his secretary, Ida, on the phone. Arrange a time to meet in chambers."

"Yes, Mr. Stone," the young woman replied, starting for the door.

Before she had taken a second step, Stone called out, "Hattie, don't let all my yelling and screaming obscure the lesson to be learned from this little event. Never, never give a shrewdie like Kirk an edge. Any edge. Because you don't know what that bastard has in mind. Got it?"

"Got it, Mr. Stone," Hattie Fielder replied. She could not resist pointing out, "From what I hear around the office, you were the one who trained Kirk."

"All right, all right," Stone shot back. "On my tombstone it will say, 'He trained David Kirk.' You'd think that was the *only* thing I did in my twenty-four years in this godforsaken place." Then he admitted somewhat grudgingly, "Boy, when

I train them I train them good. And if you listen and watch, I will do the same for you, young lady. I mean young *woman,* of course. Now, get on the horn and arrange that meeting.''

Since David Kirk was on trial in Federal Court, defending a bank official who had been charged with laundering the proceeds of a drug enterprise, the meeting in Judge Malachi's chambers was set for five-thirty on Wednesday afternoon.

Stone was already pacing in the judge's waiting room when Kirk arrived. They found Malachi in chambers, shed of his black robe, wearing an unbuttoned vest and just wetting the end of a fresh cigar. Before he even acknowledged their presence, he carefully bit off the tip, lit up, took a deep enough puff to assure that it was quite satisfactory, pleasing, in fact. While admiring his cigar he remarked casually, ''Boys, I understand we have some kind of dispute here.''

''No dispute, Your Honor,'' Stone replied sarcastically. ''Unless you consider flouting the statutory requirements a dispute.''

Malachi turned his wheelchair just enough to not quite face David Kirk. ''Well, 'Counselor,' what do you have to say to that?''

''The statute may require notice of intent to plead mental disease as a defense,'' Kirk began.

'' 'May' require?'' Stone interrupted. ''*Does* require! And there are no specific exceptions!''

''Exactly why we are here, 'Mister' Stone,'' Kirk replied. ''Because the statute does not take into account one important fact. Unless an attorney uses that defense frivolously, he must be able to support it with sound, adequate medical and psychiatric proof. Which in the case of my client took much more than the legally specified thirty days.''

''Come on, Davey,'' Stone replied, ''another of your little

fun and games. Right? I have never seen a psychiatric diagnosis that could not be made in a week, two weeks. And I have seen them all: schizos, paranoids, manic-depressives. But none of them took forty-nine days to diagnose.''

Prepared for the inevitable reaction, David Kirk replied, '' 'Mister' Stone, I'm afraid that your experience in the field of mental disease is too limited to encompass the problem we now face.''

Challenged, Stone defied, "Which is?"

"I would prefer to discuss that with one of your psychiatric experts," Kirk said.

"*You* would prefer. Well, Davey, *I* would prefer to discuss it right here, right now, in the presence of Judge Malachi, whose decision will ultimately prevail!"

From within a cloud of cigar smoke Malachi intoned, "You heard the man, Davey."

"Your Honor, making a diagnosis of this complexity takes many sessions and considerable explanation."

"You already told me that, kiddo. What the hell are you getting at?" Malachi demanded angrily.

"I am forced to plead that my client is suffering from a mental condition that robs him of the necessary element of intent to commit the crime with which he is charged."

"Davey!" Malachi rebuked, his irritation blatant by now. "Get to the point! Exactly *what* mental condition?"

"My client is suffering from Multiple Personality Disorder," Kirk announced.

Howard Stone threw up his hands. He turned away from the judge's desk and started to circle the large room, holding a conversation with himself.

"Multiple Personality Disorder. Did you hear the man? He has no shame, no shame at all. Would any other attorney in the whole state of New York dare to present such a bullshit defense? That rough-sex plea, that was a doozie. And the one where he claimed the murderer didn't stab the victim but the victim accidentally ran into the knife, that was another. But this . . . Oh, boy!"

Stone turned back to face Malachi. "Aaron, are you going to allow him to get away with this?"

"Howie, he has the right to plead any defense he chooses."

"And you have the right to cut him off at the knees right now. Just deny him the extension," Stone urged.

Malachi sat thoughtfully in his wheelchair while he contemplated the smoke that trailed up from his cigar.

"Your Honor—" Stone prodded.

"So, what is *your* position, 'Counselor'?" Malachi demanded.

"It is twofold," Kirk began.

"Give it to me one fold at a time," Malachi ordered.

"In the first place, since amnesia is a basic element of the condition of Multiple Personality Disorder, my client's inability to recall any of the facts involved in this crime renders him unable to assist in his own defense."

"Bullshit!" Stone interjected.

"Howie, it is my right to express all the opinions in this case," Malachi rebuked. Turning to Kirk, the old judge said, "Bullshit, Davey. Pure and unadulterated. Now, you had a second fold, I believe."

"Amnesia also raises the question of whether, at the time of the commission of the crime, my client knew right from wrong. We do not know what he knew at that time. Nor does he. Therefore he is not legally responsible," Kirk declared, determined to reserve the matter of alter Max for the trial itself.

Malachi nodded gravely, giving Kirk a momentary sense of having scored his points. Instead of arriving at a decision, Malachi said, "Excuse me, boys, but nature calls." With that, he rolled his wheelchair toward his private lavatory.

During Malachi's absence, Stone continued to shake his

head in disbelief and carry on his one-man conversation. "If there is anyone who has Multiple Personality Disorder it is not the client but his attorney. Talk about weird. I have seen my share. But nothing like this. I mean, this is chutzpah in the first degree. And he thought that Malachi, of all judges, would buy it."

Kirk waited patiently, not even attempting to respond to Howie Stone's monologue.

Soon Judge Malachi rolled back into the room.

"Boys, you won't believe it. But in there I got one of my bright ideas. Actually two bright ideas. First, I thought, I know what our friend Davey is up to. He has got himself a movie deal. Or at the least a television deal. Michael Douglas will play David Kirk in one of those thrilling movie epics where a brilliant, honest fighter for justice defends a victim against the system. And, as an added twist, to get the movie companies hooked, he ties in with it another *Three Faces of Eve*. But, instead of Joanne Woodward, we have Meryl Streep playing the part.

"You see, Howie, in order to practice law these days you have to understand the movie business. With Michael Douglas in the lead we need a woman to balance the picture. So we make Cory into a woman."

Malachi turned back to Kirk. "Am I close?"

"Your Honor, there is no movie deal. And no tricks. This is a legitimate diagnosis and defense. As I will demonstrate to your satisfaction at the time of trial. I stake my reputation as an attorney on that."

Howie Stone chuckled as he said, "I like His Honor's movie idea better."

Indignantly, David Kirk turned to Stone. "Damn it, Howie, I was there. I saw the proof with my own eyes, heard it with my own ears. Christopher Cory suffers from Multiple Personality Disorder. Put me under oath and I will swear to that myself."

Touched by Kirk's declaration, Judge Malachi interceded, "Davey, you didn't let me tell you the other idea I got in there. Such a fertile area for ideas."

He puffed on his cigar, discovered it had gone dead. He relit it, puffed a few times and declared, "Davey, under the new law in the state of New York, the DA no longer is required to prove the defendant sane. *You* have to prove him *insane*. So I am going to give you a break. I will allow our friend Howie to appoint a psychiatrist to examine your client. If he comes up with a report which says that it is *possible* your client has this multiple thing, I will allow you permission to file, even though time has expired."

"Thank you, Your Honor. Nothing could be fairer," Kirk replied.

But Stone interjected, "Let me remind you, 'Counselor,' once you plead mental disability, all your psychiatric records and findings must be presented to us!"

"And you'll have them," Kirk promised, anxious to get out before Stone could reopen the discussion.

Kirk had not yet reached the door when Malachi's gruff voice warned, "And let *me* remind *you*, 'Counselor,' if you are planning one of your usual games, I will burn your ass during the trial."

Seventeen

Within two days, David Kirk's office was notified to present Christopher Cory for examination on the following Monday at the offices of Dr. Helmut Klinger, which were located in the Psychiatric Department of St. Luke's Hospital up on Morningside Heights.

When Kirk returned from court and was handed the message, he immediately called Dr. Michal Scott.

At the mention of the name, Scott exclaimed, "Oh, God, not Klinger."

"Why? What's wrong with Klinger?" Kirk asked.

"He's one of the old fogies who virtually does not admit to such a condition as MPD," Scott said.

"How can he possibly take such a position?" Kirk asked.

"You'll see when we meet him," she pointed out.

"I didn't think you would want to take the time."

"Knowing Klinger as I do, I'd better be there too," she insisted. "I have witnessed too many battles between him and John—Dr. Beaumont—to miss this."

———

Late on Monday afternoon, to suit Scott's crowded schedule, David Kirk, Chris Cory and Dr. Scott arrived at Dr. Klinger's office.

At first glance, Kirk found Klinger to be a pleasant old man, short but robust in stature, with inquisitive owllike eyes behind thick-lensed glasses. He sported a trim beard, which reminded Kirk of classic photographs of Sigmund Freud. When Klinger greeted them, he betrayed the vestiges of a European accent. Later Scott would remark to Kirk, "He not only strives to look and sound like Freud, he wants people to think he is the old man's successor."

"Well," Klinger greeted them, "ah, I see you have brought Dr. Scott along. How do you do, my dear? It seems we have not met since . . . well, since the most unhappy occasion of dear John's memorial service. How you must miss him."

Kirk detected that there was a history of personal discord between them which Klinger enjoyed but Scott resented.

"Well, now, to the business at hand," Klinger said, turning to Christopher Cory, who had remained silent through the preliminary greetings, unaware of any conflict. "And this is the patient, I assume?"

"Dr. Klinger, Christopher Cory," Kirk introduced them.

"Ah, yes, I recall seeing his picture in the newspapers. And, from what I have been informed, the subject of a most interesting diagnosis." He cast an impish smile in Michal Scott's direction. "So we shall see. Mr. Kirk, would you ask your client to step outside for a moment?"

Once Cory left, Klinger became much more direct. "Dr. Scott, from the material you sent me I understand that under hypnosis you were able to evoke an alter personality. Is that correct?"

"Yes, yes it is," Scott replied.

"May I ask if this so-called alter personality came out on its own, or did you have to suggest he come out?" Klinger demanded.

"Hold on, Klinger!" Kirk interposed. "I myself had a previous telephone conversation with the alter. And I have also seen him under hypnosis."

"Aha! You see, Mr. Kirk, how easily people, even intelligent people like yourself, can be fooled," Klinger enjoyed saying. "Perhaps I should acquaint you with this so-called phenomenon termed Multiple Personality Disorder. And I am sure Dr. Scott will corroborate everything I say. Right, my dear?"

"That depends on what you say," Scott replied.

Kirk noticed that she flushed in anger.

"Anytime you disagree, speak up, my dear," Klinger invited genially, yet with the same undertone of rivalry that Kirk had detected earlier.

"My dear Mr. Kirk, we psychiatrists and psychoanalysts practice a profession that is given to as many fads and fancies as those of the women's fashion industry. We, too, have our styles that come and go. Who now believes in the traditional psychoanalysis of a generation ago? Not many. A fad comes and is gone. So it is with MPD. Today a fad, tomorrow gone."

"I deny that," Scott interrupted sharply.

Klinger smiled at her condescendingly. Kirk realized the old man was trying to demean her by treating her as a misguided student.

"Everywhere we turn these days they are finding Multiple Personality Disorder. Books, movies, television. It is the rage. Like rap music." Klinger chuckled. "It would not surprise me to have someone propose a civil rights law that demands that each alter have the right to vote."

"The point, Doctor?" Kirk urged.

"The point is that I am very skeptical of any diagnosis of MPD. Put a patient with some mental disturbance under hypnosis, suggest he produce an alter, and he will manufacture one. On demand. That is why we have so many cases now. To please doctors who like such diagnoses."

The flush in Scott's cheeks grew deeper and more pronounced, but in the interest of Kirk's position and his obligation to Chris Cory, she maintained a very trying silence.

"Dr. Klinger," Kirk asked, "do I understand that you do not accept such a diagnosis under any circumstances?"

"Oh, there *are* cases, very, very few cases, in which MPD is a legitimate diagnosis. But in a case like this, who knows?" He turned to Scott. "My dear, if I remember correctly, John had certain tests he applied to discover if a patient was truly under hypnosis. Did you apply those?"

"I did!" Scott replied firmly.

"And you were convinced that he was truly under at all times when his alter came out?"

"Beyond question," Scott replied.

"I was there. I saw it," Kirk reinforced her statement.

"Please, Mr. Kirk, no offense. But a lawyer desperate for a defense for his client is not exactly what I would call an impartial witness," Klinger said, with a certain air of light amusement.

"Dr. Klinger, you obviously have some doubts, which is precisely why we brought Cory here. For you to examine him yourself," Kirk said. "So instead of this professional bantering, let's get to it."

"Get to what?" the old man demanded. "She will hypnotize him. He will produce an alter, as he has been conditioned to do. And what will that prove? Nothing. Not even that he is truly hypnotized. After all, we have here a secondary motive. He is on trial for murder. Such a hypnotism would not impress me."

"Then, what would?" Kirk demanded.

"A Rorschach test," Klinger suggested.

Kirk glanced at Scott for some clue as to how to proceed. She answered directly, "Yes. A Rorschach would be in order."

"Then, if I arrange it, will you make your client available?" Klinger asked.

Before Kirk would agree he asked, "What will those ink-blots tell us that we don't already know?"

"Oh, a great deal," Klinger insisted. "Especially if we conduct a *double* Rorschach."

"Double Rorschach?" Kirk questioned, unwilling to jeopardize his client's rights. Kirk asked permission to confer privately with Dr. Scott in Klinger's waiting room.

"I once had a client subjected to a Rorschach, but never a double. What's a *double* Rorschach?"

"He wants to give Chris a Rorschach. Then he wants to give Max one, too," Scott explained.

"Is that possible?" Kirk asked.

"If I can induce Max to come out and undergo the test, it's possible."

"What'll it prove?" Kirk asked.

"That they either are or are not two distinct personalities."

"Doctor, Cory and his freedom are dependent on your judgment. You call the shots."

"I say let him proceed with both tests."

Once they had informed Klinger of the decision, he said, "Good. Very good. You will present him here on Tuesday next at ten o'clock in the morning."

"Here?" Scott questioned.

"Yes. I will conduct these tests myself," Klinger declared. "After all, a case this important, I trust no one's judgment but my own. So Tuesday, here. Ten o'clock."

From Scott's reaction, Kirk realized that Klinger administering both tests was distinctly not to her liking.

"Dr. Klinger," Kirk interposed, "don't you think that in view of the fact that you may have to testify later in this case, it might be better to have this test administered by some impartial person qualified to give Rorschachs and interpret the results?"

"Oh, I am quite well qualified to administer Rorschachs. Ask Dr. Scott. Even her esteemed and dearly beloved teacher, John Beaumont, respected my ability in that field. Despite our differences on other matters. Not so, Doctor?"

Kirk detected the flush rise into Scott's cheeks once more. But then she granted, "Yes, Dr. Klinger is quite expert in that field."

"Good! Then it is settled," Klinger said, obviously looking forward to the prospect.

"I assume," Scott added, "that you will have no objection to my submitting the results to another expert for a 'blind' evaluation?"

For an instant the smug smile on Klinger's lips froze, then relaxed as he agreed, "Of course I have no objection. Tuesday. Ten o'clock."

Once outside Klinger's office, Kirk asked, "What the hell is a 'blind' evaluation?"

"An interpretation and diagnosis made by an expert who has no idea who the subject, or in this case the subjects, are. Therefore he can be far more objective and unprejudiced than our friend Klinger will be."

" 'Our friend' Klinger seems to know a great deal about you and your Dr. Beaumont. The way he keeps hinting," Kirk suggested.

Michal Scott dismissed Kirk's comment with a curt, unexplained "Professional jealousy, Mr. Kirk, professional jealousy."

Eighteen

It was late afternoon.

In his private office, David Kirk and Gerry Prince were reaching the point of exasperation with an elderly alibi witness for their client. The man insisted on answering Gerry's questions with one constant refrain: "I may be eighty-two years old, but my eyes are as good now as they were when I was twenty-one years old!"

"Mr. DeBrizio, forget your age!" Gerry insisted. "Because, when they get into the jury room, the first thing those jurors will say, 'That man is too old to see what he says he saw.' Now, just answer, where was Dominick?

How do you know that? And why do you remember it so clearly?"

"Hey, Mr. Kirk, whose side is this kid on?" old DeBrizio demanded. "I'm here to tell the jury my nephew Dominick didn't do it. I don't care what they accuse him of, he didn't do it."

Both Kirk and Gerry decided that the witness was too argumentative to add anything of value to his defense when the phone rang.

Giving vent to his impatience, Kirk shouted into the phone, "Greta, what's so damned important you interrupt us in the middle of preparing a witness?"

Instead of Greta's voice, he heard the crisp voice of Dr. Michal Scott.

"Mr. Kirk, it is now twenty after five. Chris Cory has not yet appeared for his five o'clock hour," Scott informed him.

"What do you mean, he hasn't appeared?" Kirk demanded. Turning to Gerry, he said, "Get Cory on the other line!"

"I've already had my secretary call," Dr. Scott informed. "There's no answer."

"Then he's probably on his way," Kirk suggested, refusing to accept the alternative.

"I doubt that, since he lives only fifteen minutes by bus from my office."

"You think he's skipped?" Kirk asked gingerly.

"I have my suspicions. But I'd rather wait until we have more evidence."

"Look, we're just finishing up with a witness now. Please wait for me. I will be at your office in half an hour."

As David Kirk paced her office in frustration and anger, he stormed, "I warned that kid. I told him what this could mean!

134

Revocation of bail! End of his treatment here! Worse, the end of any defense!" He turned to Dr. Scott to admit, "I believed that kid. I went bail for him because I trusted him." He spoke more in regret than in anger.

Scott began to say, "I realize it's your ten thousand dollars, but I suggest . . ."

"It is not the money! I put my reputation on the line for him. And he does something like this!"

"I was about to say, I suggest we suspend judgment. In the first place, we don't know if he *has* skipped. At this moment he might be sitting on a bench in Central Park. Afraid to come here for fear I will unearth something he can't bring himself to face. It happens frequently with patients. And always when some crucial revelation is about to surface. I suggest we just wait and see."

"Don't patients generally call?"

"Usually they call the next morning, apologize and beg me not to cancel them out altogether," Scott replied.

"When he calls, get me right away. We can't sit on this too long. Don't forget we have to present him to Klinger for that Rorschach."

"Which may be the cause of all this," Scott suggested.

"He's jittery about facing a Rorschach?" Kirk asked.

"He might feel it will reveal too much."

Kirk nodded but with great concern. "I once had a client blow town for three weeks. Finally tracked him down in Vegas. Brought him back and no one was any wiser. But with Cory we have this deadline."

"Mr. Kirk, we are six days away from Tuesday. He will likely show up before then," Scott tried to reassure him.

"I hope you're right. In the meantime, no one is to know he's missing. No one!"

Late the next afternoon, when they returned from court, David Kirk called Dr. Scott. Had Cory appeared for his five o'clock hour today? No. Had he called to explain? No.

Two days gone. Kirk noted, then turned to refresh his mind on the day's testimony in their present case, but found himself too distracted by his missing client.

The following day Kirk called Scott's office twice. Still no sign or word from Cory.

"Three days gone," he raged to Gerry Prince. "Only three days left."

"And," Gerry reminded him morosely, "two of those are Saturday and Sunday. Days when he isn't even expected to see Dr. Scott."

"Man, I can just see them now. Old Malachi glaring at me, sure that I engineered this whole thing. And Howie Stone . . . his smug smirk when I have to admit my ten-thousand-dollars bail money is down the drain."

"Then he'll down two more little pills," Gerry observed. "He eats those things like popcorn."

"Not when he gloats," Kirk replied. He was silent for a moment before exploding, "Clients! Kid, if you learn anything in this office, always ask for a big fee. Clients who pay big fees respect the money they shell out. They take advice. They follow instructions. But the freebies, the ones you defend for practically nothing at the court's insistence, they're more trouble than all the others put together. Of which our Mr. Cory is a prime example!"

On Friday, David Kirk called Dr. Scott not once but four different times. Only to learn there was still no word from, no sign of, Chris Cory.

On the last call, Dr. Scott said, "Mr. Kirk, may I suggest that if I hear anything *I* call *you*?"

"Are you saying I'm making a nuisance of myself?" Kirk demanded, more than a little indignant.

"I am saying there is no reason to call. When there is, if

there is, I will call you," she said in her clipped professional manner.

Damn it, she's treating me like one of her kooky patients, he fumed silently.

Aloud, he mimicked her crisp delivery. "Yes, Doctor. Do that! Please!"

The suave lawyer, the society idol, the ladies' man, pouts like a little boy when he is frustrated, Michal Scott thought, smiling.

"Doctor, when Tuesday rolls around and you are due to present Mr. Cory for his Rorschach, what will you tell Dr. Klinger?"

"That Cory is not available," she replied very matter-of-factly. "I'm sure that's happened before in his practice."

"Not with patients out on bail facing a murder charge!" Kirk rebutted angrily.

"I wouldn't know, Mr. Kirk," she responded.

Losing all patience, Kirk shouted, "Doctor, don't you realize that the minute you say that to Klinger he will report that to Judge Malachi. Cory will be considered a fugitive and if caught he'll be back in the slammer and no longer free for treatment?"

"Yes, Mr. Kirk, I realize that. And it would be most unfortunate. But exactly what do you suggest I do about it?"

"Show some interest, some concern!" he exploded.

Even more calmly, she responded. "Mr. Kirk, I *am* interested. *And* concerned. But if I were to become emotionally involved in every difficulty of each of my patients, I would be no help to them at all."

"Yes. Sure. Of course," Kirk was forced to concede, thinking, *I suppose she is giving me the same advice.* "Well, if either of us hears anything, we'll call. Right?"

"Right," Scott agreed.

He suspected she was relieved to agree only so that she could hang up.

By Saturday afternoon, David Kirk was quite resigned to the fact that Chris Cory had jumped bail and fled New York. Fortunately, he would not have to be the one to break the news. That would be Dr. Scott's job. Then, when he was summoned to Malachi's chambers, he would meet with the old man and Howie Stone, admit that against all his advice his client had fled the jurisdiction. He was now subject to any steps the district attorney and the court felt obliged to take.

Malachi and Stone would have a great laugh at his expense. And by his expense he meant ten thousand dollars' worth. A cheap price to get rid of this annoying, time-consuming case.

After Kirk finished his Saturday stint at the office, routine during a trial, he went off to the athletic club for a much-needed workout, a few games of squash, a long, hot session in the sauna, followed by a relaxing massage.

He had split games on the squash court, then entered the sauna with a towel wrapped around his midriff, when suddenly there was a knock on the heavily insulated door.

Kirk reached the door as Gerry opened it, insisting, "Dave, you better come out here!"

David Kirk had been called out of the sauna other times in the past, but never by Gerry in such an agitated state.

Kirk stepped out into the cool air of the corridor to ask, "Okay, kid, relax and tell me. The judge turned down our motion for a mistrial in the Wolberg case, right?"

"Wrong," Gerry said. "This is weird. Eerie."

"What?" Kirk demanded impatiently.

"It was so strange that I asked him to call you here. You can take it in the manager's office."

Clad only in a towel, David Kirk hurried down the corridor as fast as he could in his paper sandals. Inside the manager's office, he picked up the phone.

"Kirk here," he announced crisply.

From the other end of the line, in a voice so soft as to be almost inaudible, he heard, "I don't blame you for being angry with me, Mr. Kirk."

He recognized the voice.

"Chris! Where the hell have you been for four days?"

"I don't know," he replied. His voice broke, his words were stifled in sobs.

"Chris! Chris, listen to me! Take your time. Get hold of yourself. Just regain control. Regain control," Kirk coaxed, while gesturing Gerry to get on the extension phone. After a few seconds, during which he could hear Cory gasp his way back from tears, Kirk said, "Now—Chris . . . tell me, where are you?"

"In a phone booth."

"I don't mean that. I mean what street. . . . Near your home, or where?" Kirk asked, gesturing to Gerry to write down any location Cory would give.

"Wait. I'll find out."

Though the answer struck Kirk as strange, he waited patiently until Cory returned to the phone.

"Water Street," he informed.

"Water Street," Kirk repeated. His hand over the mouthpiece he asked, "Gerry, is there a Water Street in New York?"

"Maybe it's one of those old crooked little streets in lower Manhattan. From the days of early New Amsterdam," Gerry suggested.

"Chris, what is the cross street?" Kirk asked.

Once more Cory said, "I'll have to see."

"Have to see?" Gerry echoed. "What the hell's going on with him?"

Cory was back to report, "Scranton Avenue."

This time Kirk was more than puzzled. He was highly suspicious.

As was Gerry Prince, who said, "He's playing games. There's no Scranton Avenue in Manhattan."

"Chris!" Kirk demanded, "Where the hell are you?"

"Scranton," he replied.

"Scranton?" Kirk questioned.

"Scranton, Pennsylvania," Cory informed him.

"Didn't I warn you not to leave the island of Manhattan?" Kirk exploded, giving full vent to his fury. "Is that where you've been for the last four days?"

He would have continued to rage on, but from the other end of the line he heard sobbing once more and muffled words that sounded like "I don't know . . . I don't know . . . I don't know. . . ."

"Chris, Chris, listen to me," Kirk tried to interrupt him.

But the young man continued to sob, saying, "I'm afraid . . . I don't know what to do. . . . I don't know how I got here. I'm . . . I'm afraid."

Kirk spoke more gently now, more reassuringly. "Chris, listen to me. Everything is going to be all right. Now, tell me, do you have any money on you?"

"I spent my last change to make this call," Cory explained.

Usually, in such a predicament, David Kirk would have advised his client to go to the nearest police station and wait there. But in this instance, since Cory's flight had to be kept secret, especially from any law-enforcement agency, Kirk advised, "Chris, go to the Greyhound bus station. There must be one in a city the size of Scranton. . . . No, never mind that," he corrected, thinking that anyone loitering around a bus station for hours would arouse the suspicion of the local police. "Tell you what, find the YMCA. Go there. Wait. I will come pick you up. It'll be three or four hours. But you wait right there. Promise?"

"Yeah . . . yes . . . I promise," Cory said.

Kirk realized Cory was sobbing once more. Then he heard the sound of a hang-up.

"Gerry, get my car, please, while I get dressed."

"You're going to Scranton yourself?" Gerry asked.

"Poor kid, the way he sounded, I'd better. And not a moment too soon."

Within the half hour David Kirk was dressed and slipping into his red Porsche in front of the athletic club.

At a controlled rate of speed to counteract his compulsion to extend his Porsche to the fullest, David Kirk started up the West Side Highway on his way to cross the Hudson and eventually pick up the interstate, which would take him into Scranton.

It was a long drive, longer than he would have chosen under other circumstances. But quite necessary. For Cory sounded on the verge of nervous collapse.

Nineteen

Two hours and twenty-eight minutes later, David Kirk's red Porsche pulled up in front of the Scranton YMCA. It was just past ten o'clock. The street on which the Y fronted was deserted. The building looked closed down for the night.

Kirk climbed the few front steps, peered in through the glass doors, scanned the desolate lobby. He saw no one except an elderly, wispy-haired man behind the reception counter and switchboard.

Kirk approached the desk. The old man was engrossed in reading a paperback book. "Excuse me, sir, but I am looking for a young man about five-ten, blond-haired."

Without waiting for a fuller description, without interrupting his reading, the old man thumbed Kirk in the direction of the worn couch, so old that the black leather upholstery appeared dark green.

Kirk could see no one, but since the couch was facing away from him, he approached it. He looked over the back to discover Chris Cory curled up and asleep.

"Chris," Kirk whispered. Cory did not stir. "Chris," he spoke more loudly.

Cory moved slowly, as if waking from a sleep of exhaustion. He moved his head in a slow, rotating motion. He opened his eyes, stared up into Kirk's face and came fully awake with a start.

"Come on, Chris, let's go!" Kirk ordered.

They did not even stop for coffee at one of the all-night service stations bordering the interstate until they had crossed the New York State line.

All the way Cory tried to talk about his unexplained adventure. "I'm sorry . . . I know what you said about not leaving New York . . . but I don't know what happened. . . ."

"Save it, Chris. For Dr. Scott."

It was with considerable relief that David Kirk drove his Porsche across the George Washington Bridge early Sunday morning. Whatever else might result from this strange adventure, the district attorney could not prove that Christopher Cory had fled the jurisdiction. As to David Kirk's obligation as an attorney and officer of the court to notify Judge Malachi of that fact, he pretended not to be sure.

At nine o'clock Kirk phoned Dr. Scott. Fortunately, she

had not yet set out on her Sunday morning run around the Central Park reservoir, so she was free to see them.

When they arrived she was in a gray running suit, piped in crimson. Her hair was neatly braided as usual, and hanging down her back. With a hint of what Kirk had been through the night before she had coffee along with a variety of muffins.

While they appeased their hunger, Dr. Scott began her interrogation.

"Okay, Chris. What happened, as nearly as you can remember?"

"I started out to pick up the morning *Times* and some milk for breakfast. I remember that because I made sure to pick up my money and my keys. But that's the last I remember. Until I was in that phone booth making the call to Mr. Kirk."

"Nothing else?" Scott asked. "Nothing at all?"

"Nothing," Cory insisted. "I didn't believe it when Mr. Kirk said I'd been missing four whole days."

Cory shook his head sadly. He wiped his damp face with the palm of his hand. His lips trembled as if he wanted to speak but did not dare.

"Tell me, Chris," Scott continued, "has anything similar ever happened to you before?"

"Like what?"

"When you ended up in a strange place and didn't know how you got there?" Scott asked.

He started to shake his head, then stopped suddenly. "There was . . . there was one time. . . . No, it's not the same."

"Tell me about it anyway," Scott coaxed.

"I was still in high school. We were doing this play, an Ibsen play. I had the lead. We rehearsed every day after school for three whole weeks. Then, the day of the last rehearsal it happened. I blacked out. I mean, I didn't show up for rehearsal. I wanted to be there. I wanted them all to see me in the role. I was good. Very good. But I didn't show up for rehearsal. Not that day or the next day or the night of the performance. It was five whole days before I came to. When I did I was a kid with a different name in a different town. And I had just got a job in the local hardware store. I couldn't tell anyone about that. I just went back home and let them all believe that I got stage fright and chickened out. If I told them the truth, they would think I was crazy. Just like you think I'm crazy right now."

"No one thinks you're crazy, Chris."

"It's your job to say that. So I won't go completely bananas," he countered.

"What happened to you is not so unusual," Scott reassured. "In a way it is a helpful episode. It gives us something to work with."

"You're not just saying that?" Cory replied, pleading for reassurance.

"Just you be here tomorrow at five for your usual hour."

Cory left. Kirk remained, anxious for explanations beyond those that appeared to satisfy his client.

"Doctor, did you mean that, about it giving you something to work with?" Kirk asked. "Or was that just to calm him? Because he's in such a highly agitated state."

"He has every reason to be. He is just recovering from a fugue episode," she pointed out.

"Fugue episode?"

"Victims of Multiple Personality Disorder are subject to fugue episodes. They suddenly go blank. Assume new identities. Work at new jobs. Create whole new personalities. Then one day, just as suddenly, their original personality comes to the fore and takes over again. They find themselves in strange places. Bearing strange names. Living lives they don't recognize. And never know how they got there."

"And that can go on for days?" Kirk asked.

"Days," Scott confirmed, then added, "weeks, even months."

"That's why you seemed so calm and in control," Kirk realized.

"It was not the first and surely won't be the last time a patient of mine experiences a fugue episode."

"Well, at least you can deliver Cory for his double Rorschach on Tuesday," Kirk was relieved to comment.

Twenty

With her usual professional promptness, Dr. Michal Scott presented patient Christopher Cory at the offices of Dr. Helmut Klinger on Tuesday morning at ten.

"Ah, Chris, good to see you again. Sit down, sit down," Klinger greeted him heartily. "I assume Dr. Scott briefed you on what is to take place here today."

Uneasy, his usually placid, handsome face now betraying his inner tension, his hands twisting nervously in his lap, Chris Cory replied, "She said something about another test."

"She didn't mention what kind of test?" Klinger asked, a bit amused.

"Said it had to do with some kind of inkblots," Cory replied.

"Exactly. A very simple test. Easy to take. Absolutely painless. I show you a series of inkblots. You study them. Then tell me what you see in them. Simple?"

"Seems so," Cory agreed, but appeared no more reassured than he had been.

"In fact, since Dr. Scott tells me you are a photographer, you might even enjoy this little exercise," Klinger explained, smiling.

Cory replied with a flicker of a nervous smile.

"Well, shall we begin?" Klinger turned to Scott. "Doctor, do you mind?"

Scott hesitated, then withdrew from the room.

Klinger produced the first card, which bore what appeared to be a blot of ink as it might have spilled from an accidentally tipped bottle.

"Now, Chris, take your time and tell me what you see, what you imagine, everything this blot brings to your mind."

Chris Cory did not respond at once. But after he studied it for more than a minute he said, "I see . . . I mean, this is a figure . . . a man. A nice man. A gentle man. He is walking along. Just walking. No, he is not just walking. He is searching. Looking . . . looking for people—people in trouble. So he can help them. He is . . . he is a helping man, like the Good Samaritan . . . but he takes on this form so he will not be too obvious. He is . . . like I said, helpful—a Good Samaritan."

"So," Klinger said. He produced the next card with another inkblot of distinctly different shape and form.

Cory studied it, then proceeded to render his interpretation.

Slowly, methodically, Dr. Helmut Klinger produced cards, each with a different inkblot. Each time Klinger carefully made accurate notes of Cory's responses.

So it went until the last card, the last blot and Cory's last answer. By which time he was perspiring heavily. He appeared greatly relieved when Dr. Klinger finally said, "Now, that wasn't so difficult, was it, my boy?"

"No, no . . . not difficult at all," Cory tried to pretend.

"The next part will be just as easy. But first we will need Dr. Scott's assistance," Klinger said.

146

He went out to his waiting room, where Dr. Scott had been spending the time correcting the galleys of her newest volume on hypnotic technique.

"Doctor, it is time now to produce your friend . . . what did you say his name was, this 'alter'?" Klinger used the word pejoratively, indicating his skepticism of her diagnosis.

"His name is Max."

"Max?" Klinger evaluated. "Strange he would choose such a name."

"He had his reasons," was all Scott would say.

"I am sure," Klinger replied with his smug smile. "Of course, it would be more convincing if you could induce your friend Max to present himself voluntarily," he taunted.

"Let's find out. Shall we?" Scott said.

Once in Klinger's private office, she instructed, "Chris, I would like to talk to Max. Through you. Max, can you hear me? Max, I would like you to make your presence known. Max? Max?"

Klinger made a small gesture, which outwardly appeared to share her frustration. But she could read in his eyes that he was delighted with her failure. She determined to make one more try.

"Max, you have come out on your own before. Do it now. Max? Max?" she persisted.

Finally she admitted, "I'm afraid I will have to resort to hypnosis."

"I understand perfectly, my dear," Klinger said, gloating just a little.

She turned back to Cory, who was looking away from her. She started to say, "Now, Chris, we will have to . . ."

Before she could utter her next intended words, Cory turned back to her very slowly. As he did, she could see, and Klinger could see, switching was taking place.

Slowly, Cory's face became a grimace. His jaw, which was normal for a man with an overbite, began to thrust forward as if he had an underbite. His lips became gnarled in a smirk. He breathed in gasps, not of exhaustion but of anger.

Klinger could not conceal his startled reaction.

"Max, good to see you again," Scott said.

Max responded with a word that was lost in a growl he emitted.

"Max, I want you to meet Dr. Klinger."

Max glared at Klinger, who tried to smile, offering his hand in greeting. Max rejected it with a look of contempt.

"Now, Max, Dr. Klinger is going to give you a test . . ."

"I am sick of tests! I want to get the hell out of here!"

As he started to rise from the chair, Scott said sharply, "Max! Sit down! And stay seated while Dr. Klinger gives you the test. To make sure, I will remain here. Do you understand me?"

"Okay, give me your test! I can pass any goddamn test in the world. Any test!"

"Dr. Klinger, I think you had better begin while he is still under control. He can become physically violent at times," Scott cautioned in a whisper.

Very gingerly Klinger arranged the inkblot cards in the exact order in which he had shown them to Cory.

"Max, this test is very simple. All I do is show you cards with random inkblots on them. All you do is tell me what you see. What you imagine these blots mean. Easy enough?"

"Easy enough," Max growled in agreement. Then he laughed. "My idiot friend Chris, how did he do? Not good, I bet. He never does anything good. A total washout. Zero. Zilch. Even when he wants to commit suicide he never makes it. One day I'm going to show him how."

Klinger was becoming more obviously uncomfortable. He tried to hurry the test along.

"Max, let's get started. Here is the first blot. Tell me what this blot means to you."

Max stared at the card, his face becoming even more grimacing and hostile, his jaw jutting farther forward until he took on the look of some early antecedent of modern man.

"Max . . ." Klinger coaxed. When that did not stir Max to respond, with a slight head gesture Klinger invited Scott to urge him.

"Max . . ." Scott assumed control. "Max, study the card. Tell us what you see there. What does that inkblot say to you?"

Max glared at her, then finally directed his attention back to the card. After staring at the formless blot he began:

"Man . . . Not really a man. More like a . . . a beast. Yeah! Godzilla. Huge. Like King Kong. Except this King Kong don't love women. Hates them. Hates all people. Grabs people. Hurls them into the air. Watches them fall. Fall to their death. And laughs. When people are crushed, when people die, he laughs. When women die, he laughs even louder. Sometimes he just squashes people. Kills them. Like flies. Like cockroaches. Never stops. He goes on killing, and laughing, killing and laughing . . . killing and laughing."

Throughout the recitation Klinger was so aghast he could hardly tear his concentration from Max to share his stunned reaction with Dr. Scott. Klinger resumed with the next card, and the next, until he had exhausted all of them with equally startling and shocking results.

The test completed, Klinger was a perspiring and quite changed man. Before Scott sent Max back and recalled Chris Cory, she directed Klinger, "I am more insistent than ever on a blind evaluation of this test. From any expert you know."

Klinger was almost relieved to answer, "Of course, my dear, of course."

Twenty-one

Four days later an envelope arrived at Dr. Scott's office from Dr. Helmut Klinger. It contained a copy of the report of Dr. Harvey Drake, a specialist in Rorschach interpretation and diagnosis.

In brief, the report on Patient C read: ". . . thus he is a close to normal individual. A bit troubled perhaps, but no more neurotic than you or I, my dear Klinger. However, as to your second patient, the one you identify as 'M,' I find him to be a violent man. A most dangerous and hostile person. A rapist possibly, even a potential murderer. In fact, this is one of the sickest Rorschachs I have seen in some time. It appalls me that he is still at large."

Klinger also sent a copy of that report to Howard Stone, the prosecutor who had referred the case to him.

With great reluctance, Stone sent a copy to Judge Malachi, who summoned both attorneys to an after-hours meeting in his chambers.

Document in hand, Malachi addressed Kirk. "Davey, I may owe you an apology. I'm not saying I will give you one. I only said I might owe you one. Frankly, when you first came in with this story I said to myself, There he goes again. Only this time our young genius must have in mind not only an acquittal but also a movie deal as well."

"I know, sir, you told me."

"It's not so far-fetched in these times when lawyers turn their trials into merchandise they sell to the media," Malachi excoriated.

Having spent his anger, Malachi picked up the Rorschach reports to consider his decision.

Finally, he spoke, "You know, Davey, at the time of Cory's arraignment you gave me no hint of what your defense would be."

"At the time I had no way of knowing. . . ." Kirk tried to explain.

"I'm not blaming you. I'm only saying that I did not pay too much attention to your client. So before I make my ruling I would like to see him. Here. In chambers. Tomorrow. One o'clock."

He then waved both attorneys out of the room to return his attention to a set of motion papers in another case.

The hastily called conference in Dr. Scott's office late that same afternoon was to prove more difficult than David Kirk had anticipated.

"Chris, we've been very lucky," he began. "I thought I would have a much tougher time with Malachi. But he is keeping an open mind on the question. All we have to do tomorrow is show up. Be polite. Call him 'Your Honor' every chance you get. Answer his questions in as few words as possible. Don't volunteer anything. I'm sure he will grant us permission to file."

"Permission to file what, Mr. Kirk?"

"Permission to file our intent to plead mental disability as a defense."

"Mental disability? That's the same as insanity, isn't it?" Cory challenged.

"We don't use that word anymore, Chris."

Cory shot up from his chair to confront Kirk. "I told you the very first time we met! I am not insane! And I am not going to sit in any courtroom and listen to any lawyer or any doctor say that I am! I will get up and deny it. Right there! And I don't give a damn if the judge holds me in contempt!"

Cory turned away to externalize his total rejection of Kirk's strategy. Which gave Michal Scott the opportunity to signal Kirk, *Let me handle this.*

"Chris . . ." Scott began. When he refused to face her, she repeated even more softly, "Chris?"

Slowly he turned back, making an obvious point of ignoring Kirk to focus on her.

"Chris, have I ever done or said anything to give you cause to distrust me?"

"No," he granted. Venting his resentment at Kirk, he added, "You're the only one I *can* trust."

"Then, sit down and listen to me."

Once he was seated again and composed, Scott began patiently, "Chris, you have to understand that when Mr. Kirk says he's going to plead mental disability as a defense, he is not talking about *you*. *You* didn't kill Alice. *Max* did. In court we will prove that you are not really the one who is on trial. *Max is.*"

"You're sure that will be clear to the jury and to the media?" Chris asked.

"I will make that clear when I testify. And remember, Chris, we have those tapes of Max that we will actually show to the jury."

"I don't want the jury to see those!" Cory protested.

"But they're a vital part of our case," Kirk pointed out.

"Ugly!" Cory condemned. "I don't want people to see me like that."

"Chris," Michal Scott intervened, "people won't *blame* you. They'll *sympathize* with you for the terror you lived through as a child."

"You really think so?" he asked.

"I'm sure of it," she replied. "So I urge you to give Mr. Kirk permission to use that defense."

After a long, unsettling silence, Cory asked, "Dr. Scott, is this what *you* want me to do?"

"I believe it's in your best interest, Chris."

Another long silence, then Cory relented. "Okay. I'll do it for you."

Greatly relieved, Kirk said, "Meet me at my office to-morrow. Twelve-thirty sharp. Wear a simple dark suit. A plain white shirt and an inconspicuous tie."

"Do I have to dress to please you, too?" Cory asked impatiently.

"Before the judge, yes. And also before the jury. I will tell you what to wear and how to act. Especially if I decide to put you on the stand," Kirk pointed out.

"You mean I'll have to testify?" Cory asked, suddenly tense once more.

"By law, you don't have to. But many times I find it helpful for a sympathetic client to take the stand in his own defense."

Cory hesitated, then agreed, "If Dr. Scott says I should take the stand, I will."

"Good. Meet me at my office and we will go see Judge Malachi."

The meeting over, Kirk got up to leave. But Cory gave no hint of going.

"Chris, our next session is tomorrow afternoon at five as usual," Scott said. "And I have a great deal of work to do."

Cory edged closer to her desk in such a manner that she rose to confront him.

"I wanted to stay only long enough to tell you how much I appreciate all you've been doing for me. No woman has ever been so kind to me before."

"You understand, Chris, it is my duty as your doctor to do that."

He smiled that disarming boyish smile he resorted to when he wanted to change the doctor-patient relationship into a more personal one.

"I know you have to say that. It's part of the rules. No personal feelings. And we certainly can't let Mr. Kirk know how I feel. That would upset him. Because I think *he* feels the same way."

"What way, Chris?"

"He's in love with you, too."

"Chris, you must stop thinking in those terms. And you really should leave now. So, please . . ."

She led the way to the head of the stairs. Just before he started down, he kissed her hurriedly. So hurriedly that instead of making contact with her lips he barely grazed her cheek. That fleeting contact seemed to satisfy him, for he went down the stairs quite jauntily. She waited until she was sure he had closed the door from the outside.

———

Later that night, after she had finished correcting her galleys over a sandwich and a cup of coffee, Michal Scott considered discussing that episode with David Kirk. She decided not to. What Chris had said about Kirk's feelings for her might be misinterpreted to be a ploy on her part. And between herself and David Kirk this must remain a purely professional relationship. The one time it had become more intimate was when he had embraced her protectively during Chris's violent abreaction. They had both experienced a moment of sexual electricity.

She determined to avoid any future situations which might encourage such feelings.

Twenty-two

When David Kirk ushered a very nervous Chris Cory into Judge Malachi's chambers, the old man took a long, critical look at him.

"Sit down, young man!"

Cory obeyed instantly.

"Are you aware of the defense your attorney proposes to plead on your behalf?"

"Yes, sir. . . . Yes, Your Honor."

"What do you think about that?" Malachi asked.

"I am being guided by my doctor's advice," Cory replied.

"Do *you* think you're insane?" Malachi asked.

Kirk felt the need to intervene. "Your Honor, I don't think my client is the one to evaluate his condition."

"Maybe not," Malachi conceded, turning his attention back to Cory. "Tell me, do you know that it is wrong to kill?"

Kirk was about to intercede once more, but Malachi cut him off with a brusque "I know, Counselor, his knowledge of right or wrong at the *time* of the commission of the crime is what counts. You can make that point at the trial. But right now I will do this my way." He turned back to Cory. "Do you know it is wrong to kill?"

Cory glanced at Kirk for a cue, until the old judge snapped, "Look at me, young man!"

Once Cory turned back to face him, Malachi asked,

"Well, answer me! You *do* know it is wrong to kill, don't you?"

"Yes, Your Honor," Cory admitted in a barely audible voice.

"And have you always known that?"

"Yes."

"You seem like a reasonable young man. A little stiff and scared at the moment, since you are facing the judge who will preside over your trial. Frankly, I would feel exactly the same way. And I am a very sane man. You may step out!"

Cory looked to Kirk, who released him with a slight nod. Once he was out of the room, Kirk asked, "Your Honor, about leave to file my notice of intent to plead mental disability or disease?"

"That young man is as sane as I am. But I will play along. You may file your notice."

"Thank you, Your Honor," Kirk said, feeling that he had just won half his case.

"Don't thank me, Davey," Malachi replied. "Part of my reason is quite selfish. About the only enjoyment I get these days is watching highly educated experts perjure themselves at a rate of about a thousand dollars a day. So, Davey, *permission* to plead insanity is one thing. *Proving* it to a jury in my courtroom will be quite another."

In conformity with the criminal code of the state of New York it was now David Kirk's duty to present his client to a panel of psychiatric experts selected by prosecutor Howard Stone. Kirk was also bound to present to the prosecution all psychiatric records, documents and test results which the defense possessed.

Thus armed, the state's experts were permitted to question, test and study Christopher Cory preparatory to trial so that they would be in a position to express their expert opinions as to his state of mind at the time of the crime as well as his state of mind at the time of trial.

The consultations were held in the psychiatric facilities of one of the large New York City medical centers. Several hours a day for five days Dr. Scott and Christopher Cory appeared at the hospital. They met the panel and, while Scott observed, Cory was put through extensive interviews, physical tests, brain scans, an MRI and various psychiatric tests.

The three psychiatrists, as well as the psychologist, whose duty it was to supervise the tests, were all of eminent standing in their specialties. Michal Scott knew them all, had attended seminars with them, had in one instance written a paper together with one of them. So the relationship between them was cordial. But she also knew that the two men on the panel were quite skeptical of any diagnosis of multiple personality disorder, making them tough opponents for Kirk to confront before the jury.

The woman psychiatrist had at one time been a student and disciple of Dr. Beaumont. It was commonly known in the profession that she had been replaced in his regard by Michal Scott. There was therefore an unspoken rivalry between them in which Scott did not participate but which Dr. Emma Congreve nurtured.

After five days of testing and consultation, the panel found no more need for Cory's presence. They were ready to appear at the trial to rebut David Kirk's contention of mental disease as a defense against the crime of murder in the second degree, with which Christopher Cory was charged.

Before the date of the trial, Dr. Michal Scott and David Kirk spent two evenings during which she instructed him on the background of each of Stone's experts. She coached him on which questions to ask, and which to guard against asking.

The most damaging piece of evidence linking Christopher Cory to Alice Ames's murder was the bloodstain found there, which was later DNA-matched with the blood sample taken from Cory at the time of his arrest. David Kirk had no doubt of his ability to shake any identifying witness who might put Cory at the scene. But he could not cross-examine a DNA test result. That was virtually unassailable. His only possible chance was to convince Judge Malachi to exclude it from evidence.

Armed with Gerry Prince's substantial memorandum citing many cases concerning the mental condition of a defendant at the time of arrest, Kirk requested a meeting in chambers to make his argument.

Malachi was in a particularly testy mood that late afternoon two days before the opening of the Cory trial. He had been to his doctor again over the weekend and had received an unfavorable diagnosis. He could not face his remaining days in useless inactivity.

"Your Honor," Kirk began, "I ask you to examine the situation at the time my client was taken into custody. A young man with no previous experience with the law. Arrested for a crime of which he had no knowledge. And totally disoriented because he was suffering severe headaches."

Stone interrupted to point out, "He was carefully read his Miranda rights. Let's not forget that."

"Okay," Kirk granted, "so he was read his Mirandas."

"Which," Stone replied, "clearly informed him that not only was he *entitled* to have an attorney present, but if he couldn't afford one we would *provide* one."

"My point," Kirk said, "is not that the specifics of the law were violated. But that under those special circumstances it was the duty of the police and the assistant DA to *insist* that he have a lawyer before continuing."

"Davey, are you inventing a new 'duty' for the police and the prosecution?" Malachi challenged. "Isn't it enough that they *offer* the man a lawyer?"

"In this case, no," Kirk responded. "Since we now discover he may not have been mentally qualified to waive his rights."

" 'Discover'?" Stone challenged. "We did not 'discover' any such thing. We have a tape of him during his interrogation. I defy any psychiatrist to say that young man was insane!"

"What about his headaches?" Kirk demanded.

"Headaches do *not* constitute mental incapacity!" Stone shot back.

"They might in this case," Kirk replied.

"Oh?" Malachi joined the battle. "Enlighten the court, my dear Mr. Kirk. Because to me this is an argument *de novo*. Headaches as a form of mental incapacity or disease."

The judge glanced toward Stone. "Howie, what I like about a certain attorney named David Kirk is that you can always expect some ingenious new interpretation of the law from him. I think he is bucking to become a justice of the Supreme Court now that a Democrat has been elected president."

"Your Honor, while at first blush . . ." Kirk tried to argue.

"See, Howie, 'at first blush.' Already he is talking like a Supreme Court justice."

Undismayed, Kirk continued: "At first blush it would appear that a headache is a trivial transitory condition. However, in the particular mental condition my client suffers, headaches are not only a presenting symptom but a severe, continuing symptom of great agony. Unendurable in some cases. So that, like Esau, who was willing, out of his hunger, to sell his birthright for a mess of pottage, my client was willing to sell his freedom for the next twenty-five years to secure some relief from his agonizing pain."

"Your Honor, you are definitely right," Stone intervened. "Kirk for the Supreme Court. It would be nice to have a justice who quotes the Bible in his opinion."

"Joke if you want, Howie, but the truth is, while my man was in agony, pleading for a doctor, for anything to relieve his pain, your boys were questioning him, taking a statement, taking a blood sample, all without the presence of an attorney," Kirk argued. "I say that was unconscionable conduct on the part of the prosecution. Your Honor, I think you will agree that my client's permission to draw his blood was given under the duress of pain caused by his mental disorder. And therefore should be excluded from this trial."

Kirk looked to Malachi for a ruling.

"I think I'd better go in there," Malachi said, wheeling his chair in the direction of his private lavatory.

While he was gone, Stone observed, "Davey, I grant you have one tough case. But invoking the exclusionary role in such circumstances? Come on!"

Soon Malachi came rolling out.

"Remarkable, boys, how a little session in there clears the mind. Davey, do I understand your argument correctly? The existence of your client's headaches constitutes undue pressure, by the police and the DA, on your client?"

"In addition, Your Honor, the very existence of his headaches was proof of his disabling mental condition."

"Your Honor, next thing you know he will be pleading premenstrual syndrome," Stone disparaged.

Malachi glanced back at Kirk. "Since we have yet to determine whether your client is indeed suffering from any mental disease or disorder, his headaches may have been nothing more than what they seemed to be at the time. Headaches. Which is not considered a disabling condition. Therefore, I will allow the state to introduce the results of that DNA blood test."

"But, Your Honor—" Kirk tried to respond.

Malachi cut him off with a curt "Davey, not today!"

Feeling the sting of defeat, yet aware that his was a highly innovative argument, David Kirk left Malachi's chambers more disturbed by the old man's attitude than by his ruling.

People v. *Cory* was now ready to go to trial.

The day before trial, David Kirk and Gerry Prince held a long session with their client about his conduct.

"Chris, during the trial, in and out of the courtroom, you are to talk to no one!" Kirk began. "Anyone tries to stop you and talk in the courthouse, say, 'Sorry,' and keep going. If they call you at home, you will say, 'Mr. Kirk is the only one authorized to speak for the defense.' Understand?"

Cory nodded gravely.

"In the courtroom, no matter what is said by anyone, the Judge, Mr. Stone, any witness, or even me, do not respond by either word or even the look on your face. You are an innocent young man, a victim of a deliberate frame-up. That's all. Understand?"

"Yes, sir!" Cory replied.

"There's a very good reason for all this. I want you to be the nicest, most white-bread guy in the world. So that when I show that tape, the jury will see two totally distinct personalities. You and Max. Men from two different worlds. That is the key to our defense.

"Gerry, take him home now and help him pick out the clothes he's to wear to court."

Gerry Prince stared at the modest clothes closet in Cory's bedroom. To his left were wire hangers bearing two simple tweed sports jackets, a worn blue blazer, and several pairs of khaki and gray slacks on pants hangers, which were intended to avoid the need for pressing. But the right side of the closet presented a complete anomaly. There were two black leather jackets adorned with bright metal ornaments better suited to a biker than to mild Chris Cory. Alongside the jackets hung a pair of black leather pants and two pairs of black denims.

As Gerry reached out to touch one of the leather jackets, Cory pleaded, "Don't touch those. Please. Don't even look at them. I hate those things. I hate what they stand for. They're not me. They have nothing to do with me."

As if imparting a secret, Cory lowered his voice. "I'd get rid of them. If I dared. But I'm afraid of what Max would do. So just . . . just make believe those things aren't here."

Gerry concentrated on selecting from the clothes on the left-hand side of the closet. He chose a proper jacket and two pairs of slacks, plus a few shirts and several undistinguished ties for Cory to wear at the trial.

When Gerry returned to the office he reported, "Dave, weirdest thing you ever saw. He *is* two different people. One side of his closet the usual stuff you'd expect for someone his age, his style. But, man, the other half of his closet, all heavy-metal stuff. When he tells Dr. Scott he can't remember buying any of it or wearing any of it, I believe him. Yet it's been worn."

"That's good," Kirk remarked, "Might come in handy during the trial."

Twenty-three

On the morning of the opening of the trial of *People* v. *Cory*, David Kirk's long black limousine pulled up at the broad steps of the Supreme Court of New York County. Before the car came to a full stop it was surrounded by media men and women armed with handheld television cameras, voice recorders and boom mikes.

As Kirk, Cory and Prince reached the long flight of stone steps, they were besieged on all sides by eager faces shouting questions.

Gerry Prince took charge. "Guys, you know when there is something significant to say Mr. Kirk will comment. He always does. As for Mr. Cory, he is under strict orders not to say anything to anyone during this trial! So, if you don't mind—"

Aware that, as always, whenever his limousine was parked in front of any courthouse, David Kirk would be available when he came out during longer recesses to keep in touch with his office by car phone, the media people no longer hounded them with questions.

Kirk, Cory and Prince started up. As they climbed the well-worn steps of the courthouse, David Kirk sensed that his young client was exhibiting signs of tension. Not unusual for a client about to face the legal process with a possible life sentence as the outcome.

As casually as he could, Kirk cast a glance at him. He noticed a slight twitching around Cory's mouth—the trembling of his lips, which seemed so pale they were almost colorless.

Kirk's great concern was that Cory might be evidencing the first signs of switching, and in the presence of so many cameras.

For an instant he pondered: *A switch on television on the evening news would be the most talked-about piece of news footage since the world-famous Los Angeles cop-beating of Rodney King. On the other hand, it might also give away the crucial demonstration we are saving for the jury. Television viewers don't vote guilty or innocent. Jurors do. Better save this for the jury.*

When they reached the top step, about to enter the court-house, Kirk took Cory by the arm so suddenly that he caught the media unaware. He hustled him into the press room just inside the entrance, then barked an order to the few newspaper reporters there: "Out!" When they started to protest, he commanded, "I said out! All of you!"

Slowly, in desultory fashion, both men and the female reporter backed out of the room.

Alone with his client, Kirk reached out to take Cory's hands. Cold. Cold as ice. He studied Cory's eyes. Moist. On the verge of tears.

"Afraid?" Kirk asked.

Unable to respond in words, Cory nodded, a single jerk of his head.

"It's natural just before a trial begins," Kirk tried to re-assure him.

Cory was finally able to summon the words. "Mr. Kirk, you have to tell them . . . convince them . . . I didn't do any-thing. Max did it. Then blamed me. Do you think they'll understand? Do you think you can convince them?"

"Yes, Chris, I think the two of us, Dr. Scott and I, can convince them."

"I was up all night . . . thinking . . . worrying . . . you read in the papers and see on television how some man was found guilty and served five, ten, sometimes fifteen years before they discover he was innocent all along. Then they set him free. I keep thinking, what if that happened to me? What if twenty-six-year-old Chris Cory went to prison for something he didn't do? Then forty-one-year-old Chris Cory is set free. Who gives me back those fifteen years? Maybe they give you some money. But no amount of money can buy back time, years, love, life. Mr. Kirk . . . Mr. . . ."

He could not continue but broke down in tears. Kirk gripped Cory's arm to encourage him. But he allowed him to cry until he recovered on his own. Then, drying his eyes and his cheeks, Cory said, "Sorry."

"'S okay, kid, I know how you feel."

Kirk used his own pocket comb to straighten Cory's disheveled hair. Then he straightened his tie and his collar.

"Ready?" Kirk asked.

Cory nodded, as bravely as he could.

Kirk opened the door to be greeted by the three irritated members of the press.

"Thanks for the use of the hall," Kirk said, leading his client toward the rotunda of the courthouse to take an elevator up to the courtroom.

To accommodate Judge Aaron Malachi's physical limitations, the uniformed attendants assigned to his courtroom were always husky young men.

Whenever he made his entrance into the courtroom in his wheelchair, a hush always followed. He disliked having his condition greeted by such a reaction, since he abhorred pity. But he had found no way around it, so he accepted the inevitable. In full sight, he and his wheelchair were lifted to the bench by the two attendants. Once he wheeled himself into place he was ready for the day's proceedings.

On this day, when the notorious trial of *People* v. *Cory* was scheduled to begin, the courtroom was full. The media occupied the first three rows. Inveterate curious trial watchers filled the rest. There was also a row of standees against the back wall. Three local television channels had requested permission to bring cameras into the courtroom. Malachi had refused. They complained that he did so because he did not wish his condition exhibited on television. The truth was, treating a trial as if it were just another piece of cheap television entertainment offended his regard for the law and the courts.

Once in place, Judge Aaron Malachi looked out at his crowded courtroom and growled, "All you people standing in the back, out!"

That order obeyed, he looked in the direction of the clerk, who announced: "People versus Cory. Docket number 965-24-34."

The jury filed in and was sworn by the clerk to render a fair and true verdict based on all the evidence and in conformity with the law in the case, as explained by the judge.

Malachi looked down at the two counsel tables before him. At the one on the right sat Howard Stone, assistant district attorney, who would present the case for the People. Alongside his notes, his omnipresent bottle of antacids, large size. On Stone's right sat young Harriet Fielder, a black woman. On his left, a young man with the dark complexion of a Latino.

Malachi observed (to himself, of course), *Howie is back to his old tricks. With two blacks on the jury, naturally he's got himself a black assistant. And a woman to boot, since the jury is split, six women, six men. With three names on the jury like Hernandez, Garcia and Lopez, he is taking no chances. So he's got that young Hispanic assistant whom I have seen*

*before. Very bright. Whose present claim to fame unfortu-
nately is not his ability but his ethnicity. Howie is like the
manager of a baseball team. He has a whole bench of assistants
from which to choose, depending on the racial elements in the
trial.*

Malachi's eyes turned slightly to the left to dwell on the
table assigned to counsel for the defense. There sat David
Kirk and his assistant, Gerry Prince. Kirk had several legal
pads ready for his notes, and also a number of legal memo-
randa prepared in the event that questions of admissible evidence arose.

Alongside Kirk sat Christopher Cory. Attired in a plain
blue jacket, white shirt and a small, figured blue tie, he re-
sembled a nice-looking, correct bank teller. Or the young
man who listens to customers' complaints at the utility-
company office. He looked anything but the vicious murderer
Howard Stone would soon try to convince the jury that
he was.

Once both counsels signified that they were ready, Malachi ordered Stone: "The People may proceed."

As Howard Stone was about to rise from his chair, there
was a stir at the courtroom doors. All eyes turned in that
direction.

The attendant at the door escorted a middle-aged woman
down the aisle to the first row. He urged the spectators seated
there to make room for her.

Puzzled by this special attention being bestowed on the
woman, Kirk was about to ask leave to go to the bench, but
Chris Cory whispered to him, "Does she have to be here?"

"Who is she?" Kirk asked.

"Mrs. Ames, Alice's mother," Cory explained. "I met
her while Alice and I were living together. She's only here to
prejudice the jury."

"One of Howie's little touches. But we have no right to
keep her out," Kirk explained.

Mrs. Ames having settled in her chair, which she would occupy every day of the trial, Judge Malachi renewed his order: "The People will proceed."

Howard Stone rose from his armchair, crossed to face the jury, well aware of his obligation. In view of the defense in this case, Stone had to present a *prima facie* case that would withstand David Kirk's inevitable motion to dismiss. Once that was denied, then Kirk would have the heavy burden of proving his defense of legal insanity. After that the jury would have to render one of three possible verdicts: Guilty of murder in the second degree. Not guilty. Or Not guilty by reason of mental defect or disease.

So Stone's strategy was to present as clear, firm and convincing a case as was necessary to withstand Kirk's motion to dismiss.

His opening statement was brief and to the point. The People would show that defendant Cory did on a certain day enter the home of Alice Ames. After an argument overheard by a witness he did kill her, using one of her own kitchen knives. Forensic evidence would show that he came prepared to commit that crime, making this a case of willful, premeditated murder.

After such a bald statement, Stone concluded by saying, "Now, the defendant may try to introduce other elements into this case. Do not be misled. Listen to the facts, and only the facts, and your duty as jurors will be clear. As will your consciences when you find this man guilty of murder."

He retreated to his chair.

The judge looked to David Kirk. "Counselor?"

Not wishing to have the jury anticipate his defense, David Kirk said only, "We will prove that Christopher Cory is not the person who murdered Alice Ames."

Malachi nodded, then directed, "Mr. Stone. Proceed."

Stone's first witness was a woman who testified that she lived on the floor below Alice Ames. On the morning of the murder she heard voices engaged in an argument in the apartment above hers. The defendant's voice, which she characterized as "real mad" and the victim's voice, which was "pleading and crying." She heard noises of a struggle, after which everything grew quiet.

Stone turned his witness over to Kirk.

David Kirk approached the witness with double purpose. Primarily he must attack the credibility of the prosecution's witnesses and hope to get a dismissal on the ground that Stone had failed to prove a *prima facie* case. Small chance. So he must take the opportunity to establish in the minds of the jury certain facts or inferences which they would later recognize as evidence of Cory's strange mental condition. With that dual strategy in mind, he faced the prosecution's first witness.

"Mrs. Miller," Kirk began, "when you eavesdropped on that little spat between—"

As Kirk expected, from his chair Stone raised his hand and at the same time called out, "Object. There is no indication the witness was eavesdropping."

"What else would the prosecutor call it?" Kirk asked.

"Counselor," Stone replied, "according to the dictionary definition, *eavesdropping* means listening in secret."

"Well, isn't that what Mrs. Miller was doing?" Kirk countered. "The two participants in the discussion were not aware that she was listening. Nor did she do anything to make them aware. I call that eavesdropping," Kirk insisted.

Malachi intruded, "Gentlemen, let's not get involved in a semantic discussion. Eavesdropping. Shmeesdropping. Did the lady hear what she said she heard? That's the question."

He turned to the jury. "Ladies and gentlemen, from time to time you have to indulge counsel in these little arguments. It's the way they make their living."

Then, impatiently, he ordered: "Mr. Kirk, either get on with it or get off it."

Kirk turned back to the witness. "Mrs. Miller, do you have any way of identifying who the woman and the man were whom you overheard?"

"Well, I know she lives in that apartment . . ." the woman started to say.

"I asked, how do you know who the woman was whom you overheard?" Kirk insisted.

"Well, if she always lived there . . ."

"Mrs. Miller, isn't it the truth that you don't really know who that woman was?"

"I know her voice. I heard it many times through the floor," Mrs. Miller protested.

"Oh, so you *were* in the habit of eavesdropping on her?" Kirk asked.

"I don't eavesdrop!" the woman protested.

"Your Honor," Stone interjected, "he is harassing the witness."

"Mr. Kirk, please?" Malachi asked.

"Your Honor, as long as it is understood that Mrs. Miller cannot identify either the woman or the man she overheard, I am willing to excuse the witness," Kirk responded.

Stone's next witness was a young actor who was sworn and gave his name as Bruce Gethers. He testified that on the morning of the murder he had left early to catch a bus to New Hope, Pennsylvania, where he was due to replace another actor in a production at the playhouse there. He had started down the stairs when he brushed by another man coming up the stairs. A man whom he could not identify at that instant. So he turned back to get a second look.

"And," Howard Stone added, "were you, on that second look, able to identify that man?"

"Yes, sir," Gethers replied.

"Do you see that man here in this courtroom?"

"Yes, sir."

"Will you point him out for the jury?" Stone asked.

"Yes, sir. He is the young man sitting there." He pointed to Christopher Cory.

"Thank you, Mr. Gethers."

Stone turned the witness over to Kirk.

David Kirk rose to cross-examine. He was halfway to his feet when he felt pinned. He looked down to discover Cory's hand gripping his sleeve. Thinking that his client was suddenly ill or feeling panic symptoms, Kirk leaned close.

In an anxious whisper, Cory demanded, "Tell him! You tell him it wasn't me! It was Max! Max!"

Kirk settled back in his chair, leaned even closer to Cory. "Never . . . you hear me . . . never give me instructions or suggestions while court is in session! I will do this my way! And I will introduce the subject of Max when I deem it best! Understand?"

Cory stared into Kirk's firm and angry eyes, then swallowed and nodded apologetically.

Kirk rose and approached the witness.

"Mr. Gethers," Kirk asked, "did you get a good close look at the man you claim is the defendant in this case? Good enough to notice what he was wearing?"

"I don't see what that's got to do with anything," Gethers replied.

"Answer the question!" Malachi ordered.

"No, I didn't notice what he was wearing," Gethers admitted.

"Then, you couldn't say if he was dressed like Mr. Cory is now?" Kirk asked.

"No, sir. I could not."

"Or if he was dressed in jeans and a sweater?" Kirk asked.

"No, sir."

"Or if he was dressed in black leather with lots of metal decoration?" Kirk asked.

Which provoked what Kirk intended—that Malachi would intervene. "Counselor, the witness has already testified that he did not notice what the man was wearing."

"Sorry, Your Honor," Kirk pretended to apologize, but he had already laid some of the groundwork for his defense.

Stone proceeded with his roster of witnesses. The actor with whom Alice Ames was scheduled to rehearse a scene that day, and who, when she did not appear, suspected that something was wrong. He insisted on having the superintendent of the building unlock her door. Together they made the gruesome discovery.

David Kirk did not elect to cross-examine.

Having established the discovery of the crime and identified the scene, Stone brought up his heavy artillery.

Detective Martinez of Homicide testified that he had been summoned to the scene. He found a small one-bedroom economy apartment in Greenwich Village of the kind that struggling young actors, writers, artists and others are able to afford while working toward their one big break. Martinez also testified that he had found a good deal of blood, as expected when death was due to a knifing.

A search of the apartment revealed that one large knife was missing from the kitchen rack. It was assumed to be the murder weapon. That knife was later found in a garbage can just outside the apartment house.

There was also found a half-torn surgical glove, which Martinez assumed, from the blood on it, was used in the course of the murder. Forensics later identified the blood as that of the victim.

Stone now asked his final question: "Mr. Martinez, based on your long experience in the police department and your years with the Homicide division, can you form an opinion as to what the presence of that surgical glove indicated?"

"Yes, sir. Clear evidence of premeditation," Martinez replied firmly. "After all, people do not go around carrying surgical gloves. That is, not unless they're doctors or nurses. The man obviously came to kill."

"Thank you," Stone said, half-turning to Kirk to invite him to cross-examine.

David Kirk looked up from making notes and pretended to be surprised by the opportunity. As if improvising, he deliberately started, "Uh, Mr. Malendez . . ."

"Martinez," the witness corrected.

"I'm sorry," Kirk apologized. "You were saying that . . . Did I get it right . . . 'the man obviously came to kill'? Did you say that?"

"Yes, sir," Martinez replied.

"And you gathered that from the presence of a surgical glove?" Kirk asked.

"As I said, people do not go around with surgical gloves unless they have a reason."

"Someone who was frightened of catching AIDS might carry surgical gloves. Isn't that right?" Kirk asked.

"I guess. But he would have to be some kind of kook to do that," Martinez replied.

" 'He would have to be some kind of kook,' Kirk repeated, since Martinez had thrown a little bonus his way. "But you said the glove proves the man came to kill."

"Yes, sir, I did."

"Have you had much experience with surgical gloves, Mr. Martinez?"

"Some," he replied, a bit defensive now.

"Enough so you can tell men's surgical gloves from women's surgical gloves?" Kirk asked.

"There is no difference between them," Martinez was quick to reply.

"Then, how did you know that the person who 'came to kill' was a man?"

"I didn't at that time. But we later identified his print," Martinez said.

"So, your original assumption could have been totally incorrect, couldn't it?" Kirk asked.

"It wasn't, though," Martinez replied.

"If, in your expert opinion, 'the man came to kill,' how come the weapon you claim he used was one of the knives that he found in the apartment?"

Martinez shifted uneasily in the witness chair. His black mustache seemed to droop.

When he did not reply at once, Kirk used the moment to remark, "Isn't it a fact, Mr. Martinez, that you have no way of knowing with what intent that person came to the scene of the crime?"

"He was there, we know that. We have his blood sample for DNA corroboration. He used the gloves when he killed her. We have his palm print. We found the weapon right outside the house."

Kirk made no effort to interrupt him. Nor did Stone. Each for quite different reasons. Stone felt that by his unfortunate question Kirk had opened the door for Martinez to spell out for the jury in sequence and detail the mountain of evidence he would introduce. Supplied by individual experts, one piece at a time, it would create a fragmented picture, which, until Stone's summation, the jury would have to put together in their minds like a jigsaw puzzle. Martinez was giving them the entire picture into which each expert's testimony would now neatly fit.

Kirk's forbearance was for a difference reason.

"So," Martinez summarized, "we have all the classic elements of the crime without even departing from the scene. Except for finding the knife outside."

"Actually a classic case," Kirk remarked. "Motive, opportunity and weapon all wrapped up neat and tidy in practically no time at all."

"Yes, sir," Martinez agreed with obvious pride.

"That will be all," Kirk said, starting to turn away. But

174

midway between the witness stand and his table, Kirk stopped and turned back to confront the witness.

"Has it occurred to you, Mr. Martinez, that maybe this case was *too* classic? *Too* neat, *too* tidy? That maybe someone arranged it all so neat and tidy in order to frame this defendant?" Kirk demanded.

"That's ridiculous!" Martinez responded. "How could anybody frame his fingerprints and his bloodstain?"

"Mr. Martinez, isn't it possible that the prints of this defendant were found at the scene, but that another person committed that murder?" Kirk asked.

"That's not the way it figures, Counselor," Martinez replied.

"Then, can you say with certainty that this defendant *did* kill Alice Ames?" Kirk asked.

"That's our best conclusion," Martinez insisted.

" 'Conclusion,' 'that's the way it figures,' " Kirk commented. "Nice words. But they don't answer the question, Mr. Martinez. I repeat, can you say now, with certainty, that this is the man who killed Alice Ames?"

"That's . . . that's for the jury to decide," Martinez replied.

"Thank you, Mr. Martinez," Kirk said. "That is all."

Twenty-four

Slowly, methodically, Howard Stone built his case against Christopher Cory without resorting to any particularly dramatic moments. He wished to convince the jury that this was a murder case pure and simple. He would leave it to Kirk to turn it into a psychiatric circus. But sanity and justice would be on the side of the People.

At the next session Howard Stone introduced the forensic expert on fingerprints to establish Cory's presence at the scene and his prints on the murder weapon he used. She brought with her charts of enlarged prints, which she mounted on an easel aimed at the jury.

In routine fashion Stone had her cite her education and experience in the field of print identification. Once qualified, Marie Wisencraft testified that she had arrived at the scene of the crime within an hour after the discovery of Alice Ames's body. That she had dusted the areas of the room most likely to reveal prints, as well as all objects that might have been touched during what had obviously been a struggle.

She was surprised at first at not finding many strange prints, which alerted her to the possibility that the perpetrator might have been using gloves. That was explained, finally, when she discovered a partial palm print on a lamp that had been knocked over during the struggle. She later found similar palm prints on the weapon that was recovered. Discovery of the torn surgical glove explained the partial palm print.

"Detective Wisencraft," Stone asked finally, did you make a comparison of the defendant's palm print with the ones you found in that room and on this knife?"

"Yes, I did."

"And what did you find?" Stone asked.

"I found that they matched exactly," Ms. Wisencraft responded. "As you can see here, and here." She referred to her charts, pointing out the enlarged prints.

"So that in your expert opinion, there is no question that this defendant was at the scene and used this knife to murder Alice Ames?" Stone asked.

"Object!" Kirk called out from his table. "Ms. Wisencraft may be able to testify as to the prints she found, but has no basis for concluding that my client used that weapon to commit a murder."

Stone smiled and shrugged, thinking, *Davey must be hard up for a line of cross-examination to resort to such a nitpicking objection.*

"Your witness," Stone said, slouching back to his table.

Kirk rose, taking with him a long legal pad, more for its effect on the witness than for its utility, since he had very few notes on it.

"Ms. Wisencraft, since Mr. Stone was generous in citing your vast experience in lifting and comparing prints of all kinds, can you tell from just a part of a palm print from which hand that print came?"

"Of course."

"Then, in this case, could you tell the jury from which of Mr. Cory's hands this print came?"

"Of course."

She angled slightly to illustrate on her charts the enlarged prints.

"Ladies and gentlemen of the jury, you can see the print which I found at the scene alongside this other print later made after the defendant was arrested. There is no doubt that the print came from his left hand."

" 'His left hand,' " Kirk repeated slowly and with great significance. "Tell the jury, Mr. Wisencraft, is my client, Mr. Cory, right-handed or left-handed?"

For a moment the witness was nonplussed. Then she admitted, "I'm sorry, I don't know."

"That's understandable." Kirk seemed to excuse her lack of knowledge. "Now, then, Ms. Wisencraft, the glove that was discovered and had been torn, could you tell whether it was torn before or during the—"

Anticipating the question, Ms. Wisencraft responded, "It was torn during the struggle. The result of sudden and undue force."

"Thank you. But I was about to ask, is it possible that that glove was ripped on purpose?"

"Anything is possible. But in this case it was undoubtedly ripped during the struggle."

Kirk went to the clerk's desk, picked up the glove that had been tagged as "People's Exhibit D."

"Ms. Wisencraft, now would you please show the jury exactly how you tell the difference between a glove that has been *accidentally* torn and one that is *intentionally* torn with ulterior motives?" Kirk demanded.

The witness stared at the glove, then improvised her response. "Well, if one were to do it intentionally, the edges might be more even. But when a glove like this bursts under sudden pressure of force, the edges would look ragged, like this."

She held the glove up for the jury to see.

"So?" Kirk remarked, as if he had learned something for the first time. "Then, perhaps you can help me with a bit of your expertise. I have here"—and he took from Gerry Prince's outstretched hand two thin latex surgical gloves— "two gloves from the same pair. One of them has been torn by applying force. The other by means of some instrument. I ask you to examine them both and tell the jury which is which."

Very gingerly Ms. Wisencraft took both gloves, studied them, then replied, "This one, the right one, was torn by exertion of force. The left one by some instrument."

"And you are willing to tell this jury that is your expert opinion?" Kirk demanded, as if it were itself an indictment of her knowledge and skill.

"Well, based on what I see . . . and without any other substantiation . . . Well, yes, yes, I stick by my earlier opinion."

As if placing great value on the moment of her indecision, Kirk carefully took each glove from her, one at a time, folded them meticulously as if intended for the archives of legal history. He placed them in his pocket and asked, "Uh, by the way, Ms. Wisencraft, when you handled those gloves, did you notice if they were cuffed?"

"Surgical gloves are always cuffed. Makes them easy to put on and take off. And keeps them tight around the wrist," she explained and illustrated for the jury.

Kirk reached into his pocket, produced the gloves, held them out to her. She took them very cautiously, examined them, then admitted, "Someone removed the cuffs from those. Cut them off."

"Yes, someone did," Kirk replied. "And you never noticed."

"I was so busy looking at the rips . . ." she started to explain.

"I'm sure," Kirk replied, taking back the gloves and returning to his table.

Up on the bench, old Malachi observed, *Slick sonofabitch. That whole megillah had absolutely nothing to do with her testimony. But the jury ate it up.*

Without stirring from his chair, Howard Stone asked, "Ms. Wisencraft, the torn glove and the exposed palm print you picked up, are they both of the defendant's left hand?"

"They most definitely are," she was relieved to reiterate.

"Thank you, that's all," Stone said, as if he had wiped out Kirk's moment of triumph.

Stone presented his next witness, Dr. Cyril Twilling, the medical examiner who had performed the autopsy on Alice Ames. He testified as to the procedures he employed to determine the cause of her death.

Whereupon Stone suggested, "Dr. Twilling, for the benefit of the jury so they may visualize your findings, will you produce your enlarged photographs taken during the autopsy? And we offer them in evidence now."

Kirk was up on his feet. "Object!"

"Counsel has already had the opportunity to examine this evidence," Stone countered.

"I object to such gruesome photographs being introduced into this trial. They are intended for only one purpose, to inflame and prejudice the jury."

Both men looked to the bench for a ruling.

"Objection denied," Malachi ruled. "And your exception will be noted for the record, Mr. Kirk."

Once the color photographs were received into evidence, Mr. Twilling used a long pointer to highlight for the jury every stab wound.

During this portion of Twilling's testimony, Mrs. Ames started to weep and continued throughout the remainder of it.

Twilling continued to describe in detail the depth of penetration of each wound and the effect on the victim. In addition, he found evidence that the murderer had started to dismember the body, but for some reason, on which he could only speculate, he did not continue.

"Perhaps," Twilling ventured, "he was scared away by a noise or a knock on the door or some other intervening circumstances."

Stone thereupon showed Dr. Twilling the knife, "People's Exhibit A," and asked, "Doctor, in your opinion, could this weapon have inflicted those fatal wounds?"

"Yes, sir," Twilling responded sharply.

"Your witness," Stone said, lumbering back to his table.

Kirk decided not to cross-examine. The longer the jury was exposed to those photographs and to Twilling's bloody recounting, the worse the effect would be on the outcome.

Stone's next witness was Gordon Harris, a technician from the medical examiner's office who was a specialist in blood studies. He testified that he had received a sample of blood taken at the scene. That he had done a DNA comparison with a blood sample of the defendant.

"And what was your finding, sir?" Stone asked.

"There was a perfect match," he replied.

"If you were informed that the defendant said that he was not in that apartment for more than four months, what would you conclude?"

"That he was lying."

"Object!" Kirk called out.

"Sustained," Malachi grumbled. "Mr. Stone, you know better than that. Don't ask a blood expert to draw conclusions like lying."

Stone did not choose to reframe his question since he had succeeded in planting in the minds of the jury that Cory had been at the murder scene at the time in question and was lying when he denied it.

"Your witness," Stone announced.

Since he had failed in his effort to exclude all DNA testimony, David Kirk advanced toward the witness stand with one objective in mind: to obfuscate the issue and thus minimize its importance in the minds of the jurors.

"Mr. Harris, I don't know about the jury, but I am a little confused. I frequently read in the newspapers about scientists who dig around in sites all over the world and come up with ancient bones and fragments of bones. How they unwrap Egyptian mummies and take tissue samples thousands of years old. Then they do DNA studies on them."

"Yes, sir," Gordon Harris responded, awaiting the question.

"If those samples, which are thousands, and in some cases millions, of years old, can yield DNA information, how can you say that any given sample is five days old, or five months old?" Kirk asked.

"That sample was handed to me as fresh blood. No more than five days old," Harris replied.

"But you had no way of actually knowing that, did you?" Kirk persisted.

"No, not really," Harris conceded.

"So that if Mr. Cory, who lived in that apartment for almost half a year, had cut himself shaving five months before this unfortunate murder, any blood he shed then would yield the same result as that you claim is a fresh blood sample. Would it not?"

Harris squirmed a bit, cast a glance toward Stone, then replied, "Yes, yes, it would."

"So that this DNA study has no bearing whatsoever on whether Mr. Cory was at the scene at the time of Miss Ames's unfortunate death. Is that correct?"

"The blood samples match," was all that Gordon Harris would say.

"I think the jury will make up its own mind as to what that means," Kirk said as he retreated to his table.

Howard Stone gulped two more pills.

Twenty-five

On the third day of trial, ADA Howard Stone presented his final witnesses.

In the morning session he called to the stand Mrs. Bertha Colwell. A black woman of medium height, a trifle over-weight, in her middle forties, she seemed a bit nervous when she took the stand. She blurted out a very forceful "I do!" when the clerk administered the oath. But once she began to testify she seemed quite at ease.

Stone led her through her background, which would serve as the reason for her attending this trial as a witness.

Mrs. Colwell had been, for seventeen years, the operator of a small cleaning, pressing and tailoring establishment in a neighborhood some ten streets from where Chris Cory lived. It was her job to check in clothes, suits, dresses, coats, and other such items for cleaning and pressing.

"Over those seventeen years, day after day, handling all sorts of people's apparel and sometimes their intimate belongings as well, have you been able to develop a sense of what those garments have been through before they come into your hands?"

"I can pretty much tell where these clothes have been and what they have been doing," she replied confidently.

"Mrs. Colwell, can you give me an example of what you mean?" Stone asked.

"Well, for example, I can tell from their dresses where some ladies have been the night before. And from certain stains, what they have been doing."

"Tell the jury exactly what you mean by that," Stone coaxed.

"Well, there . . . there are certain stains from . . . what they call these days 'bodily fluids.' When you spot those on some woman's skirt or dress you know what she has been doing. If they are slightly ripped, you also know either she resisted, or else she was in such a hurry she couldn't wait to get them off."

The snicker that ran through the courtroom was immediately squelched by Malachi's sharp gavel.

"Mrs. Colwell, are there also other things about which you have developed a sense of detection? For example, can you tell from just handling a garment if it had been washed before it came into your hands?"

"Oh, yes," she replied confidently.

At which point Stone took the folded jacket that his assistant held out to him. He offered it to Mrs. Colwell for her perusal.

"Mrs. Colwell, do you recognize this jacket?"

She examined it very briefly, then replied, "Yes, I do."

"Can you tell us *why* you recognize this jacket?"

"Yes, sir. You see, people who come to my shop are from around the neighborhood. I mean, a block or two or three. So when someone comes in with a garment and gives an address ten blocks away I know there is something unusual. So, in this case, I examined it after he left."

"And what did you discover?" Stone asked.

"This had been washed before it was brought in."

"Did that strike you as strange?"

"Yes, sir. People do not wash woolens unless maybe some sweaters."

"Now, if someone did wash such a garment and then brought it in to be dry-cleaned, what would you suspect?"

Kirk was up and on his feet to object vigorously. "Your Honor, Mr. Stone is about to ask the witness for a conclusion which she is not qualified to give."

"Sustained!" Malachi ruled.

Stone smiled a bit sheepishly. *Didn't work, but worth a try.* He had to regroup and conclude.

"Thank you, Mrs. Colwell."

Stone offered the jacket to the stenographer, saying, "I offer this as People's Exhibit L."

Assuming she was through with her stint on the witness stand, Mrs. Colwell started to rise. But David Kirk came forward saying, "Just a question or two, Mrs. Colwell."

Kirk knew he had no solid ground on which to impeach her testimony. The woman had told the truth, had no motive to do otherwise. But if he could not attack her credibility, he could at least avail himself of the opportunity to rack up a few more points for his own case later on.

He picked up the jacket from the stenographer, held it out to the witness, asking, "Mrs. Colwell, does this jacket seem to you the kind that a young man like him would wear?"

"I don't know what you mean," the confused woman replied.

"Well, look at this jacket, the leather trim, the metal decoration. Does this look like what this young man is wearing now?"

"Objection!" Howie Stone called out from his place at the table. "This 'young man' is attired for his present appearance by that eminent specialist in men's courtroom attire, David Kirk. So any difference between what he would usually wear and what he is wearing today is purely and intentionally not accidental."

"Sustained," Malachi said.

"Mrs. Colwell, have you handled many jackets like this one?"

"All the time," she replied.

"What kind of men usually bring in jackets like this?" Kirk asked.

"Well, truth to tell, those that wear this kind of jacket don't bring them in often enough. They are what we call the heavy-metal type. And usually we got to run them through two, three times, they are so filthy."

"Thank you, Mrs. Colwell," Kirk said, aware that he had left the jury puzzled about why he had asked such a seemingly innocent question.

After Mrs. Colwell, Stone introduced a lab technician from the Forensics branch of the police department. Confronted with the same jacket, he testified that he had performed certain tests which revealed that, despite washing and dry cleaning, there were still residual blood elements that matched the blood of the victim, Alice Ames.

Having proved all elements of the crime except motive, Howard Stone introduced his final witness.

Carrie Denis was a young black actress, a contemporary

of Alice Ames, a member of the same acting class and a close friend. She was pretty, petite, and with the carriage and confidence of a good actress.

"Miss Denis, how long did you know Alice Ames?"

"Ever since I got to New York. We met in acting class. We were both accepted on the same day."

"And how long did you study together?"

"Almost three years. Shared an apartment two of those years."

"And during that time did you also meet the defendant?"

"Yes, sir. Also in acting class."

"What was the relationship between you?" Stone asked.

"Not very good," she replied.

"Why not?"

"I just didn't like him, didn't trust him."

"Did there come a time when he moved in with Alice?"

"Yes. I moved out so he could move in."

"Did that upset you, having to move out to accommodate him?"

"The only thing that upset me was that he was trying to run her life. That he was jealous of her acting. Because she was very good. She would have been a star, if he hadn't kill—"

Stone interrupted. "Please, Miss Denis, we mustn't let our speculations interfere with the facts. It is for the jury to determine that."

Oh, Howie, Kirk thought, *have you no shame? Pretending to stifle such a voluntary gift from your own witness.*

"Now, Miss Denis, did there come a time when your friend decided that she no longer wanted to share the same residence with the defendant?" Stone asked.

"There certainly did," she replied. "She'd had enough of his weird conduct. She realized that he was interfering with her career."

"Exactly what do you mean, 'interfering with her career'?"

"He'd hang around when she was rehearsing, make comments, give her direction. Once she lost a job because he was secretly giving her direction and the director found out."

"Tell the jury, Miss Denis, how it came about that he was thrown out of class," Stone urged.

"Well, this one day Alice was doing a scene with Jason . . . that is, Jason Ulfeld. It was a scene from *Picnic*, that William Inge play. It was a love scene and they were really into it, I mean, it was real, you could feel it. One of the best things she ever did. And right in the middle of it, he, Chris, in his domineering possessive way, he just exploded in jealousy. Ruined the scene. Made her burst into tears. She just ran out of the studio, crying."

"And then?" Stone urged.

"She realized that he was a destructive influence over her, so she decided to give him up."

"What happened after that?"

"He kept calling, coming around, wanting to resume the relationship. And she didn't want to see him ever again."

"Miss Denis, were you close to Alice Ames during all those months after she broke off her relationship with the defendant?"

"Very close," the witness replied. "You see, she didn't want to be alone. She was afraid."

"Did she ever say that to you, that she was afraid?"

"Not in those words. But she did say she had this feeling she was being spied on. Being followed."

"By whom?" Stone asked.

"By him," she said, pointing to Chris Cory.

"Miss Denis, when was the last time you saw Alice Ames?"

"When I was called to identify her body."

"I meant before that, the last time you saw her alive?"

"The night before she was killed."

"Did she say anything that night about the defendant?" Stone asked.

"That he was getting even worse. Leaving weird messages on her answering machine. Threatening her. Things like that."

"But she still wouldn't see him?" Stone asked.

"The only time she saw him in that four months was the day he killed her."

"Please, Miss Denis," Stone pretended to rebuke her for saying that. "That will be all."

Pad in hand, David Kirk advanced toward the witness.

"Miss Denis, you don't hold a very high opinion of the defendant, do you?"

"Should I?" she responded tartly.

"Miss Denis, I'm sure that by this time the jury, having heard your animosity toward him, is wondering the same thing. *Why* this feeling?"

"Well, he was . . . was weird. I mean way out. Like, in acting class, he would do and say crazy things."

"Such as?"

"Well, this one day, shortly before he was thrown out, he disrupts the whole class. He comes in late, slips in furtively. As if he was a fugitive, on the lam. Then he opens the door again, peeks out, slams it shut and whispers, 'They're here! They're after me and they're here!' He races into a corner of the studio, crouches there and pulls out a gun. A real gun. Like he's ready to kill whoever is following him."

"And who *was* following him?" Kirk asked.

"Nobody. When our teacher blew his top, Chris said he was only rehearsing making an entrance. As I said, he was always doing weird things. He gave me a creepy feeling. So I know what Alice meant when she said she was being watched all the time."

"Miss Denis, am I correct in saying that you considered him a very strange young man?" Kirk asked.

"Strange is a small word for the way I felt about him," she replied, glaring at Chris and adding, "And still feel. When I got that call from the police, even before they told me, I knew what happened. I knew he had killed her!"

She glared at Chris. "You bastard!"

"Please, Miss Denis, try to compose yourself," Kirk pleaded gently. But he was extracting from her exactly what he wanted. "Miss Denis," he resumed with a fresh approach. "Perhaps you can help me out."

"If I can," she responded aloofly.

Howie Stone sat up a bit more alertly.

"From your description of the defendant and his conduct, I am very puzzled. Why would a nice, attractive, talented young woman like Alice Ames even be interested in him? To say nothing of living with him for months. How do you explain that?"

"Well, he wasn't like that all the time—difficult and weird, I mean," the witness explained.

"He wasn't?" Kirk asked, as if this were news to him. "How was he the rest of the time?"

"He was . . . was sort of . . . okay. I mean, he could be nice when he wanted to be," she explained.

"Nice sometimes, not nice, weird the rest of the time," Kirk pretended to sum up her reply.

"That's right," she affirmed.

"Sort of a Dr. Jekyll and Mr. Hyde?" Kirk suggested.

"Object!" Stone called out. "He is putting words in the mouth of the witness."

"A little literary reference can't hurt these proceedings," Malachi ruled.

Having succeeded in placing before the jury the precise image he needed to predispose them to his multiple personality defense, David Kirk said, "I have no more questions."

With his last witness, prosecutor Howard Stone felt confident that he had presented a strong enough case to convict Christopher Cory of the deliberate and willful murder of Alice Ames.

He rose to announce, "Your Honor, the State rests."

Whereupon Malachi glanced in David Kirk's direction for the expected motion.

"Your Honor, I move to dismiss on the grounds that the State has failed to prove a *prima facie* case."

Just as perfunctorily, Malachi ruled, "Denied! Proceed, Counselor!"

"If it please the court I would like a recess until tomorrow morning so I may notify my witnesses."

"Granted," Malachi announced. He banged his gavel to add emphasis to his word.

Thereupon, as was the custom in his courtroom, he waited until all spectators and attorneys had departed before he permitted the two uniformed attendants to lift him down.

Twenty-six

On the following morning, when David Kirk arrived in the courtroom, he found a message requesting that he join Mr. Stone in Judge Malachi's chambers before the session began.

Puzzled, mainly concerned that he was facing some sudden change in Malachi's position on admissibility of expert psychiatric testimony, Kirk went at once to chambers, where he found Malachi and Stone awaiting his arrival.

"Sorry if I'm late. But my first witness had an emergency to deal with," Kirk explained.

Malachi wheeled himself from behind his desk to form a small circle with both counsel.

"Boys," he began, "today we embark on the most idiotic venture in all of American jurisprudence. You, Davey, will present an expert who will swear up and down, and give reasons for her opinions, that your client is not only a kook but, in this particular case, a combination of kooks. Known in the head-shrink trade as Multiple Personality Disorder. Understandable. For a defense attorney, any port in a storm. And you, my dear Davey, *are* in a storm."

He turned to Howard Stone. "And you, Howie, will present two, three, four, five, however many the state can afford, experts who will swear that Davey's expert is no expert at all. That she doesn't know what she is talking about. Thus the experts will battle back and forth. Sometimes using language that I don't understand. To say nothing of the jury. Then, after we get this goulash of psychiatric opinions together, what trained, experienced psychiatrists can't agree on, a jury of laymen will have to decide."

Malachi shook his head and sighed. "If there is a crazier system than that, I am sure our Supreme Court will find it. So, the reason I called you both in was to let you know that I will have very short patience with any jerking around during this phase of the proceedings. Understood?"

"Understood," Howard Stone responded quickly.

"Yes, Your Honor," David Kirk replied.

"Okay. Now, go out and do your worst."

Judge Malachi was in place on the bench. He looked out over the courtroom and could sense the tension. Especially in the first rows, where the media merchants were eagerly awaiting the unique defense which David Kirk had promised.

To lay a proper and solid foundation for Dr. Scott's crucial testimony, David Kirk led the jury through all the steps involved in discovering Christopher Cory's condition and making the diagnosis of Multiple Personality. He did so by introducing, first, Dr. Heldeman, who testified to his findings, leading to Dr. Lipsky, who recited his conclusions, which led him to refer the patient to Dr. Charles Wilson, who explained to the jury why he referred the patient to Dr. Michal Scott.

Prosecuting attorney Howard Stone did a minimum of cross-examination for, in this trial, all else was prelude to Scott's testimony, and both prosecutor and defense were well aware of that.

Once Dr. Wilson was excused, Judge Malachi declared a lunch recess until two o'clock.

———————

At seven minutes past two, Malachi resumed the proceedings with a brisk order to defense counsel: "Mr. Kirk! Your next witness!"

Kirk left the counsel table, went up the aisle and into the corridor. When he returned he escorted Dr. Michal Scott into the courtroom.

"Your Honor, I call Dr. Michal Scott to the stand."

She came forward, stood at the foot of the witness stand for the clerk to administer the oath. She gave her name and address to the court stenographer, and took her place in the witness chair.

Meantime, Judge Malachi had swung his wheelchair about to gain a better view of this witness.

He could not help thinking, *Leave it to Davey Kirk. In the entire field of psychiatric experts, leave it to him to find one who looks like this. Oh, if only I were twenty years younger. Even fifteen. I just hope she is as smart as she is good-looking. Otherwise, I'm afraid Howie will tear her to shreds.*

His list of questions in hand, David Kirk advanced toward the witness. At which point Assistant District Attorney Stone rose to his feet to ask, "Your Honor, may I ask for a similar brief indulgence?"

Surprised and annoyed, old Malachi waved Stone on his way. Stone started up the aisle of the courtroom to where his young black female assistant was waiting. They conferred in whispers. She slipped out, was gone for a few minutes. When she returned she was no longer alone.

She had been joined by Dr. Helmut Klinger.

Looking every bit the twin of Sigmund Freud, Klinger strode down the aisle slowly, with regal bearing. He passed through the barrier to occupy the chair next to Stone.

A bit impatient with this display, Malachi grumbled with mock concern, "Mr. Stone, are you quite ready?"

"Yes, Your Honor, quite!"

Stone leaned to his left so that Klinger could whisper into his ear without being overheard by anyone close by.

Kirk had observed Stone's performance, as had Dr. Scott. They both knew that Klinger was there for one purpose only: to coach Stone on how to attack her credibility and her testimony.

Twenty-seven

"Dr. Scott," Kirk began, "would you inform the jury as to your educational background?"

Michal Scott angled slightly in the direction of the jury. "I was born in Plymouth, California. A small farming community. I went to grade school there. Then to the consolidated high school of the district."

"At what age were you graduated from high school, Doctor?"

"At age sixteen," Scott replied. "I enrolled at Yale, in Connecticut. Which I attended for three years."

"Why only three years, Doctor?" Kirk asked, aware of what her response would be.

"I completed the four-year course in three because I was anxious to get on to medical school. I was accepted at Harvard. I went on to fulfill my medical-school requirements there."

"And after that, Doctor?"

"I served my residency at New York Hospital, on the Psychiatric Service."

"And then, Doctor?"

"I became deeply interested in the study of Multiple Personality Disorder. And I was fortunate enough to become associate to Dr. John Beaumont, who was eminent in that field. I worked with him for eleven years until his death."

"Doctor, have you published any papers, books or other writings on the subject of MPD?" Kirk asked.

"I co-authored one hundred eighty-six papers on the subject, which have been published in various psychiatric and medical journals throughout the world."

At that point, Klinger tugged slightly on Stone's sleeve. Stone leaned closer to receive some whispered advice.

The moment did not pass unnoticed by either Kirk or Scott.

Kirk continued: "Doctor, have you published any other works on the subject?"

"Yes. I have completed and published three volumes of the four I have planned. I am completing the fourth now," Scott informed.

Kirk turned toward the bench. "Your Honor, may I assume we have established the witness's expertise, so I may now proceed with the rest of my examination?"

Caught staring at the witness, Malachi had to regain his composure before he started to nod his assent. Only to be interrupted by Stone, who raised his hand.

"Yes, Mr. Stone?"

"If I may, Your Honor, I would like to ask the witness a question or two before we proceed."

"Does it deal with qualifying this witness as an expert?" Malachi asked.

"In my opinion it does," Stone replied, with a hint of foreboding in his tone.

With a gesture that bespoke his annoyance as well, Malachi granted Stone permission to proceed.

"Dr. Scott, you have just testified that you have written some one hundred eighty-six papers on the subject of Multiple Personality Disorder?"

"Not wrote," she corrected, "co-authored."

"Ah, yes, 'co-authored,' " Stone appeared to agree. "May I inquire with whom you co-authored them?"

"Dr. John Beaumont, whose associate I was at the time."

"Are you telling this jury that Dr. Beaumont, an eminent,

if not *the* eminent, psychiatrist in the field of MPD, needed the help of an associate to write his papers?"

"It is quite usual for an associate to gather material, carry out tests and present that material to his or her superior and be listed as co-author."

"So that the real interpretative work, the conclusions, the thing that makes the name Beaumont so outstanding in the field is his, not yours."

"I suppose you could say that."

"And his appending your name as co-author was his way of rewarding you for . . . for whatever," Stone said.

Kirk detected a slight flush rising into Michal Scott's cheeks. She also betrayed a distinct effort to control her anger.

"I made a substantial contribution to the work. So I was, if you wish to use the term, 'rewarded' in accord with the usual practice in the scientific and medical world."

"Dr. Scott, are you aware that there is a feeling in some quarters in the psychiatric world that Dr. Beaumont did this to advance you and announce you as his heir apparent?"

"I am aware of a great deal of gossip in the psychiatric community. Most of it based on professional jealousy, of which my field happens to have its share," Scott replied.

"Dr. Scott, may I ask, since the death of Dr. Beaumont, have you co-authored papers or books with any other psychiatrist?" Stone continued.

"No, I have not. I work alone. And what do you wish to read into that, Mr. Stone?" Scott countered.

Malachi felt the need to intervene. "The witness will kindly refrain from being argumentative. And you, Mr. Stone, will kindly be less provocative. The court does not quite get the point you are driving at."

"Your Honor, I am trying to establish that a great part of the witness's so-called expertise derives from the indulgence of an old man, for reasons on which we can only speculate," Stone replied.

"Mr. Stone," Scott shot back, "I have standing in this field in my own right. True, I learned much from Dr. Beaumont. Which is usual in a professional relationship between mentor and protégé."

" 'Mentor and protégé'?" Stone remarked. "So, that's what they call it in psychiatric circles. I must remember that."

Whereupon, Stone strode back to his table.

Kirk was keenly conscious of the fact that if Stone had not diminished Scott in the minds of the jury, he had surely made her tense and combative. And concerning the same provocative situation Klinger had hinted at on a previous occasion. Kirk felt he could not risk proceeding without confronting the issue. He turned to the bench.

"Your Honor, it is now a quarter past three. Since the testimony Dr. Scott is about to give is quite involved and highly scientific, it would be best if the jury heard it all in a single session. Therefore I ask for a recess until tomorrow morning."

Always annoyed by any delay in the course of a trial, Malachi nevertheless looked to the prosecution table. "Mr. Stone?"

"No objection, Your Honor," Stone replied.

"Well," Malachi grumbled, "okay. Ten o'clock tomorrow!" He sealed it with a sharp blow of his gavel.

Puzzled by this sudden move on Kirk's part, Dr. Scott was quite furious as she stepped down from the witness box.

In a quiet but firm voice she reprimanded, "Mr. Kirk, I cleared my entire calendar for this day. Postponed four patients to be available to you. Why this delay?"

"Doctor, there is something Howard Stone seems to know, something Dr. Klinger seems to know. But that I don't. In a trial that is extremely dangerous."

"And what is that?"

The manner in which she asked the question led him to suspect she was well aware of what he was about to say.

"Dr. Beaumont."

"Dr. Beaumont is no concern of yours, Mr. Kirk."

"He is, as long as he seems to be a great concern of yours," Kirk pointed out. "I see that flush rise into your cheeks whenever his name is mentioned. For example, right now."

To avoid the issue, she countered, "Mr. Kirk, for a shrewd lawyer you are doing your client a very bad turn by distracting your principal witness with matters that have no bearing on his defense."

"Stone thinks it has bearing. Klinger surely thought so that day," Kirk countered. "What is it they know that I don't?"

"Gossip in the trade, Mr. Kirk. I would pay it no mind if I were you. I will be ready to take the stand again tomorrow at ten," she said as she started to turn away.

He reached out to catch her hand. Though her gray eyes reflected her resentment at this sudden physical contact, he did not release her.

"We must meet! This evening!" Kirk insisted.

She took a moment to consider his urgent request, then said, "My office."

"Seven o'clock?"

"Seven o'clock," she confirmed.

He watched as she started crisply up the aisle on her way out of the courtroom.

Twenty-eight

At the agreed-upon hour, David Kirk arrived at the office-residence of Dr. Michal Scott.

By her greeting, a reserved "Mr. Kirk," he knew that she was alert to the seriousness of the occasion.

He did not avail himself of the club chair near the fireplace, which she indicated. Instead, he remained standing, waiting for her to be seated.

"Dr. Scott," he began directly, "when an attorney puts a witness on the stand he vouches for her in many ways. First, he assumes that the witness will tell the truth."

She interrupted to demand, "Have I given you cause to believe that I didn't?"

"Of course not," he agreed. "But, granted the witness is telling the truth, the question then becomes, how is she perceived by the jury? Can her credibility be undermined by attacks by opposing counsel, subtle, and sometimes not so subtle. Is there something in the witness's past which if revealed will undermine the jury's belief in her testimony? So I hope you understand that I am forced to ask."

She nodded, making it easier for him to proceed.

Because she had, he felt compelled to admit, "I must also confess I feel a personal interest."

He detected a stiffening in her bearing.

"I like what I see, Doctor. I would like to know more. Much more. But I have a rule. Never mix my personal with my professional life. These past weeks I've been consoling myself that this trial won't last forever. I look forward to the time when we will no longer be professional colleagues."

His straightforward declaration caused her to relent and ask, "Do you want it all? Or just the end?"

"I'm a lawyer. Putting a witness on the stand. I can't afford any surprises. So the details are important."

"Yes. I guess you do want it all," she said, resigning herself to a burden she would rather have avoided.

"Where shall I start?" she asked. "Back in grade school? I was one of the bright ones. Always first with her hand raised to answer, even before the teacher finished the question. So, by the time I was halfway through high school, Mr. Spence—he was our principal—suggested I apply for scholarships to some of the colleges in the East. He said that was the place for someone bright. He always said, 'Back East is the place to make your mark.'

"I applied. And I was very fortunate. I was accepted by three different colleges. I chose Yale.

"After that there was medical school. Four tough years. Which I had to endure if I wanted to become a psychoanalyst. You know, of course, before one can be board-certified one must undergo a personal psychoanalysis. One day, while I was still trying to choose my analyst, we had a guest lecturer at the hospital. The prime expert in the field of Multiple Personality Disorder. I went, of course, eager to see the man whose papers and books I had studied. I guess you could say that time *I* was the groupie. I brought one of his books for him to autograph.

"He was the most commanding and distinguished man I had ever seen. Tall. Handsome. He spoke with such authority and conviction. Yet he was warm and charming. When the session was over, like a shy schoolgirl I went up. While he signed my book he looked at me and remarked, 'Specializing in psychoanalysis, eh?' The idea seemed to amuse him. I blurted out that I still needed my personal analysis. And would he, in his crowded schedule of private patients, lectures and other activities, find time for me?

"I will never forget his smile. Fatherly, benign. I felt like a little girl begging for a special toy which my daddy might say I could have.

" 'Doctor,' he asked, 'what is your name?'

" 'Scott. Michal Scott.'

" 'Ah, a biblical name. How fitting, my dear, for someone so young and lovely.' He thought a moment. 'Yes, I think I might squeeze you in. Write out your name and your number. I will have my secretary call you.'

"Mr. Kirk, to have the fabled John Beaumont agree to take me on as an analysand was quite something. It was like winning a Nobel Prize. I was to see him three times a week: Monday, Wednesday and Friday.

"After some months I became not only his analysand but his disciple as well. At first I assisted only by taping the notes he made during his sessions with multiples. And I transcribed his lectures. Sometimes he would even ask my opinion on how things went. How he handled the questions that were asked. It was very flattering to have my opinion valued by such a man.

"Eventually I traveled with him. Not too often, but often enough to have Emma . . . she's Dr. Congreve . . . become jealous of me.

"Her feelings for John were stronger, deeper than even I suspected. She not only admired him, she was in love with him. In a very sexual, carnal way. Though he never felt that way about her.

"In the early days when she did critiques of my work, she tried to undermine his confidence in me. He saw through her. And forgave her. He had great consideration for the weaknesses of other people.

"Matters came to a head when I moved in here."

Kirk's reaction caused her to explain quickly. "No, Mr. Kirk, there was never anything like that between John and me. My moving in came about when Paul died."

"Paul?" Kirk asked, startled.

"My husband. Paul and I, we'd been med students together. After graduation he was appointed to the cardiac-surgery unit at New York Hospital. So we were able to get married. Which didn't mean that much of a change. We'd lived together all through school."

She paused before she said simply, "His death was so . . . so unnecessary. So avoidable. In our student days we used to run together every morning. But his hours in surgery were so different from mine, we began to run alone, and whenever we could.

"Early one morning—Paul was running that walkway along the lower East River—he was accosted—I hate that word—he was viciously attacked by a desperate druggie. Runners do not carry money. No place for it. Keys were all Paul had. Not even identification. So . . . so when they found him it took hours before anyone could identify him. He had been killed by a rock across the back of his head. Shattered his brain. That brilliant brain. It was strange. When I saw him in the medical examiner's morgue, his face looked as handsome as it had been early that morning when I was still half asleep and he kissed me before going for his run. But the back of his head . . ."

She shuddered. Kirk felt a sudden impulse to embrace her, to protect her from her own memories.

"In my profession we give aid and comfort to those forced to face life's surprises. But somehow we are never prepared for our own."

She confessed, "I can understand much better now when patients tell me they are contemplating suicide.

"John Beaumont had me move in here. Kept me busy with work. More than I could handle at times. Until I was more tired from working than from weeping.

"But for John, I cannot say what would have happened to me. Gradually we became like father and daughter. Quite different from the gossip in the psychiatric community. Which grew even more vicious when John died. Because he left this house to me. Left me the residual of all his unpublished work. And in a way, he left me his reputation as well.

"His jealous colleagues chose to castigate it as the legacy of an illicit relationship. What they never knew, and I never want them to know, is how much of his last research was not his. By that time he was ill, far too ill to carry on the work."

She hesitated before making a very painful admission. "John had contracted ALS."

"Lou Gehrig's disease," Kirk realized.

"By the second year he had to be fed, shaved, washed. You have no idea what that can mean to a proud man. I said proud, not vain. There is a difference, a great difference. You had to know John to appreciate that. He would no longer appear in public. He would send me to fulfill his lecture schedule. Always we provided a good excuse. He was too busy finishing another book, another paper. The last twenty-four papers with both our names on them . . ."

"Yours," Kirk assumed.

"Mr. Kirk, I demand from you the same degree of confidentiality you extend to your clients. No one is ever to know about this. John was my savior when I needed one. I owe him that much. That his reputation, his image, be safe from the jealous vultures who would savage it. I am determined to preserve his reputation."

"Even at the cost of your own?"

"I would rather permit them to believe I was his mistress than that he ended up a helpless vestige of the man he once was. Especially the way he died."

Kirk refrained from asking. He sensed this was the first time she had felt compelled to unburden herself.

"That last time I flew home from a lecture in Zurich . . . I found him . . . he had put an end to his illness."

She was silent, seemed drained before she concluded, "There it is. The whole story that, by innuendo, some would turn into a nasty scandal."

"Your husband . . . how long ago?" Kirk asked.

"Eight years on February third."

"And since then?"

"Yes, there have been men. But only casual acquaintances."

"You surely do nothing to encourage them."

"After Paul's swift and sudden death, and John's slow, lingering one, I have tasted enough of death to last me for a while. A long while. If that is less than you expect from an experienced psychoanalyst, I can only tell you that it is easier to deal with the problems of others than one's own."

"Doctor, I will respect your confidence, and your feelings."

After his promise she asked only, "Am I still qualified to be your witness, Mr. Kirk?"

"Now that I am prepared for anything they might throw at me during the trial, yes."

"Then, shall I see you in the courtroom at ten?" she asked, once more cool and professional.

He could see in her eyes that reliving the last eight years of her life had not been easy for her.

"Tomorrow. At ten," he confirmed.

Twenty-nine

Promptly at ten o'clock the next morning, Dr. Michal Scott mounted the witness stand in the trial of *People* v. *Cory*.

As if nothing of a personal nature had transpired between them, David Kirk resumed his formal examination. To educate the jury and the media, he led her through a basic explanation of Multiple Personality Disorder: the terms involved, such as host and alter; the conflict between them; and what symptoms and signs a psychiatrist considers in making such a diagnosis.

Describing all the signs she searched for, Dr. Scott ended

her reply, "Finally, you have to subtly get a look at the patient's wrists."

"Why the wrists?" Kirk asked.

"To see if there are little lines, white scars that indicate if the patient has ever made any suicide attempts."

"The defendant, Christopher Cory, did his wrist reveal such scars?" Kirk asked.

"Yes. But they were not white, but red. Indicating his attempts were quite recent."

"Are suicide attempts common to people who suffer MPD?"

"Yes, indeed," Scott replied.

Thus Kirk led her, step-by-step, through her findings in Cory's case, until they reached the subject of hypnosis. At which point she said, "Instead of describing that process, it might be more helpful for the jury if I showed them tapes I made of Mr. Cory during that phase of his treatment."

"Your Honor, may we have ten minutes in which to set up three television screens?" Kirk asked.

"I look forward to this demonstration, Counselor. We will take a ten-minute recess," Malachi ruled.

With the help of both attendants, Gerry Prince rolled three television sets into the well of the courtroom. One was positioned to face the jury, the second to face the bench, the third for the benefit of media and spectators.

In the meantime, Howard Stone and Dr. Klinger were in close whispered conference, during which Stone scrawled many hasty notes on his yellow legal pad.

The television sets in place, Kirk resumed, "Doctor, will you tell the jury the circumstances under which these tapes were made?"

"The symptoms and signs which Mr. Cory presented led me to suspect he was a case of MPD. He also told me of certain experiences he had had which caused me to decide hypnosis was strongly indicated."

"And what were those, Doctor?"

"He told of receiving packages from stores in which he had never shopped. When he opened those packages he found clothing of a kind that he would never wear. What we would call heavy-metal clothes."

"Doctor, as a specialist in the field of MPD, what was the significance of those episodes?"

"It was so typical of the kind of tricks that alters play on hosts that I decided on a direct attack. Fortunately, Mr. Cory proved quite amenable to hypnosis. As for the rest, I think the tape will speak for itself."

David Kirk turned to address the jury. "Ladies and gentlemen, we are now going to darken this room. Please keep your eyes on this television screen. Give it your undivided attention."

Once the shades on the high windows were raised, blocking out any direct daylight, Kirk signaled Gerry to snap on the current.

The three screens lit up. Christopher Cory, on tape, seated in Dr. Scott's office, looking into the camera, began to respond to her hypnotizing suggestions.

As the tape played on, Dr. Klinger continued to pour suggestions into Stone's ear.

At that point in the tape where the hypnotized Chris Cory saw two David Kirks, there was a snicker from one man in the jury. But the other eleven were entranced, for they had never before witnessed a therapeutic hypnosis.

The moment arrived when the voice of Dr. Scott was heard to ask, "Chris, for days now you have been complaining about severe headaches. Twice you said, 'I feel like my head is splitting in two.' Do you recall that, Chris?"

"Yes . . . yes, I do."

"Did you really think your head was splitting in two?"

"Felt like."

"Could it have been something else?"

Cory did not respond at once, but the jurors finally saw him shake his head.

"Chris, I would like to speak to whoever is responsible for the murder of Alice Ames."

The jurors observed that Cory did not respond.

"Chris?" they heard Scott ask once more.

They saw Cory turn away from the camera.

"Chris, I would like to talk to whoever killed Alice."

Judge and jury watched as Christopher Cory's hand began to twitch. Then his entire body erupted in a convulsion. Now, as he turned to face the camera once more, the expression around his mouth and his eyes began to harden. His jaw started to protrude. His hands became clawlike and rigid.

In the dark courtroom more than one gasp was heard, several from the jury box.

"Chris," Scott's voice said once more.

Since all psychiatric material in possession of the defense had, by law, already been disclosed to the prosecution, Howard Stone knew exactly what was about to happen. To diminish its effect on the jury he called out, "Objection, Your Honor!"

"Stop the tape," Malachi ordered with obvious annoyance. "Mr. Stone? The basis of your objection?"

"Your Honor, this jury has no way of knowing if this is a spontaneous event they are witnessing or a prepared and rehearsed performance."

Malachi did not prevail on David Kirk to ask the question but addressed Dr. Scott himself.

"Doctor, you are under oath. Based on your own knowledge, is this the tape of a spontaneous event in the regular course of psychiatric treatment?"

"It is, Your Honor," Scott replied.

"Continue rolling the tape," Malachi ordered, adding, "and let's have no more interruptions or frivolous objections."

Stone was quite willing to settle for the rebuke. He had succeeded in interrupting, and to some degree minimizing, the building impact of Cory's bizarre switching from his own host personality to that of an alter.

The tape resumed with Cory in the physical guise of Max and, in the hoarse, angry voice, complaining, "Bitch! Couldn't leave it alone, could you? Damned sneaky bitch. What the hell are you doing, butting in where you don't belong?"

"Who are you?" Scott's voice asked.

"None of your goddamn business! So split! Get lost! I don't have to answer to you for anything!"

The entire assemblage—judge, jury, media, spectators—watched and listened in shocked silence to the presence of this new participant in the trial of *People* v. *Cory*. They were able to contrast this ugly person with the slender, mild-appearing young defendant who sat at the counsel table watching his vicious alter on the screen.

Dr. Scott, on the tape, led Max into his confession of how he planned to and did murder Alice Ames in such a way as to make certain that Christopher Cory would be found guilty of the crime.

At the point on the tape where Max rose up in a menacing pose extending his clawed hands ready to strangle Dr. Scott, there were gasps from various sectors of the courtroom. They heard Scott's voice order, "Max, you will sit down!" Max slowly slipped back into his chair.

The tape had run through Scott's voice saying, "You can go now. But we will be speaking again."

"Bet your sweet ass we'll be speaking again. And you won't get away so easy next time."

"Cut!" David Kirk called out.

Once the courtroom had been returned to full daylight, Kirk addressed the bench, "Your Honor, since there is another tape and of a startling nature . . ."

"More startling than what we have already seen?" Malachi asked.

"Yes, Your Honor. So I would suggest we take a break at this time. I do not wish to overtax the jury."

"To say nothing of the judge, Mr. Kirk. Yes, I think this would be a good time for a short recess."

Thirty

Judge Malachi was back on the bench. The courtroom had been restored to order.

Dr. Michal Scott resumed the stand.

"Doctor," David Kirk began, "we have seen a tape of the first time that an alter named Max came out and identified himself. Did there come a time when you were able to discover the origin of the name Max?"

"Yes, sir."

"Will you tell the jury how that happened?" Kirk urged.

Thus, question-by-question, he led Michal Scott through the need and the purpose of abreaction, unearthing the early abuse that caused a child to become a multiple.

When she became graphically specific about the abuse involved in the case of Christopher Cory, David Kirk asked, "Doctor, are you telling this jury that a six-year-old boy was threatened with castration?"

"Yes, Mr. Kirk."

"Would a child of six have any comprehension of what castration means?" Kirk asked.

"It was impressed on him by a terrifying demonstration.

The best way for the jury to understand is to view another tape I have here." She called to Gerry, "Mr. Prince, please?"

While Gerry inserted the second cassette, Klinger leaned in Stone's direction to whisper, "Isn't there some legal ground on which to object?"

"Too many objections, especially if overruled, only antagonize the jury. They think I am trying to deprive them of some vital evidence."

The courtroom once again in shadow, Gerry started the tape rolling. The jurors leaned forward to watch intently. They saw Scott regress hypnotized Chris Cory from the present through former periods of his life. Until she had brought him back to the age of six.

Now, in the language and the feelings of a terrified six-year-old, Chris related how his mother's lover warned him not to watch. Or he would cut off his doodle. To prove it, he picked up Chris's dog, a gift from his father, and, using a big kitchen knife, cut off Max's doodle, then threatened to do the same to little Chris.

By that moment on the tape, twenty-six-year-old Chris Cory had become a hysterical six-year-old huddling in a corner of the bare room crying bitterly. Suddenly he turned to the camera to accuse and physically attack Dr. Scott.

With heartrending cries of terror, and bitter anger intended for his mother but expressed against Dr. Scott, the tape came to a close.

The only sound heard in the courtroom was defendant Chris Cory sobbing.

David Kirk neither moved nor spoke, thinking, *Give the jury plenty of time to absorb this. Let them never forget this moment. Especially when they are in that jury room debating sane or insane.*

When Judge Malachi urged, "Counselor . . ." David Kirk decided not to overplay his hand. He confined himself to the two obligatory questions.

"Dr. Scott, based on your findings, can you now say with certainty that at the time of the commission of the crime, this defendant did not know the difference between right and wrong by virtue of mental defect or disease?"

"At the time Alice Ames was murdered, Christopher Cory was not in condition to know right from wrong. Since, though his body may have been there, he was not."

"Doctor, based on your findings, can you say with certainty that he did or did not have the mental capacity to form the intent to kill?"

"His alter Max had taken complete control. Christopher Cory was in no condition to form any intent, criminal or otherwise."

"Thank you, Doctor. Your witness, Mr. Stone."

Before Stone could begin what must be a lengthy cross-examination, Judge Malachi declared a half-hour recess.

As usual, David Kirk left the courtroom to go down to his limo to make phone contact with the office and sign any papers and documents Greta might have brought. He braved the media, their questions, microphones and cameras, unusually heavy since the startling testimony of this morning.

Once safely inside his limo, and while he signed the papers Greta presented, she reported, "Two special calls. CBS. ABC. CBS wants you and Cory for *Sixty Minutes*. ABC wants you alone for *Twenty/Twenty*. Barbara Walters called herself."

"Greta, you know the rule."

"Yes, sir, no interviews until the case is over."

When he reentered the courtroom David Kirk was angered to discover Chris Cory in animated discussion with an unfamiliar young woman. He raced down the aisle and brushed through the barrier to surprise them both.

"Chris! Damn it, I told you! No talking to anyone!"

Cory only smiled and said, "I think you're going to like this, Mr. Kirk."

The young woman introduced herself, "Mr. Kirk, Stella

Frank. Artland Films. I'm authorized to make a bid for the film rights to Mr. Cory's life and, of course, to the story of this trial."

"Any such talk is premature," Kirk replied. "And I consider it a highly unwelcome intrusion into my case at this stage."

"Mr. Kirk, obviously you don't understand," Ms. Frank explained smugly. "We are not talking option based on the outcome of the trial. We are talking firm deal."

"Until this trial is over, there will be no exclusive interviews. No television deals. No picture deal. Clear?"

Ms. Frank smiled. An understanding smile. As if Kirk had communicated a bargaining signal to her which she understood perfectly.

"Okay, Mr. Kirk. What'll it take now to get a first refusal when the bidding does open? And I am ready to talk big dollars."

"There is no first refusal! And I strongly resent your attempt to circumvent me by talking directly to my client at this time!" Kirk rebuked.

"Hey, hold on, Mister! *I* didn't turn murder into a profit-making business. It was your Supreme Court. *They* decided that a man could kill fifty people, sell his story, make a fortune and keep it. I'm only doing what the law allows. And so is every other producer in the business. I just happen to be ahead of the crowd, that's all."

There was little by way of rebuttal David Kirk could make to that.

The stir at the door to the judge's robing room alerted everyone that Malachi was set to return to the courtroom.

Thirty-one

Once Judge Aaron Malachi was in place on the bench and Dr. Scott was back on the witness stand, the old judge said, "Mr. Stone, I believe you were about to avail yourself of the right to cross-examine the witness."

Lean, calculating Howard Stone swallowed two more pills, then rose slowly. Taking the sheaf of notes with him, he started toward the witness.

He stared down at his notes, then, without raising his eyes to make contact, asked, "Doctor, for the benefit of the jury, who may not know a great deal about Multiple Personality Disorder, can you tell us how long this phenomenon has been recognized by the psychiatric profession?"'

"About a hundred and fifty years," Scott replied.

"Would you say it was widely recognized and accepted?"

"At the outset, no," Scott admitted.

"Were many cases diagnosed during the last hundred and fifty years?" Stone asked.

"From the outset until the last dozen or fifteen years, not many cases."

"Doctor, if we were to put that into figures, would it be correct to say that two or three times as many cases of MPD have been diagnosed in just the last dozen years than in all the previous one hundred and forty?"

"Yes . . . yes, I would accept that," Scott admitted.

"How do you account for that startling difference?"

"Diagnostic methods have improved. More psychiatrists have been trained to recognize the signs and symptoms."

"Trained by Dr. Beaumont, I assume?" Stone remarked.

David Kirk noted the now-familiar flush of anger that rose into Michal Scott's cheeks.

"Dr. Beaumont was one of the leaders in the field of diagnosing and treating MPD, yes," Scott agreed.

"So, what was once a rare phenomenon is now almost commonplace," Stone commented.

"It is distinctly *not* commonplace," Scott shot back.

"Possibly like the disease-of-the-week on television," Stone gibed.

"Definitely not!" Scott corrected.

Taking his guidance from Klinger's notes, Stone pressed on.

"Doctor, is it a widely held belief among psychiatrists that in many cases the condition is actually *induced* by the therapist?"

"First, that is *not* a widely held belief. Second, the condition is not *induced* by but *discovered* by psychiatrists," Scott replied curtly.

"From my study of the subject—" Stone continued.

Dr. Scott interrupted, "Under the helpful and prejudiced guidance of Dr. Klinger, I presume?"

"Your Honor?" Stone appealed to Malachi, as if he were being put upon and abused.

Malachi leaned in Scott's direction. "Please, Doctor. Mr. Stone is a very sensitive man. You risk crushing his delicate ego by disagreeing with him."

As part of his strategy, Stone switched subjects suddenly. "Doctor, when you were listing the defendant's signs and symptoms the day he first appeared in your office, you made special mention of scars. Scars on the inner side of his wrists. If I recall correctly, did you say those marks were not white but red? Indicating that those were fresh marks?"

"So I testified," Scott admitted.

"Did you observe those fresh scars *after* the defendant had been arrested, charged with and indicted for murder?" Stone asked.

"Of course."

"Doctor, are you aware of how many men in that same predicament attempt to commit suicide?"

"I can imagine," Scott said.

"So, Doctor, isn't it possible that what you took to be a sign of MPD was actually his disgrace at being arrested and charged with murder?" Stone demanded.

"Those scars were only *one* of many signs and symptoms Mr. Cory presented," Scott pointed out.

Stone referred again to the notes Klinger had helped him assemble. "Tell me, Doctor, did Mr. Cory present any history of time spent confined to a psychiatric hospital?"

"No, he did not."

"What about eating disorders?"

"No, no eating disorders," Scott admitted.

"What about substance abuse, use of drugs?"

"No," Scott replied.

"Doctor, aren't all those signs and symptoms of MPD?" Stone asked.

"Mr. Stone, no one patient can have *all* the symptoms of MPD and still function outside a mental institution. Which most of them do," Scott countered.

"So we must conclude that Mr. Cory had only *some*, but not *all*, of the symptoms of MPD?"

"Enough on which to make a diagnosis," Scott corrected.

"Tell me, Doctor, how do you know when a patient has 'enough' symptoms?" Stone pressed.

"That is what my training has taught me to do," Scott replied.

"Taught you by Dr. Beaumont, I presume," Stone commented.

David Kirk found himself protectively resenting Stone's deliberate and unnecessary innuendo.

"Tell me," Stone continued, "could you be so wedded to the concept of MPD because in so doing you carry on the cherished name of your . . . your mentor, John Beaumont?"

At which David Kirk rose to insist, "Mr. Stone! Confine yourself to questions concerning Dr. Scott's findings. Not to the fictitious and sinister immoral motives you are trying to ascribe to her!"

With judicial finality, Malachi intervened, "You will both do me the courtesy of restoring order to these proceedings. Mr. Stone, if you have questions of relevance to ask this witness, ask them. If not, excuse her!"

"Oh, I have a number of questions, Your Honor."

"Then get *to* them!" Malachi ordered.

"Your Honor, if I may?"

With that, Stone returned to his table to extract two pills from his ever-present bottle. He downed them both with a single gulp of water and was ready to launch a new attack on the testimony of the witness.

"Dr. Scott, what is the usual number of alters a psychiatrist is likely to discover in an MPD?"

"Several," Scott replied.

"For the benefit of the jury, how many are 'several'?"

"Two, three, four, sometimes more."

"Then, how do you account for the fact that in this defendant's case there is only one?" Stone asked.

"There is no need to account for it. It just happens to be," Scott replied.

"Isn't it true that there are some reputable psychiatrists who feel that under hypnosis a patient will develop as many alters as his doctor suggests to him?" Stone asked.

"There are some who hold with that theory," Scott conceded.

"Is is possible, then, that when your patient produced his one alter, he was actually responding to a suggestion of yours?" Stone demanded.

"I did not in any way suggest to Mr. Cory that he produce or evoke a single alter personality," Scott denied.

"Oh, no?" Stone disputed. "Dr. Klinger has gone to the trouble of viewing your tape several times. He was able to transcribe the exact language you used. May I read it to you now?" Stone made a slow, deliberate move to Klinger's side to take from him a sheet of paper from which he read, "First we hear the voice of a man, presumably Mr. Kirk, whispering, 'Can't you just ask this . . . this alter, if there is one, to come out and answer you?' And we hear your own voice, Doctor, saying, 'No.' Then, and I ask you to pay close attention to this, Doctor, you say the following, 'Chris, I would like to talk to whoever killed Alice.' "

"Yes, I used those words," Scott confirmed.

"Tell me, Doctor, when you said 'I would like to speak to whoever killed Alice,' weren't you, in essence, strongly suggesting that it was someone besides himself?"

"Of course not. If he had killed her, in response to my question, he would have said, 'I killed her.' "

"Doctor, Webster's dictionary defines *whoever* as, and I quote, 'any person at all . . . whatever person.' And you don't call that suggesting the existence of another identity? Really, Doctor!" Stone pretended to be embarrassed on her behalf.

"There was no attempt to direct the patient to produce an alter," Scott persisted.

"And if that were not enough," Stone thundered, waving the paper at the same time, "you tried to coax the answer out of him by repeating your question. By which time, your patient, no dummy he, realized what hung on his answer, so he was able to produce a manufactured alter, quaintly named Max!"

"That I would act in cahoots with a patient to manufacture an alibi is an outrageous accusation!" Scott protested.

"Your Honor!" Kirk leaped up to protest. "Mr. Stone has exceeded the bounds of cross-examination! At no time during that hypnotic session did Dr. Scott ask to speak to any alter personality. I was there. I know from personal knowledge what happened!"

Howard Stone smiled faintly. "Your Honor, you have seen that tape just as I have. In your considered opinion, have I deviated from the material on that tape?" He glanced to the jury, repeating, "Have I?"

Malachi was forced to concede to the prosecutor's question, "No, Mr. Stone, you have not."

"Then, considering the defense posed in this case, do you consider my question unfair?"

"Proceed, Mr. Stone."

"Mr. Stone, I think the jury should be made aware of another test that was applied to Mr. Cory. At the suggestion of your own Dr. Klinger," Scott said.

"Dr. Scott, I ask the questions," Stone snapped back.

Whereupon Judge Malachi intervened to rule, "Mr. Stone, you opened this subject. I believe the witness is entitled to complete her answer. Proceed, Doctor."

"As I was about to tell the jury, part of the criteria for a diagnosis of MPD is that each personality has its own unique behavior patterns, intelligence, social relationships and other attributes as well as deficiencies. For example, the host may be allergic and the alter may not. Or the host may speak one language and the alter a different one. There is even a case history of a woman with two alters, each of whom had her own menstrual period. So that she experienced three menses every month.

"To test the genuineness of my diagnosis, Dr. Klinger suggested that both the defendant, Mr. Cory, and his alter, Max, be subjected to Rorschach tests."

Stone tried to interrupt by interjecting, "Your Honor, what we have here is not the testimony of a witness, but a class in MPD."

"Mr. Stone, I think I speak for the jury when I say that the witness's response is most interesting. And also pertinent to a subject you yourself raised. Continue, Doctor," Malachi ordered. He smiled down at her, still regretting his advanced age and the limitations it had visited on him.

"As I was saying," Scott continued, "Mr. Cory was given a Rorschach test. When Max appeared, he was given the same test. Those two sets of responses were sent to an experienced interpreter, who was not told who the patients were. He assumed they were two totally different human beings. And I would like to read to the jury his conclusions."

"Your Honor, I object to the witness testifying in any but her own words."

Whereupon, David Kirk rose. "Your Honor, at this time I would like to introduce an exhibit. A copy of the report of Dr. Harvey Drake, who made the blind analysis of both tests done on Mr. Cory and his alter."

"Mark it," Malachi ruled routinely.

Once the document was received, Kirk suggested, "Your Honor, since the report is now in evidence, may the witness read the contents to the jury?"

"She may."

Dr. Michal Scott proceeded to read the contents of the entire report, which drew such vastly contrasting conclusions between Christopher Cory and his alter, Max, diagnosing one to be sane and the other dangerously insane.

Stone had only one ploy left and he resorted to it now.

"Dr. Scott, isn't it true that all the symptoms the defendant described, and which formed the basis of your diagnosis, were related to you by him?" Stone asked.

"Of course. That is the only way psychiatry can function."

"Isn't it true that there is no definitive test that can truly diagnose a case of Multiple Personality Disorder?"

"Mr. Stone, since we are dealing with levels of conscious and unconscious feelings and behavior, there is no such test. Nor do I think there ever will be," Scott replied.

Whereupon Howard Stone said, "Thank you, Doctor. You have been most helpful and enlightening."

He said this smugly and with complete confidence that, if he had not overcome the effects of those dramatic tapes, he had at least introduced the idea that this disease of Cory's was not scientifically provable. He would rely on his own experts to do the rest.

Thirty-two

Judge Malachi called for a brief recess to give the witness time to refresh herself.

The recess over, Kirk approached the witness stand.

"Doctor, during Mr. Stone's cross-examination he made quite a point of the fact that the scars on the wrist of the defendant seemed to be of recent origin."

"Yes, Mr. Kirk, I recall."

"And Mr. Stone inferred from that that the defendant might have attempted suicide because of the disgrace of being arrested and charged with murder. Doctor, would you ascribe a different reason for those suicide scars?"

"Indeed I would. Those scars were not self-inflicted in the sense Mr. Stone assumed. It is my conclusion that they were inflicted *on* him."

There was an immediate stir, not only at the prosecution table but throughout the courtroom as well.

"Doctor, are you suggesting that he had been abused by the prison staff or the police?"

"No. I am referring to the fact that alters are known to carry out physical attacks on their hosts. It is a quite common phenomenon in MPD cases."

Pretending this line of questioning had not been discussed between them, Kirk feigned surprise. "Doctor, are you telling me and this jury that an alter who shares the same body with the host would try to injure that body?"

"Yes! We have cases reported where one alter has even tried to kill another alter," Scott replied.

"Don't they realize that once they kill, actually kill, the host or another alter, they themselves will die?"

"It is what we call pseudodelusion. Where an alter can be totally unaware that to kill a host is to kill himself. But some MPD patients do it nevertheless. That is exactly what happened in the case before the court and the jury now."

"Dr. Scott, would you explain to the jury what you mean by those words?"'

"It is my opinion that the facts in this case prove that this defendant was framed."

"Object!" Stone cried out from his place at the table. "This witness is not qualified to draw any such conclusion. Her field is not law, not police work, not criminal forensics!"

Kirk shot back, "Your Honor, until you hear the witness's entire response, I do not think you can rule on this issue."

Challenged, Malachi responded, "Really? And why not, 'Counselor'?"

"Because the basis of the witness's response is not forensic in the police sense, but purely psychiatric."

"Mr. Kirk, you'd better have a damn good idea of where you are leading this witness. Else I will throw out her entire testimony. Which will leave you up a certain well-known creek, as we used to say," Malachi threatened.

Thankful for the opportunity, despite Malachi's threat, Kirk continued: "Doctor, you said that this defendant was framed. What did you mean by that?"

"The evidence on which this defendant was arrested and charged with murder is all too convenient. Too neat. Too perfect."

" 'Too perfect,' Doctor?" Kirk urged.

"The torn glove is one example. It was presented by Mr. Stone as evidence of premeditation. Because it was supposedly worn to prevent leaving fingerprints. Yet, conveniently, it rips. Leaving a palm print that is blatant evidence that the defendant was at the scene of the crime. The bloodstain which is used for DNA analysis and match, a single bloodstain. If a man really were cut in such a struggle he would have shed more than a single large drop of blood. And the knife, the murder weapon. Found in the trash can just outside the house. Too obvious. The bloodstained clothing, first washed, then given to a dry cleaner. Designed to call attention to the blood, not conceal it. It is my opinion that what we have here is a case in which a host was framed by his alter. An alter willing to condemn himself to a lifetime in prison to avenge himself on the host. A perfect example of pseudodelusion."

"Dr. Scott," Kirk asked, "is it your expert opinion that instead of being the perpetrator, Chris Cory was himself a victim?"

"That is my considered opinion. Substantiated by the tape which this jury has seen, in which Max himself said, 'I kill, he pays.' It is very clear what his intention was. And how well he succeeded. Since Christopher Cory is in this courtroom on trial for murder," Scott replied.

Kirk said only, "Mr. Stone, if you wish . . ."

A hurried whispered conference between Stone and

Klinger ensued, at the end of which Stone announced, "The People would like a recess at this time."

"We will recess for fifteen minutes," Judge Malachi announced. Then he immediately amended that by adding, "Judging from the look on Mr. Stone's face, better make that thirty minutes."

When Scott resumed the stand, Howard Stone approached, carrying a new sheaf of hastily composed notes.

"Doctor, are you familiar with the name Richard Ofshe?"

"Yes," Scott replied, a bit taken by surprise at the sudden mention of that name.

"Can you identify him for the jury?"

"He is a sociologist at the University of California, I believe."

"University of California at Berkeley," Stone added. "Now, Doctor, I read to you this statement made by Dr. Ofshe. 'The therapist starts out in search of repressed sexual abuse. Since patients want to please therapists, they cooperate with anything the therapist comes up with, aimed in that direction. So when the therapist gets the patient to actively imagine an image of abuse, saying, "Picture this happening to you," that encourages the patient to elaborate on that fantasy. Eventually the patient becomes convinced that it is not merely imagination at work, but is repressed memory of abuse.' "

"If you are suggesting that is what happened between Mr. Cory and me, you are wrong," Scott replied firmly.

"Doctor, are you telling this jury that none of your patients have ever said things or done things to ingratiate themselves with you?"

"Of course that happens. We call it transference," Scott admitted.

"Then we cannot say that Dr. Ofshe is wrong, can we?" Stone pursued.

"I say he is wrong in this case," Scott insisted. "I made quite sure never to say anything to Mr. Cory that could be interpreted by him to be a suggestion. For example, I can assure you that until it actually happened, he had never heard the term 'fugue episode' from me."

" 'Fugue episode'?" Stone picked up at once. "Until what happened, Doctor?"

At Michal Scott's first mention of the phrase "fugue episode" David Kirk was stunned. At once Stone conferred with Dr. Klinger. Though fearful of what would ensue, Kirk was powerless to intervene.

Turning back to the witness, Stone urged, " 'Fugue episode,' Dr. Scott?"

Aware of the tension in the courtroom created by her mention of the subject, she had no choice but to continue.

"A fugue episode is a period of amnesia during which an MPD person blacks out completely. For hours, days, weeks or even months. Then as suddenly comes to, to discover that, during the blackout, he lived as a different individual, doing a different job, in a different place."

"Are you telling this court that during your treatment this defendant experienced such an episode?" Stone demanded.

"Yes," Scott was forced to admit. "He was missing for five days. Until he called Mr. Kirk from Scranton and . . ."

At that word, Judge Malachi brought his gavel down sharply and announced, "Counsel and the witness will join me in chambers! At once!"

He made a brusque gesture to the courtroom attendants to lift him down so that he was free to make his exit.

"So, Mr. David Kirk," Malachi began, "your client disappeared for five whole days and was hiding out in Scranton, Pennsylvania?"

Kirk chose to remain silent until Malachi's anger cooled a bit.

"Cat got your tongue, Mr. Kirk?" Malachi demanded. "Well, I'll get your ass for this!"

"Your Honor, this was a most unusual circumstance," Kirk felt compelled to explain.

"Oh, I agree, Mr. Kirk, I agree," Malachi interposed. "Here is a defendant in a murder trial out on bail. He disappears, crosses the state line, flees the jurisdiction of the court. And you never told *me*! That little bastard should have been back in jail! And his bail forfeited! Or should I say *your* bail? Seeing as how bail was in the form of cash. Your magnanimously contributed cash."

"Your Honor, what more could I have done than what I did? I personally drove to Scranton, picked him up and brought him back."

"When I first assigned you to this case, I said, no screwing around! Remember?" Malachi roared, then, in a gentler tone, he directed his words to Michal Scott. "Doctor, 'screwing around' is a legal term for pulling some of the tricks, evasions and tactics for which our friend Mr. Kirk is noted."

Malachi turned his anger back upon David Kirk. "I could have you up before the Appellate Division so fast it would make your head spin! And you know what that would mean!"

"I did not conspire with the defendant to violate the terms of his bail. Nor did he himself knowingly or intentionally violate them. As to not revealing the matter to the court, it is an attorney's ethical duty to protect a client's confidentiality."

Malachi ignored Kirk to address Dr. Scott. "Lady, when lawyers start pleading ethics, honest people should run for the hills."

Malachi rubbed his chin, which by this time of the afternoon sported discernible white bristles. Suddenly, he said, " 'Scuse me." He wheeled his chair about and headed for his private lavatory.

While he was gone no one in the room said a word. From her eyes, Kirk could read how apologetic Michal Scott was for her inadvertent disclosure. Stone simply and silently exuded smug confidence.

Malachi wheeled himself back into the room.

"Got an idea in there. They say every cat has nine lives. "You, my dear Davey, had two. You used up one in the Corregio case. Be very careful with the life you have left. One more step out of line and you are headed for contempt proceedings before me, plus censure from the Appellate Division and possible disbarment."

"Yes, Your Honor, I understand," Kirk said softly.

"No more tricks, Davey, no more!"

———————————

As they strode down the corridor away from Judge Malachi's chambers, Michal Scott asked, "Can he do what he threatened?"

"Not only can, but given the chance, he will," David Kirk admitted. "I know one thing. We'll get no favorable rulings from him from now on."

"Yet he seems to have an affection for you," she remarked.

"Sometimes I wish he didn't. He is toughest on those he likes most. He expects more from them."

"I'm sorry I precipitated this whole thing," she apologized.

"Not your fault. I remember you said once that your business is uncovering the truth, mine is hiding it. I guess that says it all."

Thirty-three

Christopher Cory's insanity defense having been established by David Kirk, the burden fell to Howard Stone to rebut it with expert witnesses of his own.

Under the criminal statutes of the state of New York, each expert witness had been given access to Cory to examine him, test him and form their own opinions and diagnoses.

The first expert Stone introduced was Amos Ferrer. Dr. Ferrer was one of those psychiatrists who did not accept the concept of Multiple Personality Disorder. He was not only vigorous in his testimony but self-righteous as well in his condemnation of any member of the profession who felt otherwise.

Kirk saw no value in cross-examining him and thus giving him the opportunity to repeat his doctrinaire views. He decided to rely on the impact of those tapes to refute Ferrer.

Stone's second witness was Dr. Emma Congreve, who was in her late forties and still extremely attractive, if in a mature way.

In qualifying her as an expert, Stone emphasized that she, too, had been a protégé of Dr. John Beaumont.

Asked if she had read the testimony which Dr. Scott had given two days earlier, Dr. Congreve replied, "Yes, Mr. Stone, I have. And I found it typical of an immature mind. The result of a student following blindly a teacher with whom she was so enamored that she had absolutely no discernment or original thought of her own. Dr. Beaumont was a brilliant man but, like many such men, too wedded to a theory to question it. I fear that Dr. Scott suffers the same disability."

When it came his turn to cross-examine, Kirk decided not to try to shake her from her opinions but to undermine her general credibility.

"Dr. Congreve, is it possible that the opinions you have just expressed are colored by jealousy?"

"Jealousy?" she repeated with considerable disdain. "Jealousy of whom?"

"Of Dr. Scott. Because she replaced you as Dr. Beaumont's associate," Kirk stated, turning away from her to glance at the jury on his way back to his table. "No further questions."

Stone now swore in his chief and final expert, Dr. Wilbur Sloate.

Sloate qualified with eminent scholastic credentials. Stanford University, Yale Medical School, postgraduate work at two of the most famous medical clinics in the East. His present hospital affiliation consisted of New York University Hospital and the Payne Whitney Clinic in Westchester County.

"Dr. Sloate, how long did your examination of the defendant take place?"

"Three different times over a period of five days."

"Did the defendant, in your opinion, exhibit sufficient understanding of his situation, of the purpose of his visits to you and of the questions you asked him?"

"He was perfectly cognizant of his surroundings, his situation and the purpose of his visits to me," Sloate replied.

"Doctor, did you find anything during your examination that would give you the impression that within recent months the defendant had suffered any mental disease or defect?"

"Object!" Kirk called out.

"Grounds?" Malachi demanded.

"Mr. Stone is asking the witness to express an opinion on

a condition the defendant may or may not have had before he ever saw him," Kirk argued.

To which Stone replied, "Your Honor, all I asked of the witness was his expert opinion as to any *residual* effects or evidence of a previous mental condition he might have observed."

"Such as?" Kirk demanded.

"Mr. Kirk," Malachi took over, "until you hear Dr. Sloate's answer, hold your objection in abeyance! Proceed, Mr. Stone."

"Doctor, did you find any residual effects of any possible previous mental disease or defect in the defendant?"

"Aside from some very superficial scars on his wrist, I found nothing to indicate that he had any previous mental problems."

"So, Doctor, is it your opinion that at the time of his arrest he was of sufficiently sound mind to understand the charge made against him?"

"Yes. He surely seemed to understand it when I saw him."

"Doctor, one final question. Did anything that the defendant said or did during all those hours cause you to form the opinion that he was suffering from Multiple Personality Disorder?"

"I saw absolutely no indication of that condition," Sloate responded firmly.

"Your witness, Mr. Kirk."

"Dr. Sloate," Kirk began, "during your examination, did the defendant complain of headaches?"

"He did mention that he experienced some headaches," Sloate conceded.

"Just 'some headaches'? Not *severe* headaches?" Kirk pressed.

"He did say they were somewhat severe," Sloate admitted.

"And that did not impress you as a prime presenting symptom of Multiple Personality Disorder?" Kirk asked.

Sloate smiled. "Mr. Kirk, if every patient who comes to me complaining of headaches was an MPD, I'd have hundreds of them. Headaches are a 'prime' symptom of so many conditions."

"Not even in a case where the patient was referred to you with such a diagnosis by another reputable psychiatrist?"

"Yes, I read Dr. Scott's diagnosis. But she was a disciple, *the* favorite disciple, of John Beaumont. I have always considered him obsessed by the concept of Multiple Personality Disorder."

"Dr. Sloate, do I have the impression that you do not believe there is such a condition as MPD?" Kirk asked.

"Oh, there is. But it is too freely diagnosed these days. As some drugs are too freely prescribed," Sloate said, dismissing the subject.

"So that, Doctor, in Mr. Cory's case, you really didn't *look* for signs and symptoms of MPD, did you?"

"I didn't exactly say that," Sloate protested.

"What *did* you say exactly, Doctor?" Kirk challenged. "You cast aside a basic symptom like headaches. You ignore those scars on the defendant's wrists. How many other signs and symptoms did you disregard in your haste to decide the defendant was not suffering from MPD?" Kirk demanded.

"Mr. Kirk . . ." Sloate tried to protest.

Aware of the effect he was having on the jury, Kirk overrode Sloate's attempt to interrupt. "What would it take to convince you, Doctor?"

From his place at the counsel table Stone called out, "Your Honor, he is harassing the witness."

"Mr. Kirk, you will be a little less hostile in your questions," Malachi warned.

"Sorry, Your Honor," Kirk apologized. But he felt he might have begun to make inroads into Sloate's testimony.

In a less emotional tone he asked, "Dr. Sloate, I ask again, what would it take to convince you?"

"For one thing, the appearance of an alter personality," Sloate replied.

"So, Doctor, if a patient were able to produce an alter personality at the mere whim of a psychiatrist, that would convince you?"

"Not if it was—what did you call it—a whim," Sloate responded.

"Why not?" Kirk asked. "Isn't that the kind of sign you say you were looking for?"

"Mr. Kirk, there are patients who pretend being MPDs who produce alters readily. Too readily," Sloate began to explain.

Kirk seized on that. "Then, the fact that Mr. Cory did *not* readily produce an alter on demand should prove to you that he *is* a genuine multiple. Shouldn't it?"

"Mr. Kirk, a psychiatrist reaches his diagnosis based on many and various indications. It is a highly subjective process. In your client's case I did not form the conclusion that he was suffering from Multiple Personality Disorder," Sloate stated, hoping to close off any further questions.

"Doctor, is there anything *short* of producing an alter on demand that would convince you?" Kirk asked.

"Evidence! Something more than the patient's own words would convince me," Sloate said.

Kirk considered the doctor's response for a moment, then asked, "Your Honor, may I ask that we have the lunch recess at this time and that the witness be held over for further cross-examination?"

Malachi beckoned him to the bench. Kirk approached, with Stone close behind him.

"Kirk!" Malachi demanded. "What's your purpose?"

"I need an hour to gather some tangible evidence that I require for my final questions for this witness," Kirk explained.

"Questions important enough to hold this witness over?" Malachi persisted. "After all, he is costing the state money. By the hour. Right, Howie?"

"Right. And since Mr. Kirk doesn't seem to be making any headway with him, I don't see the need to hold him over," Stone replied.

"If necessary," Kirk said, "I will pay for his time out of my own pocket."

"If you're that serious, the state will stand the expense," Malachi conceded. "But, Counselor, I would like to wind up this afternoon. That will give both of you the weekend to prepare your summations and give me time to prepare my charge."

"Okay with me," Howard Stone agreed quickly.

"I'll do my best, Your Honor," David Kirk replied, though discouraged by the lack of progress he had made thus far in trying to budge Dr. Sloate from his tenaciously held opinions.

"This court will stand in recess until two o'clock!" Malachi ruled, followed by a sharp rap of his gavel.

Kirk took Gerry Prince by the arm to lead him off to the side. After some whispered instructions, he turned back to the counsel table.

"Chris, I need your keys. Your house keys."

"Why?" Cory asked.

"Sloate wants tangible evidence. Well, I want to shove some 'evidence' under his nose," Kirk explained. "I want to confront him with the difference between Max's clothes and yours."

"Okay, sure," Cory said, digging into his pocket.

———————

While having a light lunch in his limousine, Kirk began to frame some diversionary questions for Sloate so that he could

232

set him up for his final attack, confronting him with Max's bizarre wardrobe. Even should that fail to force Sloate to recant his testimony, it would certainly have a strong impact on the jury and, together with the tape of Max, should win him an insanity verdict.

Malachi had already wheeled himself back into the courtroom and was waiting for his attendants to lift him into place. The media people, and the usual spectators, were all seated. But there was no sign of Gerry Prince.

Howard Stone, Dr. Klinger and Dr. Sloate, having returned from lunch, were in intense whispered conference at the prosecution table.

Everything was in readiness for Kirk's final assault on Dr. Sloate, except for the evidence itself.

Malachi looked out over the courtroom, then focused on David Kirk.

"Counselor, are you ready?"'

As Kirk rose to respond, his second secretary, Louise Grant, rushed into the courtroom, brushing past the guard at the door. She hurried down the aisle, reached Kirk's table. Out of breath, she placed a small message slip on Kirk's yellow pad, facedown.

Whatever the message, Kirk realized, first, that it was of the utmost urgency, or else it could have awaited his return to the office. Second, the contents of the note were so highly confidential that Louise dared not risk whispering it to him in the close quarters of a courtroom.

As casually as he could, Kirk pretended to make another note on his pad, and at the same time, very cautiously, he turned up the message as if it were the down card in a poker game.

STALL FOR THE REST OF THE AFTERNOON.
BUT GET TO CORY'S SOON AS
POSSIBLE. <u>ALONE</u>.

Since the message said no more, and came from Gerry Prince, Kirk proceeded to do exactly as he had suggested. He spent two very uncomfortable hours improvising questions which Dr. Sloate had little trouble handling.

As time wore on, Howard Stone became more relaxed and confident. Judge Malachi, however, grew more enraged and impatient. Three different times he summoned Kirk and Stone to the bench.

"Counselor, why the hell did you have this witness held over? You've been wandering all over the lot and getting nowhere," Malachi remonstrated the first time.

The second time, the irate justice warned, "You're doing your case more harm than good by having Sloate repeat over and over that he does not think your client is MPD. So unless you've got some surprise up your sleeve, let this witness go."

The third time, a most irritated Malachi demanded, "What the hell is wrong with you, Kirk?"

Which gave Kirk the opening to say, "Frankly, Your Honor, I'm not feeling well and I would appreciate the week-end to recover."

Malachi glared down at him from the bench and finally ruled, "Despite my urgency to wind up this afternoon, I will grant your request."

Stone remained at the bench to concede, "Davey must be sick. I've never seen him so off the mark before."

While Kirk loaded his notes and papers into his brief bag, he suggested, "Chris, you'd better start up to Dr. Scott's for your five-o'clock. Call me later at the office."

Thirty-four

All the way uptown, David Kirk sat in the rear of his limousine pondering that strange, cryptic message from Gerry Prince.

The car pulled up at the old loft building where Chris Cory lived. Kirk rang the bell opposite the name CORY, C. and was rewarded with a buzz that automatically unlocked the door. He went in, entered the old wire-grated freight elevator and started up. When he reached Cory's floor he found the door already open.

Gerry called, "Dave! In here!"

He followed the direction of Gerry's voice and entered the small bedroom. On the bed, which consisted of a mattress on a simple movable frame, Gerry had laid out several sets of clothing. Three were of Chris Cory's usual everyday wear. Three were more bizarre sets, the kind that Max had bought and worn.

"Dammit, Gerry! You didn't need to drag me all the way up here to decide which of these to bring. Pack 'em and bring 'em all!"

Gerry Prince replied very softly, but with particular emphasis, "Dave, go into that closet."

Kirk glared at him impatiently.

Gerry repeated, "Dave! Just step in."

Kirk started into a clothes closet that was hung with Cory-type clothing on the left of the rod, Max's clothes on the right. He scanned them, then turned back to say, "I've seen this all before."

"Push aside Max's clothes." When Kirk ignored that instruction, Gerry insisted, "Dave! Push them! As far to the end as you can."

David Kirk shoved aside the clothes as far toward the right wall as it was possible to cram clothing and hangers.

"Okay. Now what?" Kirk demanded.

"What do you see?" Gerry asked.

Kirk stared at the wall that formed the back of the closet. He was about to berate Gerry for playing guessing games with time so short. As he began to turn back, something caught his eye. Skillfully camouflaged and barely discernible was a seam around an area of the back wall that created a rectangle about a foot high by three feet wide.

"Punch it, Dave. Firmly," Gerry instructed.

Kirk delivered a short, sharp blow against the circumscribed area. Instead of falling in, the panel popped out. He ignored the falling panel to stare into a compartment that had been hollowed out in the wall. He reached in and pulled out several books and a handful of Xeroxed articles.

"Take a look at them," Gerry suggested. "Take a damn good look, Dave."

David Kirk stepped back out into the light with an armful of material. He scanned the titles of the books.

Diagnosis and Treatment of Multiple Personality Disorder by Frank W. Putnam. *Multiple Personality in the Forensic Context* by Martin T. Orne. *Cause and Cure of MPD* by John Beaumont.

The rest consisted of scientific articles Xeroxed from psychiatric journals. All had references to MPD or to insanity as a defense in criminal cases.

"Sonofabitch," Kirk said softly.

"Open one of the books. Any one."

Kirk opened the Putnam book. He flipped through it. On many pages he discovered whole sentences, whole paragraphs, highlighted by yellow marking pen. In the margins alongside those sentences and paragraphs were handwritten marks and notes.

The writing was not distinct enough to decipher in all instances, but Kirk was able to read, "Interesting." And then, "Use this." Several pages later he read, "This calls for a performance? Okay."

"Performance? Is that what all this has been? Sonofabitch! Did that bastard set me up . . . set us all up? With an alibi that was phony from the word *go*? Those colorful details. That ripped surgical glove. Those headaches. Those wrist scars. All part of a 'performance'?"

Suddenly Kirk decided, "Pack this up, kid. All of it. And let's get the hell out of here!"

On their way back, David Kirk was silent and grim until he called Dr. Scott on his car phone. He waited through her usual message to leave one of his own.

"Doctor, it is vital that I see you this evening at seven. Be there!"

Thirty-five

As David Kirk started up the stairs, Michal Scott was surprised to see him carrying a small suitcase.

"Going out of town for the weekend?" she asked.

"I wish I were."

Intriguing as his reply was, it gave no hint of the emergency that had caused him to insist on this sudden meeting.

She preceded him into her office but did not take her place behind her desk. Instead, she led him to the grouping of chairs before the marble fireplace at the far end of the long paneled room where she had set up a tray table as a small bar.

"Drink?" she offered.

He refused. As she started to mix one for herself, he suggested, "You might want to make that a double."

"A double?" she repeated, puzzled. She half-turned to him.

"In view of what's coming," he added.

Her reaction demanded an explanation.

"Doctor, prepare yourself for a shock."

He described dispatching Gerry to gather samples of Max's clothing from Cory's loft.

"To display to the jury," she assumed.

"Exactly. Gerry found Max's clothes. More than enough. However, he also found something else."

Kirk placed the suitcase on the arms of one chair, then flipped up the lid. He presented the Putnam volume.

"I know this book. Dr. Putnam and I lectured at the same seminar last year. This is a very solid work on MPD and—"

Kirk interrupted, "Open it. Skim it."

Resentful of his abrupt suggestion, she nevertheless proceeded to comply. As she scanned the pages her gray eyes revealed her growing concern and astonishment.

"What do you make of it?" Kirk asked. "Especially those notes in the margins?"

She read aloud some of Cory's comments, one by one, growing more disturbed by each. Once she had skimmed that volume, Kirk handed her the Orne work on *Multiple Personality in the Forensic Context*. She skimmed through that volume more quickly.

She read one underlined sentence aloud: " 'It is virtually impossible to prove that a skilled imposter is faking hypnosis.'

She conceded, "A few very skillful malingerers and dissimulators *do* escape detection. But very few."

In the margin she read Cory's comment: " 'This calls for a performance? Okay.' "

She continued reading aloud and, by assembling Cory's margin notes, realized she had summarized the complete physical and psychiatric history which Christopher Cory had presented to her. Headaches. Depression. Amnesia. Time losses. Blackouts. Receiving clothes he could not remember buying.

" 'Bingo! Must use!' " she read aloud, which she found alongside the the description of fugue episodes.

Kirk exploded. "He had me chase all the way to Scranton in the middle of the night, like a damned fool!"

Determined to retain a more professional attitude, Scott observed, "He did present an almost perfect set of signs and symptoms of MPD."

"And don't forget his crowning touch!" Kirk added angrily. "Forbidding me to plead insanity as his defense. *We* had to convince *him*. Remember?"

Scott drained the last of her drink, then asked, "The other book you have in there?"

David Kirk presented the Beaumont volume. The instant Scott caught a glimpse of it, he could see her stiffen.

She turned it over to stare at the back of the jacket. It bore the same photograph of John Beaumont that she kept in one of the two silver frames on her desk.

"He used this portrait on his last five books. Because it was my favorite," she explained softly.

She opened the volume. These pages she studied even more intently. With each page, as she read Cory's margin notes, more color drained from her cheeks. Kirk detected a tremor in the hand that held the Beaumont volume.

Suddenly she snapped the book shut, then held it out toward him. As he took it, he asked, "Well, Doctor?"

"I must conclude that Christopher Cory is an extremely skillful dissimulator," she admitted softly, and with considerable anguish. "A complete and total fraud."

Silent, stunned, she turned away. A woman who suddenly needed her privacy. Kirk did not feel free to intrude.

Some moments later, without looking at him, she whispered, "Terrible . . . terrible what this will do . . . everyone who learns about this . . . the entire profession—"

He felt compelled to console, "I'm sure this isn't the first case in which a disingenuous patient has deceived a psychiatrist. But with your credentials, your reputation in the profession, you'll overcome it."

"Me? You don't understand," she replied. "I have sullied *him*."

"Who?"

She turned to Kirk. "John, of course! He would be furious with me. Furious. As he should be."

"Furious with *you*? Who devoted those last years to him?" Kirk countered.

"When this becomes public, they will make it not *my* failure, but *his*. Klinger, Sloate, all the others who weren't worthy to carry John's briefcase, will see to that. Jealous is what they were, and still are. Because John had it all. The brilliance. The respect of the profession. He was world-famous. When we traveled abroad you should have seen the deference that people in the field paid him. He entrusted me with that reputation. And I failed him. He would never forgive me."

Tears formed in her gray eyes and started tracing slowly down her cheeks, which were pale now, so pale.

Kirk reached out, took her hand, made her face him. She was weeping more freely. He took her in his arms and recalled vividly that moment when he had protected her from Cory's violent abreaction attack. He sensed that now her controlled, aloof, professional discipline had deserted her completely. Not merely resigned to remain in Kirk's protective embrace, she clung to him, her tear-stained face burrowing into his chest.

"John . . . John . . ." she whispered, continuing to weep. "Can you ever forgive me?"

Soon each became aware of the other's closeness. She loosened her embrace. His arms reluctantly parted to free her.

"Thank you," she whispered, starting to wipe her tears away with the palms of her hands. He offered her his handkerchief.

As she dried her eyes he comforted, "Even Dr. Orne, one of the best in the field on hypnosis, said there is no absolute way to detect a skilled impostor. And Cory is an actor. A very talented one, it turns out."

"*I failed John,*" she reiterated. "After all he did for me."

"Tell me," he said, "were you in love with him?"

"In love, of course not. I respected him. Admired him. As he deserved. Revered him, if you wish. But loved him . . ." She paused before admitting very softly, "Yes . . . yes . . . I think I did love him. But far different from the way I loved Paul. Yes. I suppose you could say that I have been widowed twice in my lifetime."

"Is that why you are so aloof from me? Or is it this place? Because this was John's place. Because he is here. Watching, judging."

To avoid answering, she said, "Please, Mr. Kirk, I didn't mean to make my problem your concern."

"I'm glad you did. It gave me a chance to discover the woman inside the totally professional doctor."

She avoided any further personal probing by asking, "The question now is, what to do about my patient and your client."

"These books, these notes. Practically a textbook on how

to commit murder and get away with it," Kirk conceded.

"What is the correct procedure? Who do you turn these over to? Mr. Stone? Or Judge Malachi?"

"Neither," Kirk said. "That's the final irony. I am forced to keep all this confidential."

"But once you enter an insanity defense, you're required to turn all psychiatric evidence over to the prosecution," she reminded him. "You made me turn over everything in *my* files."

"Because that is psychiatric material within the meaning of the criminal statute. Evidence that goes to the question of sanity or insanity," he explained.

"These books, these notes, are psychiatric material. The very basis on which he concocted his fictitious insanity defense," she argued.

"Exactly," he agreed. "*Evidence* of a fraudulent defense. As such, confidential between attorney and client."

"I must say, it's a strange profession you practice," she replied. "Where you're ordered to *reveal* one kind of psychiatric material, but forced to *conceal* what may be the most important psychiatric evidence."

"Ethics," he replied, by way of a short form explanation. "I can't join in this fraud, but I am bound to respect his confidence."

Having delivered himself of that noble professional declaration he admitted, "The hell of it is that jury is fascinated by his story. I've got them thinking they are watching a motion picture and he is the hero. The very sympathetic hero."

"We can both share the blame for that," she said.

"Yes. But I have Alice Ames's mother sitting in back of me in the courtroom day after day. Just staring at me. Sometimes I can feel her eyes burning into my back. I know that look. The Edward Trimble look. He was right."

Kirk started to pour himself a drink while confessing, "It

was my defense that set that guilty man free to go and kill again. When I first met him, in his previous murder case, I discovered he had certain bruises. Bruises he sustained in the struggle with his first victim. I had Gerry photograph those bruises. Then I claimed that they resulted from being beaten *after* his arrest. So the judge was forced to throw out his confession. That blew the prosecution's entire case. My client went free. Free to rape and murder Cecilia Trimble." He took a long drink of scotch before admitting, "Any defense attorney worth his fee would have done the same. Would have bragged about it, in fact. The cases we criminal lawyers brag about most are getting the guilty acquitted.

"Malachi was right the day he assigned me to this case. 'Davey, doesn't it ever get to you? What we've done to the system. People look on judges and lawyers as their enemies. Because we violate their basic sense of justice.' "

"Caught between ethics and justice, what do you do now?" Scott asked.

"I have to come to some decision before I walk into that courtroom Monday morning. I know one thing. I don't want to be responsible for another Cecilia Trimble."

Thirty-six

David Kirk needed time alone. Time to think. He handed the suitcase of damaging evidence to his driver, Geraldo, and started walking west to Fifth Avenue along Seventy-third, then down Fifth, almost empty, now that the usual dinner-bound, theater-bound traffic had subsided.

Geraldo trailed him, keeping the limo just slightly behind him and at the same pace.

Noble speech, Kirk thought, *that bit: "I don't want to be responsible for another Cecilia Trimble." But when you think about it, clearly, a totally emotional response. Lawyers are not paid to be emotional. The reverse, in fact. It is their function to deal with and control the emotions of their clients.*

Above all, a lawyer must not be judgmental. It is his duty to protect the rights of his client. The more guilty the client, the more he needs the skill and the vigilance of a capable attorney.

Back in law school the favorite exercise of our professor of Criminal Law was to set up a mock court to try Adolf Hitler. Once he selected me to represent him. I did. And as the professor himself said, I did a damn good job of it.

But as they say, that was then, this is now. That was theory. This is real. This sonofabitch Cory . . . with his skillful acting . . . to get him off, turn him loose on an unsuspecting world . . . he could kill again. Let some other woman reject him and he could become phony Max, do the crime, and beat the time.

The hell of it, the worst of it, we have completely fooled that jury. I can feel it in the air in that courtroom. After watching those tapes, that performance, why shouldn't that jury buy his story? God knows, I bought it. Scott bought it.

Maybe that's the trouble. The reason for my conflict of feelings now. I've defended, and damn well, killers I knew were guilty. And got them off. Why the conflict in this case?

Is it vanity? That this punk kid, this twenty-six-year-old murderer, was able to fool David Kirk? So now, out of wounded pride, I want to even the score with him?

Vanity, hell! Face it, Kirk. It's my career that's at stake. The Bar Association, and the public, still remember the Corregio case. Even though I was completely ignorant of that juror being bribed, lots of people never really believed me. To this day there are some people who think I win all my cases that way.

Give old Malachi even a hint of what I've just discovered in this case and he'll be all over me like a tent. I can just see it. His homely, craggy face, his fingers drumming on the arms of his wheelchair. He wouldn't believe me for a second. First thing, he would move to disbar me. Maybe he would even recommend that the DA go for a criminal indictment.

What a field day for the media. Howie Stone prosecuting his onetime protégé. And Howie wouldn't hold back. Not Howie. Emotions, friendship, play no part in Howie's strict book of professional rules.

What if I put Michal . . . Dr. Scott . . . why am I calling her Michal suddenly? What if I put her on the stand? Had her recant her testimony in view of new evidence? Do I have a right to put her through such a wrenching emotional experience in view of her deep and abiding loyalty to John Beaumont?

Besides, I never thought to ask her how this changes her professional obligations to Cory. Of course, there might be a different attack on this problem. I should have asked her if this devilish charade of Cory's is the work of a mind that could actually be considered insane.

That's a possibility to consider. Go to Malachi. Lay the evidence before him. Put Scott back on the stand to declare him mentally incompetent by virtue of his attempt to impersonate a victim of MPD.

Can't. That would be betraying the client's right to confidentiality. I could be censured for that. And ironically, that might be the very thing that could set Cory free. Denial of a vigilant defense. If it didn't set him free, it would at least win him a new trial and a new lawyer. Who might pick up the new claim to mental incapacity.

There must be some ruling in some court decision in some similar case that gives a lawyer guidance in a situation like this.

Even if there is, and I acted accordingly, there is no way to keep this story from the media. I can see it now, either outside the courthouse or outside my office building, the television cameras, the reporters, demanding an explanation. How's it going to look on the six o'clock news, repeated at eleven, and almost certainly on the early news the next morning? David Kirk, reputed by most people to be one of the brightest, shrewdest defense attorneys in New York, duped by a young actor?

Back to vanity again. Forget vanity! Stick to the real problem. Client's right to confidentiality. To a zealous defense. But what about a lawyer's rights? What about the danger of censure? Disbarment? Yes, what about . . .

He realized he had arrived back at his office building, and rang the night bell to summon the watchman. Once admitted, he took the elevator up to the twenty-ninth floor.

Aside from the old cleaning woman who was just finishing the offices at the end of the corridor, the floor was deserted. He unlocked the door to his own suite, trudged through the dark entryway, through the general office, past the library, into his dark private office.

He stared out of the tall floor-to-ceiling windows that constituted two of the four walls of this large room, then dropped into his desk chair, exhausted from a long day in court, from one of the most shocking discoveries of his entire career, exhausted from his confrontation with Michal . . . there was that first name again . . . his confrontation with Dr. Scott.

Only one thing to do now. Back to the books. In some case there must be an answer. Vaguely, in the back of his mind, he recalled the research he and Gerry had done when the Corregio case backfired. There was a federal case titled

Nix v. *Whiteside* that went all the way to the Supreme Court of the United States. It was about a lawyer's duty when confronted with a dishonest client.

He went into the dark library, flipped on the light, looked up the case, pulled the volume, sat down at the long table. He read completely through the case, then went back and reread Justice Blackmun's concurring opinion. Taking the volume with him, he returned to his own office and realized he needed a cup of coffee. He went out to the general office, drew some hot coffee from the machine, only to discover it was not hot. Last one out at the end of the day always shut off the machine. He turned it on, decided it would take too long, turned it off again. Then he went back into his office to resume his intensive study of *Nix*.

———————

He must have fallen asleep, because the next thing he knew Greta was knocking on his open door, asking, "Mr. Kirk . . . ? Mr. Kirk?"

He came awake. Greeted her vaguely.

One of Greta's privileges, which came with her seniority, was to give advice and orders, like a concerned mother.

"You better shave, shower and change clothes."

"Yeah. Okay. Sure." Then it occurred to him. "Greta, what are you doing in on a Saturday?"

"Gerry called. Said I should stand by. Just in case."

"Just in case what?"

"He didn't say. Now, you take that shower!"

He started toward his private dressing room, where he kept a wardrobe for just such emergencies during trials. When it was sometimes necessary to work all night in preparation for the next day's session and appear in court fresh and neat.

Shaved, showered, dressed in slacks and an open-throated shirt, he came out to find Gerry waiting.

Gerry had only one question, one word: "Well?"

"Scott confirms it. Cory is a fraud. A clever, unprincipled, skillful fraud."

"So, that's why *Nix* v. *Whiteside* is open on your desk."

"Not that it's much help."

"I know," Gerry agreed. "I remember only too well from the last time. *Nix* is certainly on point about a lawyer's obligation once he discovers his client's fraud."

"But . . ." Kirk started to say.

"But," Gerry anticipated, "unfortunately not very clear."

" 'Not very clear' is putting it mildly," Kirk said, reaching for the volume, into which he had inserted slips of yellow paper to mark significant passages. Like this line from Blackmun's opinion: 'The attorney's duty depends on several factors. Such as,' and get this, *'the stage of the proceedings at which the attorney discovers the fraud.' "*

"This couldn't have come any later in Cory's trial," Gerry added.

"Unfortunately, Blackmun ends up saying, 'Since circumstances vary so greatly from case to case, it is impossible for the court to lay down a blanket rule.' "

"Putting the burden right back on the attorney to determine what his duty is. Thank you, Mr. Justice Blackmun," Gerry declared.

"Get a load of this." Kirk flipped several pages and read a marked passage: " 'Attorneys who adopt the role of the judge or the jury to determine the facts pose a danger of depriving their clients of the zealous and loyal advocacy required by the Sixth Amendment.' "

"So," Gerry said resentfully, "according to the Supreme Court, a lawyer is duty-bound to report the client's deception to the judge . . . *however.* In the law there are always those damn *howevers.*"

"Don't knock 'em. If it wasn't for the *howevers,* people wouldn't need lawyers," Kirk reminded him.

"McKinney's!" Gerry suggested with sudden inspiration.

"Already looked it up. *Judiciary Law*. DR. 7-102, Section B. It's on my desk. Talk about *howevers*, that's the mother of all *howevers*."

Gerry picked up the black volume, read aloud the provision of the law Kirk had marked: " 'B. A lawyer who receives information clearly establishing that: 1. The client has, in the course of the representation, perpetrated a fraud upon a person or tribunal'—that surely fits—'shall promptly call upon the client to rectify the same, and if the client refuses or is unable to do so, the lawyer shall reveal the fraud to the affected person or tribunal.' That's right on the nose!"

"Now read the very last line," Kirk urged.

" 'Except when the information is protected as a confidence or a secret,' " Gerry read slowly, then admitted, "Everything we know about Cory's fraud we learned in the course of our attorney-client relationship."

Kirk nodded grimly, then reached his decision. He picked up his phone and punched in a number.

"Chris? David Kirk. I have to see you. Right now!"

Thirty-seven

Within the hour, Chris Cory knocked on the outer door of the seemingly deserted offices of David Kirk & Associates.

"That's him," Kirk said to Gerry. "You go into your office. I'll leave my intercom open so you can monitor what he says." Then he called out, "It's open!"

Cory entered the reception area.

"I'm in my office, Chris," Kirk called, in as pleasant an attitude as he could muster.

Cory appeared in the doorway. With a gesture and a smile, Kirk invited him in. Cory started across the room, his usual modest, composed self.

Until he became aware of the books and psychiatric papers which Kirk had laid out on his desk like exhibits in a trial.

Kirk studied his face. But instead of the surprise or shock Kirk anticipated, Cory only smiled and remarked casually, "Oh, Mr. Prince found these, did he?"

Kirk contained his anger to respond equally casually, "Yes, Gerry found these. Which wasn't easy. Considering how well hidden they were."

"Have to do that," Cory explained. "Mrs. Montanez. Woman who cleans for me. Terrible snoop. And she talks. Would you believe I know when every woman in my building has used one of those instant pregnancy tests? And also the result. There's not a cabinet or wastebasket in the whole building that is safe from old lady Montanez."

Throughout Cory's longer than necessary, but smoothly delivered explanation, Kirk studied Cory's boyish face, his disarming smile, the casual self-assurance.

"I can tell you one thing," Cory continued, to fill the silence Kirk deliberately maintained. "This is fascinating stuff. The hours I've spent digging into this field, fascinating."

"Chris, how long ago did you start 'digging into this field'?"

"Right after Dr. Scott diagnosed my condition. Really after she showed me those tapes. Especially that one of Max. Scared the hell out of me. So I decided to read up on it. The Putnam book first. The others just came naturally after that. The Xeroxes of those psychiatric papers were a little harder to get. But fortunately at the Medical Society Library . . . up on Fifth Avenue . . . I met this young librarian. After we got a little thing going she was very cooperative. Helped me a lot."

"That's it, Chris? You just wanted to read up on this condition you have," Kirk remarked.

"You don't know what it's like, Mr. Kirk. The patient, the real person, the host, is the only one who doesn't know. Max knew. Dr. Scott knew. You knew. Only *I* didn't. That's scary. Very scary. If you're not crazy, believe me, that can drive you crazy."

"I guess it could," Kirk pretended to agree in an effort to encourage him to keep talking.

"I sit there in the courtroom listening to those experts. They're talking about *me*. Like I was some laboratory rat. It's impossible to describe the feeling. It's like one of those out-of-body experiences. You're floating up there and at the same time watching yourself down here."

Kirk was sure that Cory had run out of his prepared lines. He stared across the desk until Cory's smile slowly began to fade.

"Mr. Kirk?"

Kirk picked up the Beaumont volume, opened to a page he had clipped, and held it out to him.

"Chris, this your handwriting in the margin?"

"Yes, sir," Cory admitted forthrightly, though he pretended puzzlement. "Thoughts that came to me while reading. Don't you do that? When you're reading a court decision or a legal opinion?"

"Indeed I do," Kirk agreed. "But I don't make notes like . . ." Kirk read from the note in the margin, " 'Bingo! Must use.' Must use? How, Chris?"

Cory's face, which had grown tense, slowly dissolved once more into his disarming smile.

"Oh, I see. Well, you've got that all wrong, Mr. Kirk. I was only anticipating."

"Anticipating *what*?" Kirk pressed.

"These days, with movie and television companies looking for reality stories, I figured they might be interested in my story. So I'd been anticipating possible scenes I might suggest for a film. That's what I meant when I wrote, 'Bingo, Must use.' "

"Alongside Beaumont's description of fugue episodes," Kirk remarked.

"Something wrong, Mr. Kirk?"

"Chris, some people might suspect this is a plot to simulate a mental condition as a defense against a charge of murder. If it is, that changes the manner in which I can continue to represent you. I can't become part of that plot. I can't be in the position of suborning perjury. I wouldn't risk that for any client."

"Oh, I can understand that," Cory responded quickly. "Especially after the trouble you got into in the Corregio case."

For a fleeting moment, Kirk had to consider: *Was Cory's a chance remark or also a part of a prepared scenario?*

"I know you proved you did nothing wrong in the Corregio case. But all the embarrassment. The need to explain to the media. Must have been hell on you. Tell you what, it's probably better for everyone if I just take my books and papers and keep them for whoever produces the film."

He was reaching to gather up his materials when Kirk ordered, "Don't touch those!"

"Cory looked up at him as if confused and asked, "Mr. Kirk?"

"Sit down!"

Cory dropped into the chair across the desk. Kirk rose and approached Cory as if he were a hostile witness.

"Cory, Dr. Scott thinks—"

"You talked to her?" Cory asked.

"Yes, I talked to her."

"And?" Cory finally asked.

"She thinks this is a very carefully orchestrated rehearsed and performed attempt to simulate a mental condition for the purpose of committing premeditated murder and getting away with it!"

Throughout Kirk's accusation Cory made no attempt to interrupt. For a long moment thereafter he sat silent. Then, very confidently, he replied, "You know you can't use any of this."

"Oh, no?" Kirk countered.

"Wouldn't be ethical. Confidentiality between lawyer and client," Cory pointed out.

He's really figured every angle, Kirk realized.

"Under the circumstances, Mr. Kirk, the way I see it, best thing for everybody we forget all about this material. You never even saw it. I just take it with me."

"That simple," Kirk commented.

"We carry on with the trial. We've about got it locked up now anyhow. That jury is on my side. I can feel it. And once I take the stand . . ."

"You're planning on taking the stand?" Kirk asked.

"That will be the clincher," Cory revealed.

"Cory, I tried to explain how limited my cooperation can be in view of all this," Kirk pointed out.

"Not if you never saw any of it," Cory countered. "Because, if it becomes known that you did, somebody in the Bar Association is going to ask that famous question: 'What did Kirk *know*? And *when* did he know it?' And we're back to the Corregio case again."

"Are you threatening me?" Kirk demanded.

"No, sir!" Cory denied quickly. "I was just concerned about what *other* people might think."

"Very considerate," Kirk commented, at the same time thinking, *This sonofabitch is as dangerous as a snake. And you don't have to listen very closely to hear the rattles.*

"Cory, in view of this situation, as your attorney, I urge

that we make a clean breast of things. Go to the judge. Lay all this stuff before him."

"You mean confess?" Cory demanded.

"I mean admit the facts, the truth, and rely on the mercy of the court to get you a shorter sentence," Kirk urged. When Cory did not respond at once, Kirk added, "I know Malachi. He's not a hanging judge. He'll take a confession into account and show leniency."

"And that's your 'advice' as my lawyer," Cory remarked with a smile. "Well, this is *my* 'advice' as your client. All this has to remain confidential. And because it does, this trial goes right on. I will take the stand. And what's more, Mr. Kirk, I will be acquitted!"

With that, Cory strode out of the office.

The sound of the outer door slamming echoed through the office. It was also Gerry's cue to rejoin Kirk.

"Man, I've heard cool and brazen. But not even a Mafia boss has that kind of nerve," Gerry commented.

"I know I should say screw the ethics. Blow the whistle on that bastard. Except that I can't."

"And he knows it," Gerry added.

"There *is* one thing I can do," Kirk determined. "And I'd better do it now instead of confronting Malachi on Monday morning."

Thirty-eight

David Kirk called Aaron Malachi at his home in Brooklyn Heights. His wife, Emma, answered. Once Kirk identified himself she greeted him, "Oh, Davey," then apologized. "Sorry to sound so personal. But that's how Aaron refers to you. What can I do for you?"

"I have to talk to the judge."

"Aaron isn't here."

"This is extremely important," Kirk insisted.

"He's in the city. In chambers. Said something about dictating a draft of his charge to the jury. I guess that would be in your case."

"Yes, I'm sure," Kirk said. "I'll drop in and see him."

"Oh, one thing, Mr. Kirk—" She sounded hesitant before she admitted, "He's a little touchy these days. I don't know what it is, but recently he's been very sensitive. So don't mind too much if he seems angry."

Within half an hour David Kirk was racing up the broad steps of the Supreme Court, New York County. He took the elevator up to the judges' floor. When he reached the thick mahogany door with JUDGE AARON MALACHI inscribed on it in fading gold leaf, he knocked. There was no reply. He tried the knob. The door was not locked. He opened it, expecting that Ida Bornstein would confront him, as she always did, being overprotective of the judge's privacy. She was not in sight. Instead, he heard Malachi dictating: "Thus, according to the applicable law in this state, which law you as jurors are bound to follow, it is your duty in this case to decide whether . . ."

By that time David Kirk had reached the open doorway to Malachi's inner chambers. As was his habit, Malachi sat staring out the window as he dictated. When Ida Bornstein turned the page of her stenographer's notebook, she was startled to catch sight of Kirk.

"Oh, my God! What are you doing here on a Saturday?" she demanded.

Malachi spun his wheelchair about to demand, "What the hell *are* you doing here, Kirk?"

"I must talk to you. It's urgent. Very urgent."

"Urgent, eh?" Malachi remarked skeptically. At the same time, he gestured Ida out of the room.

Once Ida was gone, Malachi asked, "Tell me, who is that actor in the movies? Skinny feller. Big star. Seems to have eye trouble. Always squinting. Maybe from being in the sun too long."

"I think you mean Clint Eastwood," Kirk replied.

"Yeah, That's the feller. So, as he says, 'Make my day,' Kirk. What's your trouble *this* time?"

David Kirk hesitated, then finally announced, "Your Honor, I would like permission to resign from the case of *People* v. *Cory*."

Judge Malachi glared at him.

" 'Counselor,' would you repeat what you just said?"

"I would like permission to resign from the case."

"May I ask why?" Malachi demanded, the flush of anger rising into his wrinkled cheeks.

"I'm sorry, Your Honor, but I am not at liberty to disclose the reason for my request."

"You're 'sorry'? You are 'not at liberty to disclose' your reason?" Malachi nodded, then demanded, *"Why not?"*

"Professional ethics prevent me from discussing matters of confidence between attorney and client," Kirk replied.

"Oh, 'professional ethics,' Malachi repeated with considerable disdain. "Who said once, 'When lawyers start talking ethics, honest people should run for the hills'?"

"I think you said that, Your Honor."

"*You* are one of the best examples of that that I have come across in a long, long time, 'Counselor'!"

Malachi had exploded in a voice so loud that Ida timidly opened the door to peek in to see what was wrong.

"It's okay, Ida. Just a slight difference of opinion," Malachi said in bitter sarcasm. "Our young friend here, the eminent and successful trial lawyer David Kirk, who has not had his picture in the newspapers or on television since maybe yesterday, would like to resign from *People* v. *Cory*."

Appalled, Ida breathed a whispered "Resign?" as if it were blasphemy. "Now? So near the end?"

"Now," Malachi repeated. "So near the end. And what is more, Ida, he refuses to state any reason. 'Professional ethics,' he says."

Kirk felt he had endured enough of Malachi's ridicule. "Let us say there is a difference of opinion between attorney and client as to how the defense should proceed."

"Difference of opinion, eh?" Malachi seized on it. "Considering the circumstances, I think you've been doing a pretty good job. You mean to tell me your client doesn't approve?"

"That is not the point at issue, Your Honor," Kirk protested.

"So what *is* the point at issue?" Malachi demanded.

"As I said, sir, I am not free to discuss it without breaching confidentiality," Kirk reiterated.

Malachi drummed angrily on the arms of his wheelchair. "Ida, what do *you* think?"

He turned from her to comment to David Kirk, "I always confer with Ida when I am undecided about whether to sentence a man to twenty-five to life or only fifteen. Also, when I am confronted by a smart sonofabitch of a lawyer who has some shrewd and devious plan in mind."

"I assure you, Your Honor, there is no devious plan," Kirk insisted.

"Ida?" Malachi demanded.

Never known to refrain from volunteering her opinion on matters that transpired in the course of the judge's day, this time Ida Bornstein seemed too terrified to reply.

"Well, Ida, since you don't know what is going on here, I will tell you."

Malachi wheeled himself out from behind his desk. He started slowly across the floor, following tracks he had worn in the carpet over the years.

"Remember, Ida, the day he came in here asking—did I say 'asking'?—practically begging, for permission to file a late notice to plead an insanity defense? And such a defense! Multiple Personality Disorder, no less. Remember? I finally gave in, 'Okay, file.' Well, it seems now our brilliant Mr. David Kirk has somehow decided that the effect of those dramatic tapes he played for the jury is wearing off. Maybe the jury is beginning to believe Howie's expert, Dr. Sloate. So our young friend, Mr. Kirk, has to figure out some new angle to spring his client."

Addressing his nonplussed secretary, Malachi asked, "Ida, would you like to guess what that angle is?"

"No, Your Honor, I . . . Well, not really," the woman stammered in her nervousness, for she had rarely seen the old judge in such a furious state.

"I must congratulate you, Mr. Kirk. Extremely clever strategy. You come in here and ask to be permitted to resign from the case. And I, like the old fool I am supposed to be, permit you to do so. Whereupon, first thing Cory's new lawyer does is move for a mistrial. And, under the conditions, this trial being so close to the end, I would have to grant it. Whereupon, when Howie Stone decides to retry your Mr. Cory, his new lawyer pleads double jeopardy. And what is more, the court of appeals probably upholds him. So, at state expense we have gone through this whole long charade of a trial and wind up setting the man free without a jury ever having a crack at him. Very clever. Another of David Kirk's brilliant strategic maneuvers. Have you also prepared the statement you will make to the television news people?"

David Kirk was bursting to explode in righteous indignation. *"Damn it, Aaron, you were the one who complained about people losing faith in the justice system. About so many*

*guilty men going free due to the tricks of the trade. Yet now,
when I want out of a case that I know is a fraud, you say no.
Aaron, this case, phony as it is, is winnable. I know in my
bones I can win it. But Cory is guilty. Shrewd, wily, unprincipled, and guilty. So I want no part of it anymore. Yet you
keep heaping sarcastic accusations at me as if I were the
criminal."*

Unable to say any of it without breaching his client's right
to confidentiality, David Kirk was forced to content himself
with a simple protest: "Your Honor, I give you my word
that is not true in this instance."

"So, what is true?" Malachi demanded.

"As I said, a basic difference between attorney and client
on how to proceed with the defense," Kirk insisted.

Malachi nodded thoughtfully, then replied, "Davey, my
boy, I am going to do you a big favor."

Kirk felt considerable relief.

"I am going to forget that you ever made this request. I
will assume that you are prepared to carry on this defense to
the best of your ability. Which you damn well better be.
Because, as I warned you once before, if I notice any funny
business, anything but a sharp David Kirk defense in my
courtroom, I *will* burn your ass."

He turned to Ida. "My dear, you heard none of this. It
never happened." Looking in Kirk's direction, he ordered,
"Counselor, I will see you in court Monday morning at ten
o'clock."

Thirty-nine

When Kirk returned to the office he found Gerry in the library.

"Well, Dave?"

"He did everything but sentence me to life," Kirk admitted. "And who can blame him?"

"Defending Cory, knowing what we know now, is like walking through a minefield."

Kirk nodded. But he had reached one conclusion.

"Gerry, go home."

"Dave?"‷

"I said go home. Because officially, as of now, you are off the case."

"Off *what* case?" Gerry protested.

"You said yourself, it's a minefield. So don't try to be a hero. You are off this case. Before it becomes even more dangerous than it is now."

"Dave, wait just one minute—"

"I said, you are off this case!"

Gerry was about to protest even more strongly, but Kirk anticipated him. "Gerry, I don't want your career to go up in smoke, too. So, go home. Unless you want to be fired."

Reluctantly, Gerry Prince started out. He stopped to look back, hoping Kirk might relent. But Kirk shook his head.

Once he heard the outer door close, David Kirk went back into his own office. He slipped into his desk chair, exhausted, then glanced at the incriminating books and papers laid out before him.

He reached for the Beaumont volume and began to flip through the pages, reviewing the notes Cory had made. The sentences and paragraphs he had highlighted with yellow markers. As Kirk flipped from page to page, in his mind he began to correlate each margin note with certain of Cory's actions that he could recall before and during the trial.

The entire skillful deception came alive in his mind like the rerun of a highly plotted film. Cory, the pitifully naïve and innocent young man. His headaches faked with such convincing suffering. His blue eyes which radiated such sincerity when he protested any hint of an insanity defense.

It was such a carefully choreographed and rehearsed performance, authentically contrived in accordance with the most expert available psychiatric knowledge. Small wonder Cory could play on the natural sympathy of even an experienced lawyer like himself, as well as mislead Michal Scott, who, everyone conceded, was one of the leading experts in the field of MPD.

Kirk soon realized this was a futile and discouraging indulgence, trying to explain, actually trying to justify, having been victimized. There was little consolation in reliving all that, and no escape from his present dangerous professional situation.

Pondering what steps he might now take in view of Malachi's angry refusal and his client's duplicity, David Kirk continued to sift through the pages of the Beaumont text. Pages with notes, pages with underlining, pages with highlighting. Pages with no notes or marks of any kind.

Slowly, a question began to insinuate itself into his mind.

What had caused Cory to select certain parts of all this material but eliminate others? Did he choose only those symptoms, signs and elements which, taken together, would not only present a convincing case of MPD but would also fit a character that he could play convincingly?

Howie Stone, coached by Dr. Klinger, had pointed out that Cory did not exhibit many other symptoms.

Why?

David Kirk began to peruse the volume from the beginning. This time he concentrated on those pages which bore no notes, no marks of any kind.

———————

Several hours later, he had finished with the Beaumont text. He pushed back from his desk and rose to stare down from his twenty-ninth-floor window at the crisscross streets of Manhattan at night. At this hour most office-building windows were dark. Below, cars and taxis moved at the commands of the green and red traffic lights.

After some considerable pondering, he turned back to his desk, punched in a number on his telephone.

"Cory, I think you and I had better meet. We have certain legal problems you should be aware of. So get up here. Right now."

———————

David Kirk paced his office before admitting, "Cory, we're at the point where we have to level with each other. No more secrets. I no longer like the idea of representing you. In fact, today I went to see Judge Malachi and asked to be removed from this case."

Cory sat up a bit more stiffly.

"Malachi refused. So, as long as I am forced to continue as your attorney, I feel obligated to give you my best legal advice. And the first thing I want to say is this: It is one thing to star in a courtroom performance. That might feed your ego. But it is quite another to take unnecessary risks in a trial. Especially a murder trial. My best legal advice to you is *not* to take the stand."

"But, I've already decided—"

"Cory, hear me out! According to the law a defendant does not have to take the stand in his own defense. And the prosecutor is prevented from remarking on it."

"*You* hear *me* out," Cory countered. "I *want* to take the stand. I want my shot at that *jury!*"

"That's a purely emotional decision. A personal indulgence. From a strictly legal point of view there is only one thing to consider. Will it help or hurt our case?"

"How can it possibly hurt?" Cory demanded.

"Taking the stand against an experienced prosecutor like Howard Stone is extremely dangerous. On cross-examination he is especially quick and deadly. He will tear you to shreds. With unexpected questions. With conflicting statements you made during the time of your arrest and interrogation. He'll savage you with sarcasm and ridicule. I can imagine the fun he'll have with Max. And his 'doodle.' He can blow your story right out of the courtroom. And our whole defense with it. Never forget, you are facing twenty-five to life."

Cory nodded throughout as if he had absorbed Kirk's warning, but was obviously not dissuaded.

"Taking the stand may appeal to you because it seems very dramatic."

"That's what the movie people said," Cory said.

"Oh?" Kirk reacted. "*What* did the 'movie people' say?"

"My testifying would make a terrific scene. Could be the highlight of the film." Cory proceeded to dramatize it. "The hero himself on the stand. Being cross-examined, hounded, pursued by a ruthless prosecutor like Howard Stone. They say it would create enormous sympathy not only for the character but for me personally."

"The 'movie people' actually said that," Kirk commented,

thinking, *At least now I know why he's so anxious to take the stand. Good.*

"Actually, their exact words were: 'That scene will win an Academy Award. You, Christopher Cory, speaking out on behalf of all misunderstood people. Standing up. Fighting back. Making a statement. They said I'll be like Dustin Hoffman in *Rain Man*.'"

"And you're willing to risk losing your freedom for that?" Kirk asked.

"The way I do it, there'll be no risk, Mr. Kirk."

"Cory, forgetting picture deals and everything else, I warn you, once I turn you over for cross-examination, there is nothing I can do to protect you from Stone. So take your time. Think this over very carefully."

"That's all I've been thinking about for days. I *want* to match wits with Stone. I *want* a crack at that jury."

"Okay. If that's what you've decided. After all, you have that right. An attorney can only give advice. The client always has the last word. I will put you on the stand. But in case anything goes wrong, I don't want the media second-guessing me for blowing the case. So I will need something from you."

"Oh? What?"

Kirk handed Cory a legal pad and a pen.

"I want you to write out a statement declaring that, against the advice of your attorney, you insisted on taking the stand."

Cory started to apply pen to paper. Instead of writing he asked, "What do I say? How do I start?"

"Try, 'To whom it may concern: This is to acknowledge that I, Christopher Cory, have been advised by my attorney, David Kirk, not to take the stand in my own defense. Despite that, of my own volition and on my own responsibility, I have insisted on doing so.' Then add, 'Mr. Kirk is free to disclose this statement at any time he deems necessary.' "

Cory completed writing the statement, looked up at Kirk. "Now, sign it."

Cory complied and handed back the pad.

"Monday morning I will complete my cross-examination of Dr. Sloate in such a way as to constitute a dramatic introduction to your taking the stand. Be ready."

"You can bet your life on it," Cory assured him.

As Cory turned to leave, Kirk added, "Oh, by the way, during your testimony I may find it necessary for Dr. Scott to take over so the jury can see Max in action."

"I was planning to do that *without hypnosis.* I thought it would be more startling that way."

"I think it will be more convincing for the jury if Dr. Scott handles that," Kirk advised.

"Okay," Cory agreed and started out. At the door he stopped long enough to ask. "Would you object if that movie producer came to the trial?"

"Of course not. I hope he does come," Kirk replied.

Cory gone, David Kirk picked up his phone, punched in a number. He was answered by Dr. Scott's machine.

"Doctor, I will have to ask you to clear your calendar for Monday. See you in court as near to ten as you can make it."

He hung up, then called another number.

"Gerry . . . oh, Lucinda, your husband home? Well, when he gets back tell him if he hasn't made other arrangements I will expect him in court Monday at ten."

At the call of "All Rise!" the door alongside the judge's bench opened. The crowded courtroom immediately came to order.

Judge Aaron Malachi wheeled himself in, then endured the indignity of being lifted to the bench.

He glanced down at the well of the courtroom to make sure everyone was in place. Howard Stone, Dr. Helmut Klinger and Stone's two ethnic assistants were at the prosecution table. At the other table, David Kirk, with Gerry Prince on one side and his client, Christopher Cory, on the other. The stenotypist was in place to the side of the witness box.

"Ladies and gentlemen, we shall resume. I believe that Dr. Sloane was on the stand."

Very respectfully and tentatively, the stenotypist corrected, "Dr. *Sloate*, Your Honor."

Irritable, especially so because the memory of his Saturday morning confrontation with David Kirk still lingered, Malachi agreed brusquely, "Okay, okay! I stand corrected. Will Dr. *Sloate* take the stand again?"

Sloate took his place in the witness box quite prepared for any questions David Kirk might direct to him.

Howard Stone and Dr. Klinger huddled at the prosecution table prepared to make notes that would aid Stone in his redirect examination, if indeed Stone decided it was even necessary, Sloate having acquitted himself so well on Friday.

David Kirk advanced toward the witness, his new strategy demanding a line of attack aimed solely at setting the stage for Cory's appearance on the stand. Kirk cast a glance toward the courtroom doors, stole a look at his wristwatch, then launched into his cross-examination.

"Dr. Sloate, as I recall your testimony of Friday, you were a trifle unclear on certain points and may have confused the jury. Do I summarize you correctly when I say that you believe that there *is* such a condition as Multiple Personality Disorder? But that it is rarely properly diagnosed?"

"Pretty close, Mr. Kirk, pretty close," Sloate was willing to grant.

"Since you have studied the Rorschach tests and have witnessed the tapes of the defendant made by Dr. Scott, do you still harbor doubts about the diagnosis of MPD?"

"I do," Sloate responded.

"Dr. Sloate, at the time you examined the defendant, were you aware of the fact that he had volunteered to take a lie-detector test and passed it?"

"Mr. Kirk, you could give me a lie-detector test right now, sitting here in this chair. All I would have to do is tense the muscles in my thighs sufficiently and it would give you a false reading. So, as far as I am concerned, lie detectors detect the ignorance of the layman more than the veracity of the subject."

Feeling that he had demolished Kirk's cross-examination with that response, Dr. Sloate was hoping to be excused. He looked to the bench for permission.

"Counselor?" Judge Malachi summoned Kirk for a sidebar.

Kirk reached the bench only one step ahead of Howard Stone, who moved quickly when it behooved him.

The stenotypist brought her machine closer to record the conference. Malachi waved her off.

"Kirk, what the hell are you trying to do? Are you stalling for time?"

"Your Honor, I am merely laying a foundation for my rebuttal case," Kirk said.

"You're not laying a foundation," Malachi responded impatiently. "You are digging a grave. Your client's grave."

"Your Honor, I must ask your indulgence while I present this case according to my own best judgment," Kirk insisted.

Malachi considered Kirk's request, then grunted, "Okay. But the minute I feel you are jeopardizing your client's right to a vigilant defense, as I warned you, I will intervene."

Kirk started away from the bench. But Stone lingered.

"*Davey* is not himself. *You* have given him warnings about his client's rights. Aaron, what *is* going on?"

Malachi weighed informing the prosecutor of David Kirk's request to withdraw, then decided, "Someday, Howie, over drinks at the Harmony Club, I will tell you."

Another look toward the courtroom doors and Kirk resumed his cross-examintion. "Dr. Sloate, are you aware that the defendant took and passed a galvanic skin response test?"

"Yes! I am aware," Sloate responded, becoming testy and sharp in his responses.

"Didn't *that* impress you?" Kirk asked.

"Mr. Kirk," Sloate began, with that air of indulgent condescension one accords children, "obviously you have not prepared for this case as well as you should have. In the galvanic skin response electrodes are attached to the skin of the subject. Then, when questioned, the subject's emotional response is supposed to register by a change in temperature and moisture level of the subject's skin. The only trouble, Counselor, is that by generating exciting mental images or by clenching his toes the subject can create those skin changes, thus invalidating the entire result. So, my dear young man, no, I am *not* convinced by any test that can be overcome by twiddling one's toes."

Before the laughter in the courtroom could die out, Sloate volunteered, and Kirk made no effort to interrupt him, "There are many tests for the true hypnotic state. But none that cannot be circumvented by the subject if he decides to do so and has the ability and the incentive. In this case we must scrutinize every test to which Mr. Cory was subject, because there is a secondary motive. He is fighting for his freedom. A very powerful motive to fake *any* test."

Kirk waited out Sloate's complete response before asking, "Are you quite finished, Doctor? Or do you want to get into the jury box and vote as well?"

"Your Honor . . ." Stone started to protest.

Malachi anticipated him, gesturing Kirk to the bench once again.

"Counselor, when you ask questions which invite such responses, at least have the good manners not to attack the witness when he replies. Now, I think you are wasting the time of this court, but if you insist on continuing, do so within the bounds of proper courtroom etiquette."

"Yes, Your Honor," Kirk assented.

Another glance to the courtroom doors and Kirk asked, "Doctor, is there *any* test that would convince you?"

Sloate smiled, for he obviously enjoyed jousting with a lawyer as prominent as David Kirk. "My dear man, the ancient Chinese had a test to determine if an individual was telling the truth. They required him to speak with his mouth full of rice. Their idea being that the nervousness caused by lying would inhibit salivation. Thus, with his mouth dry, and full of rice, it would be difficult for him to enunciate his words. I deem many of our modern methods of lie detection only slightly more effective and scientifically sound."

Malachi did not groan at that response, though he might have done so under other circumstances. But his pity for David Kirk was clearly written on his wrinkled, grimacing old face. He did not verbalize it, but it was in his weary gesture as he shook his head sadly, as if to ask, *Had enough, Davey?*

He beckoned Kirk to the bench with one flexing of his authoritative forefinger.

"Counselor, I don't know what you're trying to lead up to, but in protection of your client's rights I hereby *order* you to excuse this witness—"

Before Malachi concluded his sentence, a stir at the door interrupted, causing them both to look in that direction. They discovered Dr. Scott insisting to the overzealous guard that she was entitled access to the crowded courtroom.

"Davey, isn't that your expert?" Malachi asked.

"Yes, Your Honor. Dr. Scott."

"Ah, lovely-looking woman," Malachi observed, then called, "Salvatore, admit the lady!"

Michal Scott started down the aisle. Kirk went to meet her. He led her to a corner of the courtroom where they spoke in intense whispers.

Meanwhile, at the prosecution table, Howard Stone and Dr. Helmut Klinger also conferred, conjecturing on what had suddenly caused Dr. Scott to reappear in the case.

Judge Aaron Malachi drummed impatiently on the arms of his wheelchair. Through his mind ran a very disturbing thought: *Was Kirk's offer to resign just a gimmick? To set up his newest surprise tactic? With Davey Kirk you never knew.*

Having escorted Michal Scott to the defense table, Kirk approached the bench to say, "Your Honor, I now ask you to remand your order that I excuse this witness. I wish to ask him one more question."

"One more question?" Malachi challenged skeptically.

"Only one," Kirk replied.

"No follow-ups?" Malachi qualified.

"No follow-ups," Kirk agreed.

Curiosity, rather than judicial judgment, caused Malachi to grant, "Okay. One more question."

Kirk resumed his position between the witness box and the jury.

"Dr. Sloate, would you be convinced or impressed if the defendant himself took the stand and his alter appeared?"

The entire courtroom—witness, jurors, spectators, media hawks, Howard Stone, his two associates, and Dr. Helmut Klinger, but mainly Judge Aaron Malachi—were startled by Kirk's question, which promised a demonstration none of them had ever witnessed before.

Viewing an alter on tape was a safe, controlled test experience. Watching the switch occur before their eyes, with unpredictable consequences, was intriguing and frightening as well.

Dr. Sloate considered his reply to Kirk's question, then said, "That would go a long way toward settling my mind on the legitimacy of the defendant's diagnosis."

Malachi signaled Kirk to the bench. This time Stone and Kirk arrived at the same instant.

"Do you seriously intend to go through with this—this exhibition?" Malachi asked.

"If that's the only way to satisfy Dr. Sloate," Kirk said.

"Howie?" Malachi asked.

"Not only I, but Dr. Klinger, would love to see this," Stone replied.

"This court will stand in recess until two-fifteen," Malachi ruled.

Forty-one

Word had spread throughout the courthouse that David Kirk was about to present another of his unique and startling legal stratagems.

During the lunch break the television networks had flooded the telephone lines to Judge Aaron Malachi's office with calls for permission to film the event. Ida Bornstein, who had handled every emergency in that office for more than eighteen years, was overwhelmed. Finally she relayed all requests to the judge, who handled them with ease, plus a few four-letter words.

When court reconvened at two-fifteen, every seat was occupied and a double row of standees was positioned against the back wall. The only concession Judge Malachi made to this unprecedented situation was to allow the standees to remain.

Malachi opened the proceedings with a curt "Counselor!"

A few words were exchanged between Dr. Michal Scott and David Kirk before he rose to announce, "I call the defendant, Christopher Cory, to the stand."

Cory came forward, raised his hand, took the oath. Once sworn, he ascended to the witness chair.

Kirk opened with routine questions about Cory's early years, his background, education, activities before he arrived in New York to follow an acting career. Kirk then led him through his relationship with Alice Ames.

Cory admitted that he was very much in love with the budding young actress. That perhaps he had been too intense in his love and concern for her success. He realized later that he had been at fault. Thus he did not blame her for ending the relationship.

When he learned of her death, he was so emotionally overcome that he testified, "I went to the local Catholic church and lit a candle for her. Even though I am not Catholic, but because she was."

Man, Kirk realized, *that's a new one. He's really primed for this performance.*

"Chris, when did you first learn of Alice's death?"

"I was at home, my loft. Two police officers came to see me. They started asking me questions. About her. About where I was at the time, and so forth. I answered as best I could, since I was suffering very intense headaches at the time. I was begging the officers for aspirin or something, but they just kept on asking me questions. When I told them I couldn't remember anything at all about that day, they took me downtown to headquarters."

"Chris, from that day until today, do you have any recollection whatsoever as to where you were and what you were doing at the time that Alice Ames was murdered?"

"God, I wish I did. But no, sir, I do not," Cory declared fervently.

David Kirk could not resist thinking, *This sonofabitch is doing one terrific job of acting. Some people may accuse me of suborning perjury. But they won't be by the time I'm through.*

"Chris, at the time you were being held downtown, did they offer you a lawyer?"

"Yes, but being innocent, I didn't need a lawyer. I needed a doctor. For my headaches. I thought my head was going to split wide open."

"Chris, are you now aware of the cause of your severe headaches?"

"Since being treated by Dr. Scott I have been," he said.

"Chris, do you wish to expose to the jury the reason for your headaches?"

"Yes, sir. I have nothing to hide," he replied forthrightly.

Kirk turned toward the bench. "Your Honor, at this time I would like the record to show that, for the purpose of administering hypnosis to enable the witness to continue, Dr. Michal Scott will take over."

"So ordered," Malachi assented.

As David Kirk retreated, Dr. Michal Scott came forward. Between them passed a look of purpose that evaded everyone else in the courtroom.

"Chris," Michal Scott began, "to demonstrate for the jury the manner in which your problem manifested itself, I am going to have to put you under hypnosis."

"Yes, Doctor, I understand," Cory agreed solemnly.

While the jury followed the ritual intently, Michal Scott led Cory through the relaxing exercise of walking across wide, green, peaceful meadows, then counting off the steps down to the lake. Before they had finished counting in unison, it was obvious to the jurors that Christopher Cory was finally in a deep hypnotic state.

To further convince them, Dr. Scott put him through several basic commands with which he fully complied in the drowsy, soft-spoken, expressionless way of hypnotics.

That demonstrated, Dr. Scott turned to the bench. "Your Honor, I must ask you to caution the jury, and all spectators, not to react in any way, no matter what happens from now on. It could prove dangerous."

"I am sure the jury, the media and the spectators understand that. Proceed, Doctor," Malachi urged, as focused on Cory as was everyone in the courtroom.

"Chris, can you hear me?"

"Yes," he said in a flat, unemotional voice.

"Chris, I ask you, did you kill Alice Ames?"

"No, Doctor. He did."

"And who is *he*?"

"Max," Cory replied.

"Tell the jury, Chris, who is Max?"

"The other one. The bad one. Who comes out and does terrible things," Chris responded.

"Would you ask him to come out now?"

"I can't. I have no control over him."

"I am now going to ask you to go into a deeper sleep. So that Max can come out if he wishes," Scott suggested. "Deeper, deeper, deeper, Chris."

At that point, in response to a tug on his sleeve by Klinger, Howard Stone interjected in a hoarse whisper, "I want the record to show that Dr. Scott is actively suggesting the alter appear."

Malachi was so deeply engrossed in Scott's procedure that he waved a silent order in the direction of the stenotypist to make note of Stone's objection.

"Now that Chris is deep asleep, I would like to talk

through him to the person who murdered Alice Ames," Dr. Scott said.

Slowly Cory began to exhibit the first jerking stages of a clonic episode. His legs twitched. Then his arms. Now his lower jaw started to edge forward. His shoulders began to hunch up to appear bulkier, more muscular. His forehead, which had not been wrinkled before, slowly assumed deep, horizontal lines.

When, as Max, Cory turned to confront the jury and the spectators, there were audible gasps from both areas.

Suddenly, from the first row of spectators, a woman was heard to utter a suppressed "No!" followed by a burst of weeping. David Kirk swung about to see Mrs. Ames slump forward.

"Attendants!" Malachi ordered.

Both uniformed men came forward to lift Mrs. Ames to her feet and assist her from the courtroom.

Quiet restored, all eyes again focused on Max. Dr. Scott continued, "Who are you?"

"Come on, Doc, who the hell do you think you're going to fool with that 'Who are you?' crap?"

Max smiled, his mouth distorting into a twisted grin.

"What is your name?" Scott asked.

"What's with you, Doc? You know my name. You've been saying it for weeks now. Max *M-A-X*. Max! Look, if you're putting on a show for the jury and we're supposed to be strangers, okay, I'll play along. But enough of this bullshit. Whatever you want to know, just ask."

David Kirk rose from his place at the defense table.

"Your Honor, since Dr. Scott's next questions are likely to elicit responses which can prove self-incriminating, I must take over briefly."

"Proceed, Mr. Kirk."

He came forward. "Max, since what you may reveal is highly confidential and possibly incriminating, it will be necessary for Dr. Scott to have assurance that she won't later be sued for breach of professional confidentiality."

Howard Stone was up with his accustomed alacrity to protest, "Your Honor, this is a most unorthodox request!"

"Mr. Stone, this entire *procedure* is unorthodox," Malachi replied. "But if the doctor feels she needs such a statement to avoid being sued for malpractice, or whatever the hell they are suing doctors for these days, I see no reason to object."

"Thank you, Your Honor," Kirk replied. He gestured to Gerry Prince, who brought him a pad and a pen. "Now, Max, please write as I dictate."

Max grinned. "Gee, I don't know. I think I should ask for advice of counsel. Since you represent the Idiot, that's good old Chris, does that mean you also represent me?"

"You may assume so," Kirk assured.

Still grinning, Max said, "Whoever thought a high-priced legal gun like David Kirk would run a sale. Two for the price of one. Okay, Kirk, *you* say it's right, *I* will write."

Smugly, Max smiled in the direction of the jury, enjoying his little play on words.

Slowly, Kirk dictated: "I . . . Max . . . consent to . . . being freely questioned . . . by Dr. Michal Scott . . . in the presence . . . of the jury . . . during the trial . . . of Christopher Cory . . . concerning the murder . . . of Alice Ames. And I . . . will . . . hold Dr. Scott harmless from any . . . consequences."

Max laboriously wrote out the words. Kirk examined them and approved. "Good. Now sign."

Max signed with a flourish. Kirk withdrew to the counsel table.

"Max," Dr. Scott resumed, "would you tell the jury of your relationship with Chris Cory?"

"Sure. I run that Idiot ragged. I *do* things to him. And he doesn't even know it. More than once I make dates for him with people. Sometimes women. Sometimes business

276

things. When he doesn't show up they blame him. Not me. One time . . . oh, this is rich! I call this producer on the phone. Say I'm his agent. I talk him into giving the Idiot a reading for a part in his new production. I get him so sold he even rents a theater for the reading. But the Idiot, not knowing about it, he doesn't even show up. The word gets around. So nobody will give him an audition after that. Doc, I can't tell you the fun I've had with him."

"Max, tell the jury, did you also frame Chris for the murder of Alice Ames?"

"That was my best!" Max boasted. "You see"—he shifted to face the jury directly, his twisted, grinning face fully revealed to them—"this Alice, she was a real bitch. The Idiot waited on her hand and foot. Ran her errands. Rehearsed with her. Meantime, his own career is going down the drain. He's got real talent. Big talent. But he ignores that so she can have all the chances. When, after that, she dumps him, I know he won't do anything about it. No guts. What do you call a man with no balls? He's a goddamn chicken. No, a capon. So, like I did long years ago, when as a kid he couldn't take the pain—you all saw that tape of him when he was six—I had to step in and do the job for him. At the same time, I have to teach him a lesson. How? Kill her. And put the blame on him.

"All that stuff you heard from those witnesses? That torn surgical glove. Wasn't that brilliant planning? On the one hand . . . hey, that's funny, that expression, on the one hand, because what I did, on the one hand I wear this glove which I tore before I ever went there. So I make it look like I am trying . . . I mean *he* is trying to do the job without leaving prints. Which any cop or DA will tell you is proof of premeditation. On the other hand, with that tear in the glove, I intentionally leave my palm print.

"Of course, they find it. Then the knife thing. From having lived there, I knew which knife I would use. The bitch put up a little more fight than I expected. But in the end she was easy. Then, once she was . . . you know . . . I hate that word. Because I am really very sensitive. Once she is . . . let's say gone, I think he hated her so much and since he is the dramatic type, what would he do? Dismember her body. But then, as I said, being sensitive, I stopped after that one slash to her shoulder. I left. Dropped the knife in the ash can right outside the house. Making him look even dumber than he is."

Max laughed, the harsh laugh of a sadistic victor.

Max continued: "And this poor jerk, this Idiot, Chris, when the police ask him where he was when the crime was committed, what else could he say but, 'I don't remember.' At first even his own lawyer, the great David Kirk, didn't really believe him. Did you?"

He shouted those last words past Dr. Scott toward Kirk, who, he noticed, was deep in his study of two legal pads.

Apprehensive about any development not under his control, Max said, "Now I am tired of all this crap. So I will blow this joint and leave the Idiot to face the music."

Howard Stone came to his feet so swiftly he overturned his bottle, spilling pills across his table. "Your Honor, we now demand the right to cross-examine this witness! In his present form *and* in the form in which he originally took the stand."

"You will have your turn, Mr. Stone." Malachi then addressed Scott, "Doctor, are you finished with the witness?"

Kirk rose to say, "Your Honor, first I would like a sidebar. In your robing room, if possible."

Distressed by the need to endure the unnecessary embarrassment of being lifted down from the bench once more, Malachi was inclined to deny Kirk's request. But the very unusual nature of it convinced him to comply.

Once within the confidential confines of the robing room,

David Kirk addressed both Malachi and Stone. "At this time, on behalf of my client, I would like to propose a plea of guilty of Manslaughter."

"After that convincing demonstration?" Malachi asked suspiciously, for he knew the jury had been greatly impressed by what they had just witnessed.

"*Because* of the convincing demonstration," Kirk replied.

"Did you discuss this with your client before he took the stand?" Malachi demanded suspiciously.

"No, sir," Kirk admitted.

"I thought not," Malachi grunted.

Stone interjected, "Okay, Davey, let's have it. Your case has never been stronger and *you* ask for a deal? Why? *Emmess!*"

"If you say there's the possibility of a deal, let me talk to my client," was all Kirk would say.

"Considering how things stand," Stone reluctantly admitted, "yes, Manslaughter. Eight and a third to twenty-five."

"Then, Your Honor, give me fifteen minutes."

Forty-two

David Kirk opened the door to the small conference room behind Judge Malachi's bench. He allowed Max to enter. Once he closed the door, Max turned to him, curious, yet unable to restrain his look of triumph.

Kirk gestured him to be seated at the small table. He laid before him two legal pads.

One contained the statement Chris Cory had signed in Kirk's office on Saturday. The other, the statement Max himself had signed only minutes before on the witness stand.

"Notice anything, 'Max'?"

"Notice what?" he asked gingerly.

"Max, I'm not a handwriting expert. But I've had enough experience with forgery cases to know what the experts look for. The slant of the writing. The firmness. The stroke of the *l*'s. The formation of the *o*'s and the *a*'s. Suspiciously similar, these two. By tomorrow I can have expert corroboration."

"So?"

"The same person wrote both these statements. Not host and alter. Not Chris Cory and Max. But Chris Cory alone. So you can drop the pose. The party's over. What I am about to say does not relate to Max, but to Chris Cory, who is facing twenty-five to life for the murder of Alice Ames."

The twisted smile, the jutting jaw, the wrinkles across his forehead slowly dissolved until he was once again Chris Cory. But still smiling.

"That's better. Now let's get down to business. Legal business," Kirk said grimly. "Cory, you now have to make the most important decision of your life."

Cory smiled even more broadly as he corrected, "There's only one decision that counts now. The jury's. And you could see for yourself what that will be. Not guilty by reason of mental defect or disorder."

"Sure, that was a powerful act you put on," Kirk agreed. "Because it was, I am now in position to offer you a firm deal."

"I told you, I'm not in the market for any deal," Cory replied, his smile now a smirk.

Kirk persisted. "Instead of twenty-five to life, I can now promise you Manslaughter, eight and a third to twenty-five. Putting aside my personal feelings about you, as your attorney I am advising you, take the plea."

"After I just wowed that jury? No deal! No, sir!"

"Cory, I've seen cases before that looked like sure things and seen them lost. So, for your own good, listen to me—"

"No, Kirk. *You* listen to *me*!" Cory interrupted. "Did you notice that chubby little man in the second row? Taking notes so fast I thought his pen would start smoking. Do you know who he is?"

"Adam Westcott. The film producer," Kirk said.

"He's the one who's hot for the rights to my story. For a big theatrical motion picture. With the hottest stars. A forty-million-dollar production.

"Another producer offered to find a young Jack Nicholson to play me. But Westcott said he would cast *me* in the role myself. I've got a whole new career now. I am not going to blow it with any plea bargain."

He turned away angrily to indicate the finality of his decision. Then, seized by another thought, he half-turned back in a softer, conspiratorial attitude.

"You know, Kirk, you could do yourself a lot of good, too. Represent me in the negotiation with Westcott and we split. Seventy-thirty. Even though I could get any agent in town to handle this for only ten. But the way I figure, there's so much here, I can afford not to be greedy. We can both do very well."

Over the years David Kirk had received more than one unscrupulous offer from a client, but none delivered as brazenly as this bribe.

Cory mistook Kirk's failure to respond at once as a sign of interest rather than contempt.

"Look, I'll suggest Westcott get Nicholson to play you. He's a good type for it. Strong, powerful. Good-looking."

Kirk did not respond, wondering how far Cory would go. He was not disappointed.

"Or, if you'd rather, I could suggest De Niro. Or Robert Redford. Even Paul Newman. I think he was nominated for an Oscar once for playing a lawyer. There's no telling what this can lead to."

"I'm beginning to see that," Kirk said.

"So forget this handwriting business. Just put me back on the stand. If you think Max has been terrific up to now, wait till you see what he does when Stone cross-examines me. Then all you have to do is sum up and we're home free."

And, David Kirk thought, *the irony is that this young, arrogant sonofabitch is right. He could carry it off.*

"Cory, even if you win, you're not 'home free.' Instead of making a film you'll be confined to a mental institution. That's the law!"

Cory's smug grin spread into a broader, more self-confident smile.

"That's the beauty of my plan. Look it up."

"Look what up?"

"*Cure!*" Cory announced with great confidence. "Part of my plan. From the beginning. MPD? What I'm supposed to have? It's curable. Sometimes in only a year. In my case it will be less. Because, Kirk, if I can be convincing playing crazy, you can bet your ass I'll be terrific playing cured. Just in time for Westcott to have a shooting script. And for me to play myself. So, all in all, we got it made. Because I did my homework, Mister. I really did it. That's why now, all you have to do is take your thirty percent and become the hero of a big movie to boot."

From the very beginning he planned it, Kirk realized. *Covered all the bases. Including how he would profit from her murder. He may not be insane in the legal sense, but, man, this is one twisted mind. One dangerous mind!*

"Believe me, Kirk, I can carry it off. I've done it thus far. And damn well, you must admit. So just play along, Kirk, play along. Because the way things stand now, Stone doesn't have a chance in hell of getting a conviction. Then a few months in the nuthouse and I am free. Plus something else."

"What else?" Kirk asked, curious as to what more this strange mind could have conjured up.

"By the time the picture comes out, I will be a celebrity. Donahue, Oprah, all those shows will be after me. I'm even going to get a lecture service to line up a tour for me. 'Multiple Personality Disorder. And how to cure it.' Why not? After all, here I am, a living example."

Cory laughed.

"Can't you see it, Kirk? How I shock the hell out of audiences with that pathetic story of my little dog, poor, dear Max, and the terrible thing that happened to him. The possibilities are endless! And you're telling me to cop a plea? Kirk, I may be crazy out there in the courtroom. But not in here. No, sir!"

"Cory, once I introduce these two pads into evidence, your act will be exposed as a scheme to commit premeditated murder," Kirk pointed out.

Cory continued to smile, then began to shake his head even more confidently.

"So, you were going to use those two handwriting samples. Well, Mr. David Kirk, Esquire, big-shot lawyer, you can't introduce them into evidence. You will be violating confidentiality between lawyer and client!"

"Cory, maybe you should have spent a little time in a law library, too," Kirk replied.

For the first time the smile on Cory's face seemed not quite so beaming and self-assured.

"If you had, you would have discovered something. Yes, confidentiality prevents me from introducing your books that Gerry discovered. As well as your notes in the margins. Because we came upon them in the course of our attorney-client relationship."

"You got those handwriting samples the same way!" Cory protested.

Kirk nodded, then pointed out, "But there's a difference. A very big difference."

Very gingerly, not sure if Kirk was bluffing, Cory asked, "What difference?"

"Taken together, these two handwriting samples constitute a test," Kirk started to explain.

"Test?"

"Like your double Rorschach. One of you, one of Max, side-by-side. These are *another* psychiatric test. And as such they are now part of your psychiatric file. Since we pleaded insanity as your defense, I am not only *permitted* to turn all psychiatric material over to the prosecutor, by law I am *required* to do so."

"But you won't," Cory contradicted confidently.

"Don't bet on that, Cory," Kirk warned.

"And let the whole world know that a young, unknown actor was able to fool brilliant defense lawyer David Kirk?"

"I'll risk that," Kirk replied.

"And that I fooled so completely the famous MPD expert, Dr. Michal Scott. I don't think so. You care too much for her to hurt her."

Kirk realized that Cory had verbalized what he himself had been aware of but which his strict personal rules of professional decorum had not permitted him to admit.

"Think about that, Kirk."

Kirk studied the impudent challenge on the face of the young imposter.

"Cory, regardless of any risk to Dr. Scott or myself, either you take the deal or I will hand these over to Howard Stone."

"You bastard!" Cory exploded. "You double-crossed me. Deprived me of my rights!"

"What rights? Your movie rights? Your lecture rights?" Kirk demanded.

"My constitutional rights! I demand to see the judge!"

"Fine! I can arrange that," Kirk agreed quickly.

Cory was unable to reply.

"Well, Cory?"

Cory turned away. He went back to the table to stare at the two handwriting samples.

"Cory? Deal or no deal?" Kirk persisted. Then he warned, "Malachi won't wait forever."

Slowly Cory turned from the table to face Kirk. Instead of the grave attitude Kirk had expected from a man facing years in the state penitentiary, Cory was smiling defiantly once more.

"Cory, what's your decision?"

"Put Max back on the stand."

"No plea?" Kirk asked one last time.

"You told me the client has the final word. Well, I say, put Max back on the stand."

Kirk studied his rebellious young client, thinking, *Okay, you arrogant, blackmailing bastard, if that's what you want.*

"Let's go," Kirk assented.

He started for the door. Cory did not follow. Kirk looked back to discover him in the clonic stages of his switching process. While he did so, he explained, "Learned it in acting class. How to get into the role."

Slowly, gradually, he assumed the posture, the facial distortions, the attitude of the Max who had entered this room.

"Now, Kirk, that jury is waiting for me!" he announced in Max's strident voice.

Forty-three

Resentful of the lengthy interruption in the trial's most dramatic testimony, the media hawks and the spectators had clustered into small noisy groups speculating on the cause of the unexplained delay.

The sudden order "All rise!" sent them scurrying to their seats.

Looking even more dour and irritable than ever, Judge Aaron Malachi rolled into the courtroom only minutes after David Kirk had informed him of his client's refusal to accept the plea bargain. Both attendants sensed the judge's seething fury as they lifted him into place. Once ensconced behind his desk he glared out at the last straggler who hastily reached his seat.

"Mr. Kirk, will you ask your client, whoever he happens to be at the moment, to resume the witness stand?" Malachi requested grimly.

David Kirk gestured to Max, who came forward with considerable alacrity.

Judge Malachi then gave the order "And will Dr. Scott continue with her examination of the witness?"

Kirk interrupted his whispered conference with Michal Scott to announce, "Your Honor, I will carry on the examination of my client."

"Anything to get this case into the hands of the jury as expeditiously as possible," Malachi declared.

David Kirk approached his client-witness.

"Max, when we recessed you were telling the jury how you often played tricks on the defendant, Christopher Cory, to annoy him, embarrass him, endanger his career, and eventually to make him appear guilty of the murder of Alice Ames."

"Yeah. So?" Max replied defiantly.

"Is it your testimony, then, that Christopher Cory had no knowledge of how Alice Ames died?"

"Until Dr. Scott started playing with his mind, I never let him know *anything* I did."

"So, when he told the police that he knew nothing of the death of Alice Ames, he was telling the truth?"

"He was."

"When he denied being in her apartment at the time she was killed, was he also telling the truth?"

"He was," Max declared.

"Therefore, if I understand you correctly, are you also saying that Christopher Cory not only had no knowledge of that crime but at no time did he have the intent to kill Alice Ames?"

Stone was on his feet at once. "Object! Whatever qualifications this witness may possess, he is not qualified to express an opinion as to the criminal intent of the defendant!"

"Sustained!" Malachi ruled. He also beckoned David Kirk to the bench.

"Okay, Kirk, you've gone about as far as you can legitimately go with this witness. So, unless you have a new and relevant area to explore, I suggest . . . and I use the word *suggest* to mean I damn well insist . . . you stand aside and give Mr. Stone the opportunity to cross-examine him."

"*Both* of him!" Stone made sure to point out.

"There is only one other area I would like to pursue," Kirk replied. "But since it is highly technical and very tricky, I would like an understanding with the prosecutor that he withhold his objections until I have finished."

Malachi looked to Stone for his reply.

"Your Honor, may I remind the court that eminent counsel asked for the right to ask Dr. Sloate 'just one more question.' Which led to the spectacle we are now witnessing. If Mr. Kirk wishes to proceed, he will do so without any cease-fire from me."

"You heard the man, Kirk."

"I will do the best I can under the circumstances," Kirk conceded.

Throughout the sidebar, Max had been smiling confidently at the jury, and at the members of the media. At the same time he had been straining to hear what was being said at the bench. He had gleaned very little, but enough to suspect David Kirk and his planned attack. Confident that he was skillful enough to overcome any strategy Kirk might have in mind, Max greeted him with a smile when he returned to resume his questioning.

"Max, you have said that at all times *you* are aware of everything that Chris does. But *he* is not aware of what *you* do."

"That's how I keep control." Max turned to the jury. "I am the ventriloquist. He's the dummy."

"Then, you know that two days ago in my office, Chris Cory made a written statement in which he insisted on taking the witness stand against my advice."

At once, Malachi interceded with a rap of his gavel so sharp that it threatened to split the block of wood on which it rested. With an imperious gesture of his forefinger, he commanded Kirk to approach the bench.

"Counselor," the judge demanded angrily, "do I detect you are about to reveal confidential dealings between attorney and client?"

"With my client's complete consent, Your Honor."

"Since, in a sense, your 'client' is not even present in this courtroom at this time, I would like some verification of such an unusual consent," Malachi ruled.

Kirk turned to Gerry, who came forward with the yellow legal pad on which Cory had written his statement.

As Kirk handed up the pad, Malachi asked, "Counselor, as an officer of this court, do you vouch for the fact that this indeed was written by the defendant in this case?"

"I do. And I call the attention of the court to the last sentence."

In a guarded voice, Malachi read aloud, " 'Mr. Kirk is free to disclose this statement at any time he deems necessary.' " Glowering at Kirk, he added, "I do not like the idea of attorneys exacting such agreements from clients. However, proceed, subject to future developments."

"Max, would you examine this statement and say whether it is the same one you saw Chris sign?" Kirk resumed.

Max took it, scanned it and nodded.

"For the record, respond by word, please."

"Yeah, yeah, this is the statement he signed," Max declared impatiently. "I said to myself at the time, There the Idiot goes again. You see, *I* knew what was going on, but *he* was too stupid to realize. As ususal."

"Now, Max, do you recall that just a short time ago you wrote a similar statement relieving Dr. Scott of any breach of professional confidentiality?"

Kirk handed Max the second pad. One quick glance and Max replied, "The jury saw me sign this. So what?"

He glanced in the direction of the jury, slowly shaking his head in annoyance to convey his amusement with what he considered merely a trivial diversion. Whatever strategy Kirk was planning, Max knew he held the trump card.

"Max, would you examine both these statements side-by-side?"

With a glance to the jury, inviting them to share his shrewd handling of the situation, Max took both pads. He made an exaggerated pretense of examining them from various angles. He held them up in a way to catch the daylight from the high courtroom window, then he favored an angle closer to the jury box. Finally he settled back in the witness chair for one last long look of intense scrutiny.

"Examined. Now what?"

"Max, does anything strike you about these two writings?"

"Nothing in particular," Max responded.

"Study them closely. Especially the *l*'s and the *o*'s and the *a*'s. Also, the general slant of both writings."

Max made a pretense of studying them once more, then asked, "Yeah, so?"

"Do you detect a resemblance between Chris Cory's handwriting on this pad and your handwriting on this other pad?"

"Yeah. There's a resemblance. So what?" Max defied him.

"Max, are you aware of what that means?" Kirk asked, laying out each word carefully.

"Yes, I am," Max replied smugly.

"Would you explain to the jury?" Kirk persisted.

Max's smile broadened as he faced the jury. "Lawyers," he derided as he began. "Instead of asking a question straight out like the rest of us poor slobs, they ask long-winded legal-type questions. That's because they are usually paid by the hour. Now, what Mr. Kirk is trying to get at is simply this: If both of these . . ." He brandished the pads in the direction of the jury. "If both of these handwritings seem to be the same, then Chris Cory does not suffer from Multiple Personality Dis . . ."

The judge brought Max's answer to a sudden halt with a sharp rap of his gavel that sounded like a pistol shot in the crowded but hushed courtroom;

"Mr. Kirk!" Malachi shouted, demanding his presence at

the bench. Once both counsel were before him, he asked in a hoarse whisper filled with fury, "Counselor, are you about to impeach your own witness and client?"

"Yes, Your Honor," Kirk stated frankly.

"Then, ethically you had no right to put him on the stand in the first place!" Malachi rebuked him angrily.

"Your Honor, due to the unusual circumstances in this case, I must either treat him as a hostile witness or else be put in the position of suborning perjury," Kirk explained.

Grudgingly, Malachi replied, "I grant that this is a case replete with unusual circumstance. But to impeach your own witness, who is your client as well . . . In my long experience I have never presided over a case like this."

"I remind the court that you refused me permission to resign from the case," Kirk replied.

Aware of this fact for the first time, Howard Stone demanded, "Aaron, what the hell is going on here?"

Malachi gestured Stone to contain his outrage, while ruling, "I will allow counsel to proceed. But, if this is some trick, he had better start preparing his defense before the Departmental Disciplinary Committee of the Appellate Division right now!"

Permission granted, though conditioned by a grave threat to his professional future, David Kirk returned to confront his client.

"Now, Max, if you will please complete your response to the last question?"

Max laughed. "Counselor, you legal eagles take so long schmoozing at the bench that I forgot the question. Let alone my answer."

Some of the jurors chuckled along with him.

"Will the stenotypist read back the question and the witness's partial response?"

The woman peeled back a layer of tape in her stenotype machine.

" 'Question: Would you explain to the jury? Answer: Lawyers . . . instead of asking a question straight out like the rest of us poor slobs, they ask long-winded legal-type questions. That's because they are usually paid by the hour. Now, what Mr. Kirk is trying to get at is simply this: If both of these handwritings seem to be the same, then Chris Cory does not suffer from Multiple Personality Dis . . .' Interrupted by gavel."

"Now, Max, will you complete your answer?" Kirk insisted.

Instead of being embarrassed or hesitant, as Kirk had expected, to his surprise Max replied, "Delighted!"

He paused as if to prepare, then began, "What you are getting at is this. If both these writings seem to be the same, then Chris Cory is not a real multiple but one personality. Which means that I, Max, do not exist. Which, as you can see, is not true. Like me or not, Mr. Kirk, here I am!"

Max turned to face the jury. He spread his arms wide and, though seated, gave his impression of an exaggeratedly respectful bow in their direction.

Kirk permitted him his dramatic moment, then asked, "Max, are you aware of the *legal* effect these similarities could have on the outcome of this trial?"

"I know the effect you would *like* them to have!" Max exploded, suddenly shrill and loud. He rose from the witness chair to accuse, "You and Dr. Scott want this jury to believe that because these handwritings seem to be the same, Chris Cory is guilty of the murder of Alice Ames!" Turning to the jury, he charged, "His own lawyer, his own doctor, conspiring against him!"

By this time Malachi was rapping his gavel with the rapidity of a machine gun, while Kirk tried to override him by calling out, "Your Honor, it is crucial the witness be permitted to complete his response!"

Meantime, Max appealed to the jury, "You see! Even the

judge is trying to shut me up. Well, I won't be shut up! As for these . . ."

He held out both pads toward the jury.

"Handwriting? Similarities? Bullshit!" His anger turned to a smug smile. "A trap that I set. A trick that *I* played. And big-shot lawyer David Kirk, famous specialist Dr. Michal Scott, they fell for it. Hook, line and sinker. Do these two handwritings look the same? Of course they do. I planned it that way!"

Contemptuously, he flung both pads in the direction of the defense table.

Despite the electric atmosphere created by Max's violent action, David Kirk proceeded in a calm, subdued voice to ask, "Max, would you explain to the jury this ingenious 'trap' of yours?"

Glaring at Kirk with a look of impatient disdain, he turned his full attention to the jury.

"Ladies and gentlemen, remember Dr. Scott asking me about all the things I did to frame the Idiot for the murder of Alice Ames? Palm print. Blood sample. Weapon. Torn glove. Remember? What do you think this handwriting is? Same thing! I knew all along what Kirk was after. So I gave it to him. Two handwriting samples as nearly the same as I could make them."

"And why would you do that, Max?" Kirk asked.

"He still doesn't get it," Max remarked to the jury, with an indulgent smile.

"Because, Counselor, if both those handwritings seem to be the same, they were both written by Chris Cory. So, there is no Multiple Personality Disorder, and no defense. Therefore Chris Cory is guilty. Exactly as I planned from the very beginning!"

After a defiant glare at Kirk, which challenged, *Try to top that if you can!* he made a formal bow to the jury and slipped back into the witness chair. He cast a quick glance in the direction of producer Adam Westcott, who looked up from hastily making his notes. Westcott's nod of approval was all Max needed to confirm his triumph.

Aware of growing disapproval and impatience from the bench, David Kirk resumed, "Max, I'm sure the jury is grateful to you for your enlightening testimony. How cleverly you planned to entrap Chris Cory. How skillfully you wove your airtight web of incriminating evidence. Especially this latest and final achievement in your plan, matching handwritings." Kirk brandished both pads at him. "However, Max . . . didn't you forget something??"

Max sat up a bit stiffly. He appeared slightly less smug and much more alert.

"Max, didn't you forget to inform the jury that in true cases of Multiple Personality Disorder host and alters not only have uniquely different habits, different abilities, even different allergies, but also different *handwritings?*"

"That's exactly what I meant."

"Ah, then we agree," Kirk said as he turned to his counsel table. "Mr. Prince, would you please bring the witness a fresh pad?"

Gerry came forward with a clean legal pad. He handed it to Max. Kirk took out his gold pen, unscrewed the cap and held the pen out to his witness.

"Max?"

Max stared at the pen, stared at Kirk, then unconsciously pulled silently back in his chair.

"Max, here. This is your chance. Your chance to prove who you are. All you have to do is write a few lines. In your own different and distinctive handwriting when you are *not* trying to imitate Christopher Cory. Max?"

Kirk held the pen closer. Max pressed farther back in the witness chair. He looked to the bench.

"Your Honor, I object. He's not allowed to do this. Is he?"

"The witness will comply with counsel's request!" Malachi ruled.

Finally, Max reached for the pen as if it were radioactive.

"Go on, Max! Write! Any words you wish. In your own distinctive handwriting!" Kirk urged. "Show the jury! And the court!"

After a furtive glance at the jury, Max embarked on a determined effort to scrawl random words across the yellow page. He attempted to make wide, deliberately exaggerated strokes. But the more he strove to suppress the natural strokes and formations of his usual handwriting, the more rigid and unsteady his hand became.

"Max!" Kirk prodded.

Max glared at him, then applied himself with greater determination, making strokes that were even more bizarre. Until his hand began to lose control. Finally it began to draw jagged strokes on the page, like a needle on a seismograph tracing a severe earthquake.

"Max?" Kirk demanded.

His hand trembled so that now he lost control of it completely. At the same time, his persona of alter Max slowly started to dissolve, like a wax mask melting. The grotesque features dripped away. His out-thrust jaw slowly receded. The weakness that had always endowed him with his bland, innocent appearance became visible once more. The carefully created and rehearsed persona of alter Max had deserted Chris Cory completely.

Unable finally to control his anger and his fear, he leaped to his feet, hurled the pen at David Kirk and shouted, "Damn you! You're my lawyer! It's your duty to defend me. Not convict me! Not convict me . . . not . . . not . . . convict . . ." His voice was swallowed up in a sob as he began to weep.

He stood before the jury and the courtroom as Christopher Cory. Trembling, lips twitching, bathed in the sweat of fear, guilty by his own actions and admissions of the pre-meditated murder of Alice Ames.

David Kirk could not deny feeling a surge of pity for this shattered young man. But justice had been done.

He had no time to dwell on it, for Judge Malachi was urging, "Counselor?"

"I have no more questions for the witness," David Kirk said softly.

"Mr. Stone?" Malachi asked.

"The people have nothing further to add, Your Honor. Except to request that bail be revoked and the defendant remanded to custody at once," Howard Stone stated.

"So ordered!" Malachi declared.

Forty-four

Seated behind his desk in chambers, Judge Aaron Malachi held the two pads which David Kirk had placed before him. After he studied both handwriting samples he looked up at Kirk and Dr. Michal Scott.

"Counselor, when did you first become aware of your client's fraud?"

"The evening before I asked to resign from the case."

"Naturally you couldn't reveal your reason. Even to me."

"He was entitled to confidentiality. But not to have me act as his co-conspirator," Kirk replied.

"You did try to get him a plea bargain. . . ."

"I was still his lawyer. I had to do everything I could for him," Kirk replied.

"His performance on the stand raises a new ethical problem."

"I trust you'll appoint another attorney to handle the appeal," Kirk urged.

"Afraid not, Davey," Malachi replied.

"I don't think I can be forced to represent Cory any longer," Kirk argued.

"It's not that, Davey. But now that this trial is over, I have a date. With a surgeon."

"Aaron?"

"My sonofabitch of a doctor was poking around again. He found something. Something 'suspicious.' Which is his way of saying 'very serious.' Says it can't be delayed. So some other judge will have to appoint new counsel for Cory."

"God, Aaron, I'm sorry to hear . . . I mean . . . I . . ."

"Don't try, Davey. No matter how eloquent you are before a jury, you don't know how to say this gracefully. Nobody does. And even if you did, I wouldn't know how to listen gracefully. So just go."

Kirk was about to reply, but Malachi anticipated him with a soft "Davey, no. Just go, please."

———————

As David Kirk and Michal Scott passed through the waiting room they found Ida Bornstein in tears. Embarrassed, she sniffled and attempted to speak.

"Ida, we know. He told us."

The woman was relieved not to have to explain.

———————

As Kirk and Scott started down the wide stone steps of the Supreme Court Scott said, "Cory passed all his other tests so

297

well, none of us, not even Klinger, thought to give him the handwriting test. What put you onto it?"

"Beaumont."

"John Beaumont?" she asked, puzzled.

"Cory used Beaumont's book like he was shopping in a psychiatric supermarket. Picking up a symptom here, a symptom there. A fact here, a fact there. Differences between hosts and alters. Each having a different life-style. Wearing different clothes. Speaking in different voices. Different vocabularies. Until he could play the role of an utterly convincing victim of Multiple Personality Disorder. So I asked myself, what about those facts and symptoms he *didn't* pick, *didn't* underline or *didn't* comment on in the margins?"

"Such as different motor and manual skills between host and alters. Like handwriting?" Scott suggested.

"Exactly."

"But John . . . Dr. Beaumont . . . pointed out that handwriting differs in only fifty percent of MPD cases."

"I had to gamble that Cory didn't know that. Evidently he didn't."

"*Will* he get a new trial?"

"Probably," Kirk conceded. "But at least I won't have another Cecilia Trimble on my conscience."

They had reached the bottom step, where Kirk's limousine waited.

"Drop you?" he asked.

She hesitated, then said, "That would be convenient."

" 'Convenient,' " he commented.

"And . . . and thoughtful," she granted.

" 'Thoughtful.' At least we're making progress."

Once the car was on its way north on Centre Street, Kirk said, "You realize that even if Cory appeals, it won't involve us?"

"That'll be a relief," she confessed.

"It also means we're no longer colleagues."

She glanced at him out of the corner of her eye. His response confirmed what she had suspected.

"The best time to call is before eight or after six," she said.

"And get that cool, precise, professional voice on your answering machine?"

"That's my alter. You will find her host much friendlier, I assure you."